The
LAST
HAND

Also by ERIC WRIGHT

The
LAST
HAND

ERIC WRIGHT

THOMAS DUNNE BOOKS
ST. MARTIN'S MINOTAUR
New York

THOMAS DUNNE BOOKS.
An imprint of St. Martin's Press.

www.minotaurbooks.com

Library of Congress Cataloging-in-Publication Data

Wright, Eric.
    The last hand / Eric Wright.—1st ed.
      p.   cm.
    ISBN 0-312-28330-X
    1. Salter, Charlie (Fictitious character)—Fiction. 2. Police—Ontario—Toronto—Fiction. 3. Toronto (Ont.)—Fiction. I. Title.

PR9199.3.W66 L37   2002
813'.54—dc21   2001051295

First published in Canada by Dundurn Press
First U.S. Edition: February 2002

10 9 8 7 6 5 4 3 2 1

FOR LIZ AND TERRY BYRAM

The
LAST
HAND

S alter reached out to hold onto the dock as he got ready to step out of the boat; in his other hand he carried his weekend bag and two fishing rods. He waited until Seth, his son, was also holding onto the dock, then let go and slowly stood up straight. Stepping cleanly from the boat to the dock is nearly as important in disembarking from an aluminum dinghy as from a canoe. If you lean forward, you push the boat away with your back foot before you have completely stepped up onto the dock. All this Salter had properly in mind, but the dock had been rebuilt since the previous year and was slightly higher than his leg remembered, thus it caught his foot as he swung it forward, dumping him face down on the dock, bending back his wrist as he hung onto his bag and his fishing rods, bruising his knees and his hip, and abrading his cheekbone.

Seth said, "Jesus, Dad. Take it *easy*," as if Salter had fallen as the result of failing to complete a handstand at his age.

Salter lay on the dock for a moment, then raised his head, said "Shit" and grimaced comically at Seth in an effort to reassure his son that he felt more foolish than injured. He climbed onto his knees. "They raised the fucking dock," he said, trying for a mock-serious tone that would make light of his fall.

"I guess," Seth said, missing the jocularity and therefore slightly shocked at the obscenity. "Be careful going up the ramp. The river's gone down and it's kind of steep."

"I'll crawl up it, shall I?" This, too, was meant to be a joke but there was enough irritation in his voice to make Seth flinch slightly, and Salter scrambled to get the right tone back. "Or I could wait until next spring when the river comes up again," he said, smiling. And then a wave lifted the dock slightly, causing him to stumble, not quite to fall.

Seth grabbed him and held him steady before Salter could brush him off. Now Salter tried for one last pleasantry. "Don't tell your mother," he said. "I promised her I'd lay off liquor after I set fire to the barn that time."

Seth laughed politely and started to unload the equipment from the boat. Salter put his bag on top of the cooler, adjusted the rods in his hand, picked up the cooler and walked up the ramp to the marina parking lot. When he tried to haul back the sliding door on the mini-van he found that he had sprained his wrist when he fell.

Seth got behind the wheel without any argument from Salter, who licked the blood from his knuckles and thought about the incident and the pattern it was part of, about what the pattern showed about other patterns in his life lately; in the process, he uncovered some things he had not been aware of.

Tripping up like that could happen to anybody, of course; it wasn't the tripping that bothered him but the failure of his reflexes to respond in time to soften the fall. He had had the same experience at the cabin. Once a year Salter went fishing, using this cabin located three hundred twenty kilometers north of Toronto, so he had a clear measure of the rate at which he deteriorated year by year. It seemed a lot this time. The rock, for example. To get to the cabin from the shore you had to climb up about thirty feet of incline, rock which in winter lay under the ice and acquired a thin mebrane of black moss. This dried in the sun and became as adhesive as a well-laid tennis court, but when it was wet it was as slippery as a coat of grease. Even Seth slowed down, moving warily, getting footholds on the tiny patches of pink unmossed rock and seeing the places on the black moss which would support a light, brief step as he skipped to the next patch of dry rock. Once Salter had been able to do that, but this year he had been roundly defeated; every tentatively placed foot shot out from under him when he tried to stand and he had had to grab Seth's hand repeatedly to avoid sliding into the river. Finally he took the alternate route up to the cabin, along the beach to the path through the brush and the little set of granny steps that led up to the slab of rock the cabin rested on. It was like using the ladies' tee. And the route up to the outhouse, which he had once admired for the way the owner of the cabin, a colleague of Salter's in the Organized Crime Unit, had made nature yield up a path over roots and around rocks without laying concrete, now seemed a fifty-yard booby trap guaranteed to break your ankle in the dark.

So some nimbleness had gone? As they drove up to the chip wagon at Point au Baril, Salter was inclined to shrug it off until he opened the car door to jump down and found no answer when he called on his legs. Stiff? After sitting for fifty kilometers? Less than half an hour?

"It's okay, Dad," Seth said, uncoiling himself from the driver's seat like a limbo dancer and turning towards the chip wagon as he descended. "I'll get 'em. Small or large fries? Salt and vinegar?"

Salter finished standing up. Not decrepit; just bruised, surely. He had fallen more heavily than he thought. Be gone in a day. "You want some coffee?" he asked.

"I can carry it."

"They don't sell coffee at the chip wagon. You have to go to the gas station. I'll get it. Cream and two sugars, right?"

"Yeah, sure, but I could get it after . . ."

"No sweat." Salter judged his legs safe and ready now. He gave them their orders and walked with hardly any jerkiness to the gas station to pick up the coffee.

They ate their chips at the picnic table and capped the rest of their coffee to drink along the highway. Back, seated in the van, Salter said, "Here, I'll hold your coffee until you get settled."

Instead of answering, Seth pulled out the little tray under the dash. Two cup holders popped up, ready to take their coffee. "See?" Seth said.

"Right. Right. I never use it myself."

3

"How long you had this van? Three years?"

"About that."

"And you never used this tray?"

"I forgot it was there."

Now he probably sounded senile. Christ! He was only sixty. Still playing squash, wasn't he? And generally beating the little gang of semiretired seniors he played with, lawyers and accountants mostly, men undistinguished—even unsuccessful—by the standards of the sharks of their professions, or they would not be playing at his club but at one of the grand ones suitable for entertaining clients from out of town. These were contented, self-deprecating family men who lived in Leaside or near the Old Mill and said "Golly!" when their opponents hit a good shot. Salter himself still leaped and ran and dived for the ball when it came his way, his body reacting on the court as well as when he was fifty, unaware of any need to compensate—it did so for thirty minutes, anyway, which was all the members of his age group lasted. Three games.

Up to a point: because two years ago he had faced a new tragedy on one of the few occasions he had behaved prudently. In the course of a routine visit to his optometrist he had let her know, bragging a little, that he still played squash without glasses. She was appalled, delivering a lecture on the possibility of a smashed eyeball that could result from being hit by a squash ball that exactly fit the eye socket, never mind the wounds that your opponent's racquet could cause. Salter humbly bought some goggles—all his opponents had been using them for years—even paying a hefty premium to get prescription lenses. The first time he used them he found himself in an unfamiliar universe, like someone on a mood-enhancing drug. His perception of distance especially was awry, and that, combined with the conscious-ness of this new structure strapped to his head, caused him to jump back too quickly and too far in pursuit of an overhead ball and smash his shoulder against the back wall, which was much closer than he had judged. That night, one side of his body was dark blue with a rosy edge where it met the uncompacted flesh in the middle of his chest. The diagnosis was a rotator cuff injury. But in a month his normal coloring returned and he started to play again, finding that in spite of the clicking sounds and the feeling that he had exchanged some of the small bones in his shoulder for a bag of marbles, he found his game was about the same, and when he discarded the three-hundred-dollar goggles in favor of a six dollar pair with plain lenses that didn't interfere with his peripheral vision, he could still play at about the old level. That was a great relief, because playing squash was now about the only activity that completely wiped out the world for thirty minutes a week.

In the mirror, without his reading glasses on, he thought he looked pretty good, and he was able to dismiss the fact that well-mannered high school girls, especially black ones, now occasionally offered him a seat on the subway. To them, everybody over thirty is doddering, right? He had a bit more trouble with the knowledge that several times lately he had been offered seniors' discounts in dry-cleaning stores and cinemas, again, especially by West Indian women, but here too he was able to surmise that all white men in their prime must look old to young black women, the white skin only shrouding the skull beneath.

Salter tried to tell himself that he was being silly. He had been feeling his age for as long as he could remember, but he was still not about to join the growing band of his peers seeking eternal youth in Viagra and hair transplants and weight lifting. Accept what is natural to the age, he told himself, and discard or at least stare down the rest. So, sure, be a bit more careful stepping out of boats and lifting rocks. But don't worry if you can't remember the movie you saw last night—not just its name but anything that happened during the whole two hours, even the genre. War? Song and dance? Jane Austen? Ah, fuck it. Look, talking to Seth over the weekend he had found, effortlessly, the name of Petrucchio from *The Taming of the Shrew*, a play he had seen only once twelve years before. It was all in there somewhere.

He went into a light doze and woke up as they passed the sign for Honey Harbor with the real problem on his mind, the problem of whether he was finally all washed up, and what he should do about it. And now he made the shift from pondering his condition to real-izing he was not alone in being aware of the damage. Now he con-sciously brought to mind (instead of unconsciously repressing) all the small signs that he and his deterioration were being daily discussed by his nearest and dearest, by his acquaintances, and certainly by his enemies. Now he realized that Seth had gone to some trouble to come fishing with him, silent as to the inconvenience, although Seth's need to fish had decreased steadily since he was twelve. The very smoothness with which the weekend had come together indicated a conspiracy which had begun as soon as Salter had announced he wanted to go fishing, and expected to go alone. What Annie had seen then, Salter realized now, was a vision of her tottering husband surrounded by large rocks and larger waves, breaking an ankle on his way up to the outhouse at night, and thus trapped until daylight when a passing boat might see his feeble signal. So Seth was recruited without fuss because they had all been discussing behind his back for some time the roles they would soon be playing in alleviating his advancing senility. Right?

Which led him once more to the realization that the same thing was happening at work. Salter was head and sole member of the Special Affairs Unit and worked on special assignment directly for the deputy chief. The unit had been created to deal with some specific unusual situations, such as investigating crooked politicians who were members of the Police Commission. Salter had handled several such sensitive cases, and in between times he had assisted Homicide, which was always understaffed. But for a year now, although the unit had remained in existence—in name, at least—he himself had been in fact the deputy's personal assistant. His *office* assistant, his office boy, earning his pay by doing the deputy's desk work and listening to the deputy, who liked to talk his ideas out before he went public. Even this role had shrunk lately, and Salter now came to the conclusion, about fifty kilometers south of Barrie, where Seth pulled in for gas, that Deputy Chief Mackenzie was waiting for him to accept the fact that under the rules this was Salter's last year—sixty was the limit for active police work—and he became filled with anxiety.

He had even sought out former Staff Superintendent Orliff, his old boss, who, though long retired, still kept in touch because he was a political animal and that's what he liked to do. But in the matter of Salter's situation, beyond flicking away as paranoia the idea that there was any kind of conspiracy to keep Salter in the paddock, Orliff had no advice or understanding to offer. "You've gotta retire this year, that's the rule. Unless you're a deputy, you have to be street-ready, which means not over sixty. In the meantime, Marinelli doesn't need you, and Mackenzie likes having you around. If you were ten years younger, the chief would try to get his money's worth out of you. But my guess is that if they think about you at all, yeah, they're glad Mackenzie is looking after you until you go away. Nobody's got it in for you, but if you make a nuisance of yourself, you'll finish up in Public Relations."

So there it was. Salter played a little golf in the summer, and squash twice a week, and he could not imagine what he would do with the rest of his time if he stopped work. His situation was thus frightening, and banal.

2

"T hat it?" Deputy Chief Mackenzie asked. A big man, sitting at attention.

"Those are all the new ones."

They were in Mackenzie's office, the deputy chief and Staff Inspector Marinelli of Homicide. At the back of the room, Salter was sorting through some files while he listened to Marinelli's report.

The two new homicide cases sounded routine; they were outstanding only because the investigation had not proceeded far enough for the squad to have arrested anyone. One victim was a middle-aged welfare case, found bludgeoned in his room, almost certainly the victim of a robbery. The other was a teenage boy stabbed on a subway platform during a gang brawl. Marinelli did not anticipate any difficulty in finding either of the villains. It was simply a matter of talking to the witnesses, of shaking them hard enough. In both cases a lot of people knew who was responsible, and one of them would give up a name soon—within days, probably. There was no risk to the public.

"That lawyer who was stabbed?" Mackenzie wet a meaty finger and turned a page in his desk diary. "Getting anywhere?"

"The Vice Squad are working with us on that one . . ."

"I know, I know, I know. What's it been now? Two weeks? Three?"

". . . we haven't come up with anyone yet."

"Family lawyer wants us to find a prowler, someone just looking for a hit. Wrap the case up quick." Mackenzie phrased his remarks economically, eliminating all the inessential words. Salter believed the mannerism had its roots in a desire to sound businesslike, even military, back when Mackenzie had been a sergeant.

"You in touch with this lawyer, sir?"

"I take his calls." Mackenzie straightened an already straight back.

"What's his name, sir, in case he calls me?"

"Holt."

Marinelli waited for him to continue.

"Holt," Mackenzie repeated. "I thought he might know something about the victim that the family don't want to get out. Something they don't want the world or us to know about. Thought I might get a smell of it, save you some time."

"And?"

"They think a casual prowler. They *hope* it was. Any sign of a prowler?"

"We've come up with a hooker, or what looks like one, a woman who was hanging around that night. Maybe that's what this lawyer thought we'd find."

"What's a hooker look like?"

"Blond wig, big silver boots—you know."

"Maybe peddling her ass door-to-door?" Mackenzie's expression changed from thoughtful and receptive to creased with amusement, then immediately returned to quizzical, changes that seemed not to be generated by emotion or thought, but switched on intentionally while the deputy considered something else. "Eh?" Mackenzie now said sharply, returning to wanting an answer to his question. "Any of the hookers work like that? 'Avon calling'?"

"It would be news to us." He grinned politely at Mackenzie's joke.

"And me. Still. What have you done?"

"The Vice Squad has trawled Jarvis and the other main areas for a whisper, but they haven't got one yet. They know a lot of the pros and they've showed the victim's picture around, just in case someone knew him. I mean if there's a hooker going to his apartment, then he probably would have had her sent, and she might not be the only one he's had sent up. But we haven't had a smell."

"What about the guy. Found anything?"

"Not much. Famous for his integrity, everyone says. Sat on all the law society's ethical committees, things like that. Well-known in the trade, but not famous to the public, because his practice was civil, didn't go near the criminal courts if he could avoid it. No known enemies. Married and divorced some time ago, but no bad blood there, either. Granite Club, like his father before him. His mother recently died, and there was just him and a sister. Didn't work too hard; spent a lot of the summer at his cottage in Muskoka; traveled a lot, mostly with those wine-tasting groups, organized booze-ups, tasting the local porch-climber. You know."

"Faggot?"

It was a routine question. The files contained plenty of pictures of bodies of naked middle-aged men with stab wounds.

Marinelli shook his head. "No sign of that. Anyway, the hooker kind of rules that out, doesn't she?"

"These days? Who knows?" Mackenzie snickered. "What do you plan to do now?"

"Keep looking for Pussy-in-Boots. We'll find her. Should be easy to spot."

From across the room, Salter chimed in. "Maybe she's taken her boots off by now."

Marinelli smiled courteously at Salter as if acknowledging his right to make an irrelevant comment during a serious discussion, then turned back to the deputy chief.

"You need any help?" Mackenzie asked.

Salter walked across the room to search his raincoat pocket for tissue.

"We're always shorthanded, sir. But no special problem. I'll get back to you." Marinelli stood up and left the office, nodding to Salter on his way out.

Salter watched him go. Over the last six or seven years he and Marinelli had become comfortable with each other without becoming friends. Salter had worked on several homicide cases from his base in the Special Affairs Unit, the last case at the specific request of Marinelli.

When the door closed behind Marinelli, Salter said, "If he needs any help . . ."

"He'll manage. You heard him."

Salter closed the file drawer and walked to Mackenzie's desk. He sat down in front of the deputy chief. "What's going on?" he asked after a long silence.

Now Mackenzie looked up from the document he was pretending to read. "What?" he asked. "What? What?"

"Question. What the fuck is going on?" Salter had worked for Mackenzie for several years, and with the door closed he could set aside the deputy's rank while they talked.

Mackenzie said, "Far as I know, nothing's going on. That you don't know about, that is. Why? What's up?"

Salter saw that the deputy was trying to think, and waited ten seconds before he continued. "Last week Marinelli was complaining about being undermanned. Now you ask him if he needs help and he says no. He knows I'm in the room. What I hear is that he doesn't need *me*."

Mackenzie sniffed hard. "Sit down, Charlie."

"I am sitting down."

"Yeah, right. Okay. First, nothing's going on right now. Okay? But this gives me a chance to say something on the topic." Now he gathered himself and hunched forward. "You're a bit of a lone wolf, you know that, Charlie?"

What Salter heard was Mackenzie calling him Charlie for the first time, while he fished around for something to say, and he didn't like it. He waited for the unpleasant thing that was coming.

Mackenzie continued. "You don't get to hear all the scuttlebutt around the canteen, do you? Kind of out of touch. You have any buddies on the force?"

"This is where I *work*," Salter said. I *socialize* with *civilians*." It was the response he had ready for whenever the topic cropped up. In truth, Salter had never been sociable. Golf was the only thing he had in common with most of his colleagues. Although he was on good, respectful terms with several middle-rank officers he had worked with, including Marinelli, none of them had been inside his house.

"So I understand." Mackenzie touched his tie and rolled his shoulders to settle himself inside his jacket, then cleared his throat. "Keep your life private. That's your privilege, but it cuts you off."

"From what? The politics? I'm close to retirement. I work for you. Why do I need to be plugged into the grapevine? My ambitious days are over. I've been lucky to work for guys who knew how to look after themselves, and who looked after the people who worked for them."

"Orliff?"

"He was the latest, yeah."

"Did Orliff start the Special Affairs Unit?"

"Yeah."

Mackenzie nodded. "When I took over, I liked the idea of keeping the unit, and you as head of it. Gave me a resource that no one else knew enough to question, put a little flexibility in my budget. Someone to talk to, as well. You've been good to have around."

"So what's changed?"

"How do you mean?"

"I haven't had an assignment outside the office for six months."

"I needed you here, Charlie. You've got a good head for administration."

"I'm not administrating. I'm a clerk. Your office manager."

"Want a transfer? They're looking for someone in the archives, down in the basement."

"Sorry. But something *is* going on. Isn't it?"

Mackenzie resumed. "Face it, Charlie, look at yourself. Realize how people see you. You've handled some pretty high profile cases in the last few years. Your name crops up around the Police Commission table. You're a threat. People are jealous. They don't want you around, taking credit."

"I make Marinelli feel threatened? I don't believe it. He's got more sense."

Mackenzie looked less sure of himself. "Not Marinelli himself, per se. People who work with him," he offered. "You're too big for their boots."

Salter said, "If you don't mind my saying so, this is all bullshit. What's *really* going on?"

Mackenzie gave up. "Nothing. There's nothing going on, Charlie.

Nothing at all. I could give you a long list of the problems they have working with you, but they don't amount to a pinch of coonshit; no more than they have with each other. Like, for instance, you aren't up to this new computer system we've got, are you?" Mackenzie scratched his forehead as he searched his mind. "Haven't had a refresher course for five years, have you? Been looking at your file. Things change. Here's a f'r instance: You know how DNA works?"

"Everyone knows how DNA works."

"Yeah, right. What about the latest bugging devices? Forensic accountancy? You know when to call in the experts? There's all kinds of stuff to stay on top of."

Twenty seconds went by. Salter looked out the window while Mackenzie watched him. Then Salter said, "When I was working on the homicide case at Bathurst College, I didn't know we had a liaison officer for native people in trouble. And if I'd been more comfortable with the new toys—" he pointed at the computer screen "—I probably would have automatically looked up the people I suspected on the CPIC file and found out that the guy I wanted to arrest had the perfect alibi—he was in jail that night—and saved myself a couple of days foot-slogging. That kind of thing?"

"More or less." Mackenzie grabbed at the example gratefully. "Yeah. Yeah. More or less. Basically, yes."

"So I've not kept up-to-date enough for the hotshots in Homicide, that it?"

"Sort of."

Salter stood up. Mackenzie said, "I still need you here, Charlie."

"Good."

He left the office and turned down the corridor to Marinelli's room. As he walked in, the phone rang.

"Yes, sir," Marinelli said into it, looking steadily at Salter. "He just came in." He put up a hand to signal Salter not to leave.

"Jesus Christ," Salter said. He sat down in front of Marinelli's desk.

"I'll talk to you later," Marinelli said into the phone. "Or he will."

"Mackenzie?" Salter asked, when Marinelli put down the phone.

"Who else?"

"How long have you been discussing my case?"

"Don't be an asshole. What case? You were in the room when he asked me if I needed help. You overheard me saying no. We don't need any help."

"Not from me, anyway."

Marinelli said nothing.

"Why not? Anything specific?"

"Ah, come on. All that happened was that you caught a small signal that wasn't meant for you."

"It was about me."

"Don't make a mountain out of it."

"Just tell me the size of the fucking molehill."

"Okay. You ready for this, this big news I have for you? This secret everybody is whispering? It's nothing special. Not even very interesting. You're not about to be nailed finally for stealing the coffee money back in eighty-nine. None of the women clerks has complained that you've become a bum-pincher. It's just that my guys don't want you on their team; they don't want you backing them up. I know, I know, you've handled stuff on your own, but all those cases were special, and we haven't had any lately. You asked me, so I'm telling you. Look around the office out there. Who do you see over forty? To those guys you are an old guy with some good stories. Not an old fart, no. They know I respect you. They know I was glad to have you handle a couple of cases. But that was yesterday. Nowadays if they see me having lunch with you it makes them uneasy. They think I'm consulting you, for fuck's sake, and they get uptight." Marinelli took a moment to look indignant on his own behalf.

"All of them?"

Marinelli said reluctantly, "Mainly Stevenson, my number two. He got a little stressed when I wanted to borrow you from Mackenzie this spring to help out with the threat to that Balkan politician. I told Stevenson you had experience in threats to royal visitors and he said that was ten years ago. Techniques have changed. You know what he said? He said he had a college degree with a minor in crowd surveillance."

"He's got *what!*"

Marinelli grinned, relieved. "He does have a degree, Charlie, from some police college in Wisconsin. He's not the only one. Anyway, I put him in charge and we handled it without you, and nobody got assassinated."

"Fine. So I shouldn't sit around waiting for you to consult me because it isn't going to happen anymore. That what you're saying?"

"Charlie, we're sitting here now because you caught me telling Mackenzie we didn't need any help, after I'd told him already, a little while ago, why we didn't need you when the Balkan guy was visiting. Mackenzie's on your side, wants to save your feelings. But for the sake of my guys, I'd prefer to think of you as . . . taking a back seat.

"You haven't gotten very far with that lawyer case, have you? The guy who was stabbed."

Marinelli looked irritated, then shrugged. "No, we haven't. And I don't think we will, yet. We're not baffled, though, as in 'Police Baffled,' nothing like that. We'll find her. You know that."

"Might not be soon enough for that gang breathing down your neck."

Marinelli looked out the window, waiting for Salter to go away.

After a few moments, Salter said, "I'm glad you told me. I'll stay out of your hair from now on." He stood up.

Rising with him, Marinelli said, "Charlie, it's no big deal. Christ, you must have seen it coming. Let's have dinner. Please. Your wife's away, you said last week. Let's have a steak. Tonight. No, tomorrow. My treat. Barberian's. Meet you there at six. Okay?"

"Better not walk over together, eh? Stevenson might see us."

"Oh, fuck off. I'll call by your office at five-thirty."

Salter walked back to his office and sat at his desk, uncertain what to think about. He had always prided himself on keeping his illusions under control, ever since the time twenty years earlier when his then-boss and mentor retired and he learned that he had enemies of whom he had been entirely unaware, who showed their faces then for the first time. And here he was again.

How long had it been going on? Surely not all that long. It was three years since he had undertaken a case entirely on his own, the investigation into the death of a dean of a local community college. Stevenson, the number two in the Homicide Unit, had been around then, but Salter had not been as aware of him as he might have been. Stevenson was probably in the room when the deputy congratulated Salter on his handling of the case. Salter couldn't remember.

But what had he done since then? Passed the time of day with Marinelli was all. Strolled down to Marinelli's office when he heard of something interesting happening, listened to the chat. Marinelli had always made him feel welcome, until now. But what had it looked like to the others? That Marinelli was consulting him? "Let's ask Salter?" And after that, maybe, "Salter thinks . . ." "Salter says . . ." Ah, shit.

Even now he was probably glamourizing himself. It wasn't Salter of Special Affairs they resented, but that old guy in the the deputy's office who Marinelli was constantly having to be agreeable to that irritated them, especially Stevenson, the number two. Marinelli could have just left it at that. You're past it, Salter thought. Or that's what they think. From now on—or, rather more likely, for a year already—they were waiting for him to go away.

Now he got angry. It need not have come to this. Somebody might have said something sooner. Now what? Retirement; the word had been in his head for a long time without needing to be confronted. Suddenly the need was there, not to retire on the spot but to pick a date—three months? Six months? Why wait?

He bought a copy of the *Star*, glad as ever that there were enough newspapers in Toronto that you could read one over breakfast and buy another for the subway, and another for when you had to eat alone, downtown. He walked down to the Atrium for a corned beef sandwich and a mug of beer.

The stretch along Yonge Street between College and Dundas was as grungy and lively as it had been for at least forty years, filled with street people, permanent and temporary; kids from the suburbs; homeless kids and their elders; beggars; tourists who think this *is* Toronto; people washed up from the Eaton Center—the giant bazaar that is the mecca of Ontario country folk and shoppers from upstate New York—and students from the nearby university. The area was about to be remodeled—The Gap was there already—but it was still a street of electronics stores, record shops, T-shirt stores, video arcades and currency exchanges. The sidewalks at dusk were crammed with the people from South Porcupine, slightly excited by the energy of the crowd, holding onto each other as they made their way to the safety of the next McDonald's. Salter liked this scene; it seemed to him what a downtown should look like to folks up from Binghamton, or down from Pickerel Lake—lively, slightly cosmopolitan (there was a pornography bookstore), raffish without being dangerous. And a lot more interesting to stroll along than the street of burghers he was retiring to.

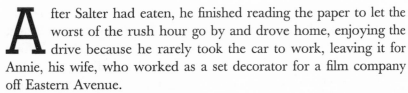

After Salter had eaten, he finished reading the paper to let the worst of the rush hour go by and drove home, enjoying the drive because he rarely took the car to work, leaving it for Annie, his wife, who worked as a set decorator for a film company off Eastern Avenue.

Seth was watching television. "Did you eat yet?" he asked, as Salter walked in. "I thought you might want some company with Mom away."

Salter felt abashed at Seth's consideration. "You should have given me a call. What are you doing here, anyway? Mum call to ask you to keep an eye on me?"

"She asked me how you were managing, so I thought I'd better find out before she asked me again."

Seth was an actor, at the level at which he could reasonably audition for a job as principal actor at the Stratford (Ontario) Shakespeare Festival. As far as Salter could tell, he was a good actor, the kind who caught your eye when he was onstage. He had carried spears on Canadian television and played some significant parts in Toronto's equivalent of Off Off Broadway, the dozen or so theaters located in old synagogues and meat-packing plants and derelict taverns.

Technically, he lived at home with Salter and Annie, but for the last few days he had not been around; lately, he had often been absent, sleeping over, Salter assumed, with his girlfriend, Tatti, who lived in a tiny, one-room flat on Bloor Street, near Bathurst.

Tatti was from Grenoble, a lumber and farming community a hundred kilometers north of Montreal, and she had left home to attend a CGEP, one of Quebec's community colleges. There she had tried to study fashion but soon found herself in Montreal, drawn to theatrical costume design. She had served an informal apprenticeship backstage in the city's little theaters, put together a portfolio, come west to Toronto to make her fortune and there met Seth.

To Salter she sometimes seemed like a trim child of about fourteen instead of the twenty she was. She had a skin like cream-colored chamois tinged with pink along the tops of her cheeks; straight, short hair the color of bamboo; slightly crooked teeth and about a sixteen-inch waist. Her chin very nearly receded, making her overfull cheeks give her the look of a chipmunk, and when she smiled her cheeks bunched up and pushed her eyes shut. Salter thought on first sight that she was the ugliest pretty girl he had ever seen, or the prettiest ugly girl. At any rate, he gave himself credit for finding such a plain girl, if not bewitching, then enormously easy to look at and be with.

Salter said, "I'm sorry. I ate downtown. I think there's some frozen fish and chips . . ."

"That's okay. I'll scramble some cholesterol. Go ahead. I'll make us some coffee."

Salter went upstairs to change out of his suit, eager to take the opportunity of sharing any kind of time with his son. With Annie and his other son, Angus, away in Prince Edward Island, where Annie's family lived, Salter was getting a foretaste of the empty house of the future, and he was becoming frightened that his family life was ending before he was ready, just when he was finding his sons interesting.

When he came down, Seth had cooked his eggs, and Salter poured some coffee and sat down opposite him at the kitchen table.

"So," Salter said, "You can tell your mother I'm okay. What shall I tell her about you?"

Seth said, "Tell her I'm finding it hard to get by . . ."

This was a problem Salter could handle. He was now sure that he and Annie had more money than they needed, and he had begun to try to shuck off the Depression mentality he had inherited from his own father, to the point that Annie, descended from the Prince Edward Island establishment and therefore much better trained than he in the ways of handling surplus money, had had to speak to him about his habit of offering money to the boys at every opportunity. But she wasn't here now.

"I don't doubt it," Salter said. "You need something to tide you over?"

"No. I want to live on what I make. *We* make. We both do." He waited until the pronoun registered. "Tatti's a terrific manager. She figures we could make it if . . . if we lived together."

Salter wondered if this meant just what he had feared. No more Seth? No more Tatti? The empty house, finally? "She doesn't spend much on clothes, I would think," he said.

"She makes all her own."

That wasn't what Salter meant. He meant that he had only ever seen Tatti in one outfit, a sort of brown wind sock, a woolen tubelike garment that fitted her neat figure perfectly. Salter entirely approved of this garment, but it was only one outfit, unless she had several, identical. "Then what are we talking about? You spend half your nights at her place already. You want to move in with her full time? You're a big boy, twenty-two? Do what you want. How about her? Does her mother know?"

Seth smiled, recognizing that his father was babbling in search of something light and witty.

Salter had already gone down this road with Angus, but he was still unsure how to act in response to the changing times, the new world of his sons' sexual relationships. He had tried, a year or two too late, to have the proper little chats as they reached adolescence, and after that he concerned himself with the age of consent. (A colleague of his had told him once that as soon as his sons were aware of sex, he decided that they should understand how to practice safe sex, so he had bought a package of weiners and some condoms, called the boys together and showed them how to roll a condom over a weiner. "There," he'd said. "Understand? Always practice safe sex."

"Right, dad," the boys had said—Salter suspected the next bit of being apocryphal, added for the sake of a good story—"We understand. Never go on a date without a hot dog. Right?")

When first Angus and then Seth reached the age of having eighteen-year-old girlfriends who did not become pregnant, he considered that his job as a father was done, and done well. Neither of the boys had ever consulted him about sex, thank God. Salter understood that they had had hours of expert instruction in school during the time that used to be set aside for religious studies. He had made no comment (except to Annie) when first Angus and then Seth had found lovers. Just so long as . . . etc., etc., which included their being entirely responsible for any consequences, not hurting anyone's feelings, and, for a long time, not forcing Salter to be aware of their activities.

When they were growing up there had been a few formal conversations around the Salter hearth that turned on personal morality, and the boys had slid successfully into adulthood with inherited assumptions about right ethical behavior without any specific citations of Judaic or Christian codes.

Questions of public morality were far more likely to generate heat, because Angus had graduated with his eye on the good life, a firm believer in the necessity of capitalism and his ability to profit from it, while Seth, apparently not sharing Angus's needs nor caring much for his toys, had sidled to the left and spent his time and energy looking for other satisfactions. He never actually joined those who came to the door on bitter January nights seeking money to save the forests, or the wetlands, or the lakes, but his instincts just seemed more charitable than Angus's. Yet Angus, while saying that panhandlers ought to get jobs, was the one who had the most trouble refusing money to an actual poor wretch wrapped in a blanket in a shop doorway, holding out a thin, dirty hand.

Together the two boys constituted the usual problem for theorists of the origins of human character, because, identical in genetic makeup as well as in nurture, only the possible effect of being born first or last allowed any room for a theory that would account for the difference between them.

"Does Tatti's mother know what?" Seth asked in response to Salter's last question.

"I was joking. You know. Pretending you were still a kid, keeping a neighbor's daughter out late. She's a grown-up, too. Nothing to do with her mother who her daughter sleeps with, is it?"

Seth looked as if he had been slapped. "This isn't about fucking, Dad. It's about living together, being with each other."

For a moment Salter felt almost admonished, but in another moment had bitten back an apology, because as well as the idyll Seth had constructed, of course it was about fucking. "I just wondered if her mother would see it that way. Where's she from? Grenoble? Old Quebec family? Very traditional values they get from the Church about what is a good girl, by which they mean one who doesn't sleep with her boyfriend. I just wondered."

"They're Catholic. Is that okay?" Seth said it quietly, but it was a challenge. No one talked much about religion in Salter's house. Salter had inherited a wispy association with Anglicanism, an association that would last him to his funeral, so that he felt slightly less uncomfortable inside an Anglican church than in a religious building of any other denomination. Annie had left her own, much stronger Anglican connections behind in the Maritimes; she had had the boys christened because her own mother expected it, but there ended the lesson. When Annie's mother visited from Prince Edward Island, the two women went to church and Annie came home cheered by having been able to sing a couple of favorite hymns again, but she never went on her own. Now Seth was genuinely asking, in the absence of any information that he could remember: were the Salters, as a family, anti-Catholic?

"If you're planning to get married, son, I'd've preferred a Jew," Salter said, adopting a mock-solemn stance as a way of being serious as well as a defense against it if he sounded silly. "The next best would've been one of those evangelical women you see on TV, the black ones from the U.S. South. See, most of the Jewish women I know are better cooks than . . . our people, mine, anyway. And a singing black daughter-in-law would liven us up. Apart from those, I don't have any preferences. What's the difference? For a while, you could tell the Catholics by the size of their families. Then they stopped having big families any more, never mind the Pope. Tatti like that?"

"We practice birth control, sure . . ."

Salter moved to cut off any further discussion of his son's sex life. "Good." As he said it he realized again that this kind of thinking regarded pregnancy as if it were a sexual disease, to be avoided by practicing contraception, and he gained an insight into how it might sound to a devout Catholic; yet, certain that he could not offer any alternative, he changed the subject, or rather, pursued the original question. "Is there enough room?"

"Where?"

"At Tatti's. I thought she lived in one room over a store near Honest Ed?"

"Yes. No. There isn't enough room in her place. She just has a single futon. We would have to find somewhere else."

"Can you afford it?"

"We could get a small place for five hundred a month. Tatti's working pretty regularly now, and I made eighteen thousand last year. I'm hoping to beat that if I get the call from Stratford. If that happens we'll still need a place here because of Tatti's work, and I'll buy an old car and commute. I think I would get off two days in six, something like that. Is there a problem?" he ended, looking at Salter's face.

Salter had begun to pick at one of the elements of his unease, one he tried not to think about, certainly not reveal to his son. It had to do with the function of marriage. At some time he had heard marriage described as "a trap baited with sex that is snapped on consummation," which it certainly had been to some of his father's generation, and this attitude had left its mark on his own. But not many, these days, got married just to get laid regularly, did they? And yet the times, which had eliminated this necessity, and with it a lot of wedding night misery, also got rid of something else: the positive, romantic side celebrated by, as far as Salter could remember, some early poets, though not many in the last two hundred years.

Salter had no doubt that Seth's life in this arena was much to be preferred over the anxious fumbling experience of his own generation, but did that mean that the whole Old World of sacraments, and blessings-on-your-union, and virginity and all that was simply mumbo-jumbo, created and perpetuated by a gang of self-loving celibates who had no direct interest in the matter other than making a living out of it?

2 4

"What are you thinking about, Dad?" Seth asked, reminding Salter that he was waiting for an answer.

Salter said immediately, "I was just thinking that I will miss you around the house. Does your mother know what you're thinking of doing?"

Seth blushed faintly. "I already talked to her. She said when she comes back, if we still don't have a place she'll help us look for one." He changed the subject. "How are things at work, Dad? Everything okay?"

"Sure." The response was automatic. "Why?" Salter and Seth had lately started to move into a newer adult relationship, Seth taking upon himself the right and duty to ask after Salter's welfare, one adult to another. Salter found it exhilarating to discover Seth as a friend while being conscious that it was one more diminishment of his paternal role. Soon, he would be left with just the money.

"Mum mentioned something."

"What? When?"

"Before she left. I asked her when you were going to retire."

"What did she say?"

"She said you had to quit soon. How do you feel about it?"

Salter looked for the honest answer that would reinforce this new bond between them without alarming Seth or depressing himself. "I'm nervous," he said. "I don't have any plans. I don't know what happens next."

Seth grinned. "Read 'Ulysses'," he said.

Salter's year and a half at university provided the reference. "I did look at it once. I didn't get far. I couldn't see why they banned it."

"That comes at the end. I didn't mean the novel, the poem. Tennyson."

"What's that about?"

"Ulysses at sixty, picking up his oar for the last time, maybe, but still heading out to sea."

"Good poem? Readable?"

"Terrific."

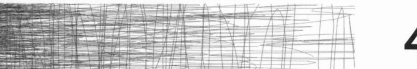

4

There was a time, in the sixties, when Harry Barberian's steak house was one of the few Toronto restaurants that out-of-towners, especially show business people on the road, recommended to each other. In those days Toronto had a French restaurant, La Chaumiere, a spaghetti house, George's, and a fish restaurant, The Mermaid, several steak houses and, of course—the backbone of Canadian dining since the last spike was driven into the Trans-Canada Railroad bed—the dining rooms of the major hotels, the railroad hotels. And the Park Plaza. Most of the other eating places in those days competed in offering the cheapest breakfast in town.

Now there are sixteen Yellow Pages of restaurants offering a range of cuisines from couscous to curried goat, a choice as varied as that on the West Side of New York below 120th street. Most of the dining rooms of the sixties are gone now, but Harry Barberian's has kept its place of honor among the local steak-eaters, and visiting actors still recommend it to each other.

An earnest discussion of how long the restaurant had been there, and how much a twelve-ounce rib steak had cost the first time they had been there, and when that first time was in each case, took Salter and Marinelli through the awkward time, until the predinner scotch took hold and they could come to the point, whatever that was.

Marinelli coughed, adjusted himself in his chair, sipped his drink, moved his knife and fork slightly, and said, "Thanks for coming along, Charlie. Gives me a chance to show my appreciation for all the help you've been over the last few years. And still to come, I hope. How old are you now?"

"Sixty."

"Uh-huh. I figured about that. You know Harry Wycke? Used to be in Homicide years ago, then moved to Community Affairs? Retired last year. You know him?"

"I use his cabin for fishing."

"Yeah? Well, I bumped into him the other day. He lives near me. He thought you'd reached mandatory retirement already."

"This year."

"But you *could* retire now, couldn't you?"

"Any time in the last eight years."

"Why don't you just take the money and run?"

"You think I should? If I was a senator I would stay around for another fifteen years."

"Yeah, and you'd get a living allowance for the days you weren't in Florida, too. But most normal people look forward to putting their feet up by now. They plan for it."

"I've got a pension, my wife has her own money, and my kids are independent, more or less."

"Sounds good. How's your dad?"

"He died last year."

Marinelli looked for a new start.

"You hear some people talk about nothing else," he said finally. "Can't wait to retire."

"Some of the jobs people have to do I'm not surprised. But I'm already doing everything I want to do. I don't have any hobbies except squash, and the old buggers I play with will last my time. I need something to do, you know? What I'd like is to start all over again, retire to a little town, be the one-man police force. They used to have them in this province. My first act would be to lock up the gun, be the first police force in Canada that goes back to the truncheon. That has to start somewhere. If any armed bandits come to town I'd send for the Mounties."

Marinelli smiled to acknowledge that he recognized Salter was talking playfully, though maybe from a serious impulse. "There haven't been any one-man police forces in Ontario for a long time, Charlie. You could open an agency."

"Sit in a car all day taking pictures of guys faking injuries for insurance companies? Let's change the subject. What are you up to these days?"

"Me and June joined the local tennis club. They've got a bubble so you can play all winter. I've put on two pounds a year for the last ten years. I'll be up to two hundred and fifty by the time I'm your age. I figure a couple of tennis matches a week and no desserts and I should be able to hold my own. Otherwise, I . . ."

"I mean, what are you working on?"

"At work, you mean?"

"Yeah. Are you busy?"

"We're always *busy,* Charlie, you know that. There's always a backlog of stuff we can get on with."

"Mackenzie doesn't tell me everything. Open files?"

"Sure. I make the new guys read them. Once in a while they come up with something we ought to look at again. Nothing very dramatic."

"How often has it happened that one of these old cases got solved? In your time."

"Just once, actually. But I live in hope."

And then Salter couldn't resist it. He had provided Marinelli with plenty of openings, but now he tried the direct route. "How about that lawyer who was stabbed. Got any farther with that one yet?"

"We still figure it was a hooker."

"But you haven't found her."

"We will. Someone will whisper her whereabouts to us. One of her buddies when she's trying to beat a rap of her own. You know how it is, you keep the pressure on and someone comes forward eventually."

"I was thinking about her, after I heard you tell Mackenzie about her. I was wondering, did you consider the possibility that she may not be around anymore?"

"Skipped town, you mean? We've put out a bulletin across the country. Someone will turn her in."

"Maybe she doesn't exist." There. It was out.

Marinelli laughed. "At least three people saw her. She'll surface eventually. Oh, yeah, she exists, all right. We'll find her."

"There might be another way of seeing it," Salter offered, but Marinelli cut him off.

"If there is, we'll get there. Now I'd better head off. No, no. This is mine. I asked you. Let's do it again, on you. Before you quit for good."

Salter thought, I'm being put in my place. All I did was make a chatty remark, could have been helpful, because they are looking in the wrong place for the wrong person. But he came ready to keep me off their grass. So fuck him.

The phone rang in both offices, and Salter picked up the call. "Deputy Chief Mackenzie's Office. Staff Inspector Salter speaking."

It was the agreed-upon formula to take care of Salter's calls directly and to create a buffer for Mackenzie. The deputy's vanity did not require that someone should answer his phone; he just liked Salter to do it because it gave him time to think if, say, the prime minister was on the line.

The constable at the reception desk in the rotunda said, "I have a Mr. Gregson here, would like to have a word with the deputy chief."

"Tell him to write a letter, ask for an appointment. Tell him the deputy's in a meeting," he added.

A pause. "He says it's urgent. He says that he's Mr. Calvin Gregson. He says he was just passing by and thought he would drop in to talk about a pressing matter. Shall I send him on his way, sir?"

"Hang on." The name Calvin Gregson rang a bell. Salter pressed the hold button and walked to the door of the inner office. "Calvin Gregson, sir. Want to see him?"

"Who's he? Oh, shit, him. What's he want that's important enough to walk up here for? Better find out. Tell him I'm in a meeting. Be free in ten minutes."

Salter relayed the message, adding, "I'll come down and get him."

Mackenzie stood up and went over to the tiny mirror on the back of his closet door. He smoothed his hair, bared his teeth and knocked the dandruff off his shoulders. "Right," he said.

"I'm here on the kind of mission that a leading criminal lawyer should never attempt, Hal. I want to find out what is happening in the Lucas case. You know, the lawyer found stabbed in his apartment? And if you tell me nothing is happening, I'm here to ask why not? And to tell you about a little problem that's just cropped up."

Calvin Gregson, at fifty, one of Toronto's and therefore the country's leading criminal lawyers, threw a two-thousand-dollar raincoat at a chair and sat down in another, loosening his tie.

"What's that, then?" Mackenzie straightened his own tie and made sure his cuffs were even as he placed his hands on the desk and looked down at himself. He was pleased with his suit; he had bought it at the Bay, where he bought everything he wore. It always paid to buy quality, though you could go too far. He thought Gregson looked like a tailor's dummy. An Italian tailor.

"Lucas's sister, Flora, the member of the Provincial Parliament herself, is expecting a visit from a reporter on the *Daily Dominion*—you know, the new media crusader for truth on the block? And not *any* reporter, by the way, but the one the *Dominion* bought a couple of weeks ago from a Vancouver paper. The *Dominion* offered him a piss-pot full of money I hear. I wonder if the day isn't coming when everybody will be traded like sports stars? You know, if *The World* gives a reporter an iron-clad, two-year contract with an option, then develops him until he's worth as much as Fulford, say, could they put him on the block with a big price attached? Interesting. He'd need a lawyer to represent him, wouldn't he?"

Mackenzie, hearing through Gregson's patter the sound of someone trying to ingratiate himself, relaxed slightly. "What's the guy's name?"

"Gavin Chapel."

"You know him?"

"Oh, yes, indeed, Hal, and so does everybody in Vancouver.

31

Chapel isn't a reporter; he's a 'Special-to-the-*Dominion*,' award-winning shit-disturber, the one who will write the stories when you guys fuck up."

So this was it. Mackenzie tried not to look as bothered as he felt. He clasped his hands together, leaned forward, and searched for something casual to say. Although he had not had time to assess Gregson's news, it was obviously full of portent. The fact that Gregson was sitting in Mackenzie's office at all, never mind the "drop-by visit" bullshit, was significant in itself. Gregson's time was too valuable to squander.

Mackenzie knew him, of course. Gregson had many times defended people accused of major crimes, often successfully, and always spectacularly, so that criminals with serious money tended to seek him out. Occasionally—when he was deeply irritated at some particularly casual misuse of the law by the police in their eagerness to get a conviction—he worked for nothing. Usually these were cases in which Gregson's presence was enough to tip the balance in the defendant's favor when an awed jury or judge was called on to choose between the police version or the defendant's version of the story in, for example, a case of police brutality.

Gregson made no secret of the fact that he practiced law for money first, then fame. He had both already, and was now rich enough to tithe himself (as he called it)—not by giving to Grace-Church-on-the-Hill, though he did that generously enough—but by donating a portion of his time to people who couldn't afford him.

"You retained by the family?"

"Not for a fee, no."

"I've already had one conversation with this other lawyer, guy named Holt. Now you. What's up?"

"I'm helping out Flora, his sister. She's the only family he had."

"The MPP."

"The attorney general after the next election. I want to keep her on my side." Gregson grinned and winked, though whether to indicate his cunning, or to give the lie to what he was saying, Mackenzie couldn't tell.

"She throwing her weight about? Should I be worried?"

An actor faced with Mackenzie's last line would have a lot of room for interpretation. Mackenzie's own delivery was sufficiently poker-faced that he might have been consulting Gregson, wary of Flora Lucas's clout; *or* speaking sarcastically, indicating that no female politician, especially a *provincial* politician, was going to bother him, *or* asking Gregson if Flora Lucas had raised questions he should take seriously. A really good actor would try for all three possibilities.

"Insofar as Flora Lucas is a member of the Provincial Parliament, an M dot P dot P dot, she is not about to let you feel her full legislative weight, no . . ." Gregson, necessarily something of an actor himself, was much given to the dramatic pause, but the first flourishes of any speech were only the preliminary capework performed while he gathered his thoughts.

". . . but insofar as Flora is a woman, the sole survivor of an old Ontario family, distinguished in her lineage and proud of the family name, she is determined to do everything in her power to bring the killer to justice, and to preserve her brother's good name."

Mackenzie had an elementary knowledge of city and provincial politics; elementary, but adequate to the job of keeping his nose clean. He knew who Flora Lucas was; he also knew she was a Liberal, whereas Gregson, he was pretty sure, at one time had been a bagman for the Progressive Conservatives. So what was going on? "So she hired you?" he asked.

Disconcerted by his failure to make Mackenzie smile at the self-parody he had been trying for, Gregson nodded slowly. "I know what you're thinking, Hal, and that is a reasonable assumption, an assumption anyone would make, must make, and it makes no difference if it is true or not. But no. My own interest, as I suggested, is entirely personal. Allied with Flora's, as I mentioned, but my own still. Lucas was, not a *friend*, but a crony. I liked him. We went to the track together once or twice. He had a box at Woodbine. And though I believe the details of his private life are irrelevant to your investigation, they might not seem so to your people and to a salacious public eager for libelous anecdotes. My visit here is to assist you in finding the culprit, while leaving undisturbed irrelevant facts about Lucas's private life, however interesting."

Mackenzie, feeling patronized by Gregson's style, and no longer wary of Gregson himself, came alive. "For Christ's sake, Calvin, get hold of yourself. Why are you talking like this? I mean, I know what you are talking *about*, but come out of the courtroom, will you? Or is this the way you talk in bed, too?"

"I was just relaxing in your company, Hal, forgetting myself."

"Bullshit. You were trying to impress me. Let's take that for granted. I'm impressed by you. Have been for twenty years. And even more lately, ever since that stage carpenter who killed the actor got off with two years for manslaughter, thanks to you. You impress me, always have. No need to keep it up. Now, what are we here for? What's this new development?"

"Gavin Chapel, the tribune."

"Thought you said he worked for the *The Dominion*."

"I meant the tribune, the herald of the people, not the paper he works for."

"Ah." Mackenzie wrote it down on a pad. "My daughter gave me a big dictionary for Christmas, on a wooden stand. I'll look it up. So what's he up to?"

"First of all, he's after your ass."

"Tell him to get in line," Mackenzie said, while he considered whether he had allowed Gregson too much familiarity for all his million-dollar-a-year income. He didn't want to show any kind of concern, not to Gregson, and he mulled how to let the lawyer tell his story without appearing to be too interested. He had recently discovered the difference between "uninterested" and "disinterested," and he tried now to speak out of a disinterested curiosity, the curiosity of a man whose ass was totally protected. "Going a goddamn strange way about it, isn't he? Does he think he can get Flora Lucas to help him raise a stink? That's not her way, you say."

"You know her?"

"I've read about her. And seen her picture. About fifty? Tall, kind of plump, quite well-featured?"

"She's forty-eight. . . .

"Keeps herself in shape, too. How come she never married?"

"She was once. He died."

"Yeah?"

"Yes. I've known her for many years. I went to Jarvis with one of her old boyfriends. Her last . . ." Gregson either searched for the word or paused to let Mackenzie know it was coming. ". . . lover was a doctor who worked for Doctors Without Borders. He worked with a group in Africa, trying to keep kids alive. He is or was Greek. He disappeared. Flora met him when she went to Bosnia in the early days to find out what had happened to the money she had raised to assist child refugees."

"You've answered that one, then. Can we move on? This reporter?"

"I called Flora a couple of days ago. There haven't been too many sex murders lately, so he was casting around, looking for something to write about, and he stumbled over Lucas's case. One thing led to another, and he dug and came up with one or two things he thought she should know. Things no one else knew, except you, of course."

"Like?"

"You know what I'm talking about?"

"Not yet."

Gregson sighed. "Okay, then. Chapel spoke of what you are keeping close to your chest. About Lucas's visitor that night."

Mackenzie shrugged and waited.

"To start with the facts, then—you're going to make me spell it out, aren't you, you bastard?—okay, the night Jerry was stabbed, he had a visitor, a woman who looked to the neighbors like a hooker. Someone the police have so far not mentioned."

"Not to you or to the media, no."

"Point is, Flora is afraid of what Chapel will find out about this woman. She's concerned, though not in the way you think. She doesn't care about Jerry's sex life. They were so close she probably knew all about it."

"Let's go back over it. She doesn't care, his sister, that maybe he was killed by a prostitute?"

"It wouldn't bother her. He just got unlucky, or made a bad choice, that's all. But she doesn't want it turned into a sex scandal saga, which Chapel will do. Two or three weeks of newspaper speculation, which will eventually involve her and—this is for your ears only, Hal—the discovery that her last boyfriend was a Greek doctor who disappeared in the Sahara. The connection is not public. It's nobody's business but her own, but she *is* a politician, and therefore who she's slept with lately is interesting, and it's a rotten prospect for her."

"And?"

"And?"

"And now she wants to lean on us a little, which she's not supposed to do, so she's asked you to bring the message. As you say, it wouldn't do her any good in the Ottawa Valley to have her connected with the Greek doctor."

"But, Hal, would you believe that her real motive is to protect her privacy? The assumption these days about a woman in her position is that she's a lesbian; the assumption in sophisticated circles, that is, not in the Ottawa Valley. Would you believe that she would rather they think whatever they like than that they should actually know about her private life, which is much less interesting? We're talking about a . . . *lady* here, Hal, not some MPP trying to keep her nose clean while she angles for a cabinet job."

"So what do you want from me?"

"I'd like to be able to tell Flora that you've moved the investigation onto the front burner to try to get it solved. You know, put your best men on it, as they say."

"You can tell her that. I can speak to Marinelli. I can't shut this reporter up."

"I'll try to speak to someone on the masthead. Get them to lay off for a couple of weeks."

"That how long it will take us?" Again, Mackenzie's tone gave the remark several possible interpretations. "I guess *I* could talk to someone on the—what did you call it?—the masthead, too, but that would use up all my influence for about a year. Can't her connections handle it?"

They considered each other for a few seconds. Mackenzie continued. "The editors or the publishers or owners—they're all in your club, aren't they?"

Gregson laughed. "That's not exactly how it works, Hal. Okay, I'll think of something."

"Have a word with the premier. He must know someone who can help." Mackenzie leaned away from his desk, openly jeering, adopting the voice of the man on the street who believes all the people at the top are hand in glove with each other, protecting each other's interests. Not that this discounted what had already been understood between them. Mackenzie simply wanted to put a limit on their collaboration, so he leaned back.

Gregson picked up his raincoat, grabbing it in the middle as if he intended to dump it in a garbage can on his way out. "Find her, please, and get her out of sight."

Like a goddamn actor, Mackenzie said later, to Salter.

"You know him?" Mackenzie asked, when the door had closed on Gregson, and Salter had reappeared. "You collared that stagehand who killed that actor, didn't you? Gregson got him off easy."

"Two years. Apart from that, I've never come up against him, but I know about him, sure. He gets himself in the papers and on TV giving his opinion on capital punishment, stuff like that. He likes the spotlight."

"Dresses like it, that's for sure. Real prince."

"What did he want?"

Mackenzie considered the question for several seconds. "I'm not sure. Says he's looking out for Flora Lucas. You know? The politico? But he's not the family lawyer. I've already heard from that one. Gregson implied they are afraid that if the investigation goes on too long it will damage her chances in the election. She's tipped for A-G, did you know that? Gregson made goddamn sure that *I* knew it. But that's not the point. Point is, I don't think Gregson was being totally up front. I think there's something else." Mackenzie laced his fingers together and hunched over the desk, thinking. "Something, maybe, about Lucas that all the guys in Gregson's club know, but are keeping quiet about to protect his reputation. Maybe hers, too. Funny. As a lawyer, getting a client off, he's worth a million a year, but offstage, like, he's a lousy liar. I must tell Marinelli."

I could leave a letter on Mackenzie's desk tonight, Salter thought, telling him that "compelling personal circumstances" had made it necessary for him to leave a few months early. They would go for that.

He could drive down to the Island and surprise Annie.

It was ten years since he had taken that drive. Get up at five and get the hairy part, the 401 through Montreal, out of the way by lunchtime. Then south through Quebec for a couple of hours, enjoying the Frenchness of the villages, the first surge of pleasure because you were on a trip to foreign parts. Then over the border into Maine—or was it Vermont?—the tiny thrill of being abroad confirmed by the American practice of decorating their houses with flags. This, the flags said, is the U.S. of A., the land where peameal bacon is called "Canadian;" where you can get Michelob on tap, and where the diners in the villages open at six in the morning, unlike Canadian diners, whose owners consider eight o'clock an enterprising hour to begin selling coffee.

Once he had gotten as far as Bangor in one day, six hundred-odd miles, but now four hundred was his maximum, so the trip took three days, which, on reflection, was a bit long.

Maybe a fishing trip, then? But Seth was too busy, and he knew of no one else free to go fishing on a day's notice.

So perhaps he would stick around.

From the first overheard mention of the hooker he had had a hunch, an insight into her significance, an insight without which neither Marinelli nor anyone else would get very far. And so, very soon—he had seen it all before—Marinelli's squad would focus too early on an obvious suspect as they put together a case that would collapse in court (or worse, convict an innocent woman). Then, the whole case in shambles, the witnesses scattered, the crime scene polluted, someone would have to start from scratch to find the real culprit—a task made infinitely harder by having the job already botched. Salter felt as if he were at the races, certain of the winner of the next race, but without the money to play his hunch. An idea formed. First he would have to get up to speed on the investigation Marinelli's detectives had started. At one time he might have had to mount a small, classic espionage operation on the files and desk drawers of the Homicide Division, probably after the detectives had gone home, but nowadays all the information he needed was on the computer. All he would have to do would be to bring it up and print it. And instead of following the investigation into the victim's background, he could just spend an hour with *Who's Who* and get all he wanted.

Next he had to talk to some of the people the homicide detectives had interviewed, for which he would need an excuse—a different excuse for each one would be best. And as he began to try to think of ways of doing this without it coming to the ears of Marinelli and Mackenzie, Salter realized that there would come a point at which someone, Mackenzie probably, would hear about what he was doing and ask him what the hell he thought he was playing at, and that would be that.

He saw that he had been creating a little fantasy, that the idea of conducting his own investigation was out of the question, and so sank back into frustrated glumness and returned to thinking about driving to the Island.

But unknown to Salter, without any help from him, the world was already rearranging itself to his benefit.

5

Former Staff Superintendent Orliff, Salter's old boss, was a small, neat man who had laid aside the blue suit of his police days for a leather jacket, a denim shirt and chinos, but he kept the black shoes, the tidy haircut and the well-pressed look.

He had been retired for six years, but had not disappeared. He supplemented a handsome pension by advising American movie companies making films set in Toronto, especially crime stories. His job was to keep the gaffes out of the script, to make sure Hollywood's Toronto police did not call each other "Captain" or "Lootenant," and to explain Canadian criminal law as it affected police procedures.

In practice Orliff found himself going beyond his police expertise into the larger culture, eliminating references to the election of senators, for example, and pointing out that there was no such thing as "Canadian" food if you left out butter tarts and back bacon; the term as it is used in restaurants in Windsor just means "not Chinese."

He had cards printed after it was clear that there was an ongoing demand for his services. "Advisor on Police Protocol" was how he described himself. He was frequently asked why he didn't call himself "consultant," and his reply was that a consultant claimed to know how things ought to be, whereas an advisor just knew how they were.

Orliff and the lawyer Calvin Gregson met over coffee in the food court of the College Park shopping center, chosen by Gregson because he had occasionally seen Orliff drinking coffee there, and the traffic back and forth to the law courts on the second floor would make their meeting unremarkable to anyone who saw them together. It was better to be seen bumping into each other in public than to be noticed dining together in a quiet restaurant.

For Orliff's part, it was his favorite daytime spot for drinking coffee, on the pedestrian route between the courthouse and Police Headquarters, the place where he was most likely to bump into old colleagues and keep up with the gossip, even if he was no longer active.

Orliff arrived first. He watched Gregson approach, and leaned back, his hands behind his head, staying seated as if they met each other every day.

"So what's up, Calvin? I can call you Calvin, can't I? I will, anyway. It's nice being retired, you don't have to worry about upsetting anyone with things like that. Hey, you going away for the weekend? You look dressy."

Gregson looked blank and shrugged, the gesture of someone who pretends not to understand the question, and who finds it faintly offensive anyway.

Then Orliff got it—Gregson's new look registered. It was the suit, a beautiful silvery grey tweed, narrow in the waist. It didn't look to Orliff like a lawyer's suit, not a Toronto lawyer, at any rate. What was Gregson up to?

Gregson said, "Calvin will do. Not Cal, if you don't mind. That sounds like the driver of a chuck wagon. And what do I call you?"

"Use my old nickname. Nobody has since I was a PC."

"What's that?"

"Figaro."

"As in Barber of?"

"That's *right*! I got called that when I was horsing around one day. Five different sergeants were shouting at me at the same time to do this, do that, so I started to sing. "Figaro here, Figaro there, Figaro high, Figaro low, Feeeegaro!"

"And the name stuck."

"Until I made sergeant. Then it just got said behind my back. But lately I've been having lunch with my old buddies, those who knew me as Figaro, and they still use it. For a joke. I don't mind. It was my joke first."

"Figaro." Gregson waited, but there was no more to come. "You don't mind if someone overhears me calling you Figaro?"

"It would just mean we go back a long way. A little farther than we do. So. Why are we accidentally meeting like this?"

"I need your advice."

"Wow! Or maybe, even, Gee! I thought you were just being sociable for old times' sake. But you need something! Not about the law, I hope? You making a movie? What else do I know that you don't? I know. 'Who do you go to these days to get a traffic ticket fixed?' Right, Calvin?"

"The Lucas murder. You know about it?"

Orliff brought down the front legs of his chair and took a sip of his coffee. "These days you could run the same newspaper by me twice a week and I wouldn't know the difference except for the births and deaths column. There were two in the *Globe* last week I knew. Deaths, not births. Remind me who Lucas was."

"A lawyer found stabbed in his apartment in the Annex. Presumably by someone on a casual break-and-enter."

"A couple of weeks ago? I remember something. What's happened?"

"Nothing. They've made no headway at all, as far as I can tell. I talked to your Deputy Chief Mackenzie, and he just says the unit is overworked."

"It always is. But let's get to the point. What's so special about this case? To you?"

"Lucas was a crony of mine."

"A crony. What's that mean? A buddy?"

"Not a close friend, no. We used to go to the track together. I *am* a friend of his sister, Flora." Gregson waited for the name to register. "Flora Lucas," he amplified.

"I was nearly there. The MPP. How do you know her? I've never heard of her in connection with us."

"You wouldn't. She's absolutely solid. There's nothing self-serving about her. A wonderful woman, real old-fashioned public servant."

"They're nearly extinct. She's loaded, too, though, right? That helps. If you're going in for good works, I mean."

"Old family money."

"Old enough to be dry-cleaned by now, however they made it, you mean. Never mind the sister, how far back do you really go with Lucas, Calvin? Law school? Upper Canada College? Or did you work your way through law school?"

But Gregson was up to this kind of taunting. "My father was head of the law school. Didn't you know that? I didn't even have to apply. Before that he was solicitor general of this province. 'Course, he'd already made a potful in private practice. How about you? Raggedy-ass newsboy were you? Scraping together the pennies to get through college?"

"We were all right. My dad was a cop, see. It's our strongest tradition, getting your kid on the force. Started in the Depression, when we didn't hire anyone who wasn't connected. Like your club, I would think. Things have changed lately; some of our guys took a look at your fees and encouraged their kids to go to law school. Kind of like construction workers not wanting their own kids to mix concrete.

Gregson leaned back, making clear he was going to wait until Orliff was through. Then he said, "If I take the silver spoon out of my mouth and stick it up my ass, can we go on?"

Orliff laughed. "Don't mind me. I'm just enjoying retirement. So what's the agitation about Lucas's death? They'll find the killer on the streets one of these days."

"There's a reporter around stirring things up."

"That's good, isn't it? That'll get Mackenzie going."

Gregson leaned over the table, trying to close the gap between them. "Let me tell you what a reporter might be interested in. The night Lucas was killed there was a woman around his apartment block."

"Who? Do they know who?"

"They can't track her down. Point is she was pretty obviously a hooker. The police know about her, though they haven't found her, but hardly anyone else knows yet."

"Just you and Lucas's sister and a few cronies? I'm getting the point. So far you've been able to keep this woman out of the headlines, but now this reporter might find out about her."

"He has already. *That's* the point. Now he has a story. Why have the police gotten nowhere, with such an obvious suspect to look for? Is there a reason why the police can't find her, he's wondering. What's going on, he's wondering."

"So what *is* going on, Calvin?"

"Huh?"

"I mean now, between you and me. What do you want from me?"

"How do I get Mackenzie to get moving? Find the killer before everyone starts speculating about Lucas's kinks?"

Orliff laughed. "And if it turns out that he *was* a little kinky? Not that paying for sex qualifies under that heading anymore, I wouldn't think."

"Then so be it. But it won't. He wasn't."

"You only went to the track with him, though, didn't you? How can you be so certain?"

"Okay. I'm not. Let's say I'm ninety percent sure."

"And the other ten?"

"He was always a very private person. Even Flora says so. Although I'm sure there's nothing in it, there was room there for a—well—a secret life."

"As opposed to just a private one?"

"Yes, and that's the point. This hooker may be a sign of it. Certainly she's right out of character for the ninety percent that I knew. Now, if there *was* something there, it is probably none of your business, either."

"Me? I'm retired."

"You know what I mean. Your people."

"So what do you want Mackenzie to do? Specifically."

"Catch Jerry's killer and leave his life alone."

"And me?"

Gregson took a breath, and for the first time checked the adjoining tables to make sure they were not being overheard. "You have Mackenzie's ear these days? You always used to."

"I've been retired six years. I don't have anybody's ear except my grandson's."

Gregson looked over at the elevators, now disgorging a clutch of policemen and lawyers from the courts upstairs. "You just hang around here like an old firehorse, listening for the bell?" Gregson made a chuckling noise.

"Look, Mr. Gregson . . ."

"Calvin."

"Sorry. It's an instinct I have, to keep my distance when I feel a hand on my leg. Let me tell you what I'm really doing here." Briefly he explained his role as an advisor to the film industry. "Right now there are fifty-three film companies with permits to shoot scenes in Toronto, so I'm onto a good thing. At the moment I'm waiting for Sergeant Kuntz, who deals with issuing permits to film companies who need to park equipment trailers while they are shooting a scene. Sergeant Kuntz is in court right now, as a witness on some other case, and I'll catch him when he comes down. I'm not sitting here hoping to arrest someone. I'm retired. I never did much of that, anyway. Now as to Deputy Chief Mackenzie, I do bump into him from time to time and we do have a chat about the things we still have in common, yes. But I don't have any influence."

"Just tell me how to do it. I want the case handled carefully," Gregson said urgently, his detachment gone.

"Why?"

"I don't want innocent bystanders hurt."

"It's a good thing I'm retired, Calvin, or I'd find your assumption that without your personal intervention innocent bystanders always get hurt in a homicide case offensive, and tell you to go fuck yourself." Orliff grinned. "But I don't have to take it personally anymore. By innocent bystanders, you mean Flora Lucas."

"And some of Lucas's friends."

"Ah."

"Don't say 'Ah' like that. I'm not after a cover-up. I don't want anyone turning a blind eye to anything illegal. I just want the case wrapped up as quickly as possible before the press starts playing detective."

"What about this reporter? He's already got a juicy little story, you say. He could go to press tomorrow."

Gregson sucked in his breath, nodding. "I think we bought a little time. The owner of Chapel's paper is sympathetic, and he's already told the staff that nothing must be printed until he says so, until he is sure."

"Chapel, like in 'church'?"

"Gavin Chapel."

"New to me. You mean he's got to find the killer before he can write up the investigation? That's a new one."

"Not exactly. No speculating, no fishing, that's what the owner's ordered. But sooner or later if the police don't release the story that the reporter already knows, about this hooker, word will get out, and the other papers will come sniffing around . . ."

"So you want someone to take charge who understands the need for what, discretion?"

"Someone who isn't out for brownie points."

"I never understood why that was such a no-no. Everybody's out for brownie points, except us retired guys, surely? But how long can this reporter be kept chained up?"

"Two weeks."

Orliff considered. He had no reason to like Gregson, who had caused him and his colleagues a lot of trouble in the past, but it was a delicious situation. Orliff's major talent had always been internal politics, ever since he had been made a sergeant thirty years before, and Gregson's dilemma seemed eminently manageable. The solution had been forming in his head since the beginning of their conversation. Having Gregson in his debt would be nice. He'd be able to call the lawyer up anytime.

"You don't figure to talk to Mackenzie yourself?"

"I already sort of have. I get the feeling if I went back he'd tell me to fuck off."

"So would I if I were him. Still. Okay. But what I need from you is some kind of guarantee that this is on the up and up. If there's a skeleton in Lucas's closet you know about, that I *ought* to know about, and I stub my toe on it, I'll get in touch with that reporter, tell him about this conversation. So is it on the up and up? I don't conspire to break laws, as they say."

"Of course it is. What do you *think* I would be asking you . . ."

"Okay, okay. Just tell me you want this killer caught, no matter who it is."

"That's what I want."

"I'll talk to Mackenzie, then. When I've figured out what to say."

"When will you call me?"

"You want me to report back? To you? You aren't paying me. This is pro bono publico stuff you want from me, like you're doing. Do I have the words right? No. You'll hear soon enough."

"Sorry. Of course. And thanks."

"Don't mention it. Ever. You and me, I mean. Not to your cronies, and most of all, not to your local MPP. Take the credit yourself. Just owe me."

Gregson looked startled and opened his mouth, but Orliff was rising, waving to someone a few yards away as he nodded to dismiss Gregson. Then he stopped, looking down. "What's with the boots, Calvin? Sorry, I'm being rude, right? Offensive. Sorry. But I haven't seen anyone in dress boots since my son left college. You developed weak ankles?"

"As a matter of fact, they aren't dress boots, Figaro. They are riding shoes." He pulled up his pant cuff to show Orliff that the boots stopped at the ankle. "The point is, you should never ride in shoes with laces. They might catch in the stirrup if you get thrown."

"That right?" Orliff scratched his head to find something to say that wasn't raucous and offensive. "That would be a real problem, I guess. Depends how you get to work. Comfortable, are they? Around town?"

"Of course. That's why I wear them."

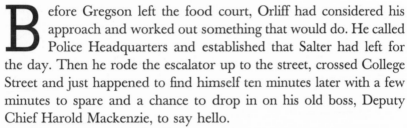

6

B efore Gregson left the food court, Orliff had considered his
approach and worked out something that would do. He called
Police Headquarters and established that Salter had left for
the day. Then he rode the escalator up to the street, crossed College
Street and just happened to find himself ten minutes later with a few
minutes to spare and a chance to drop in on his old boss, Deputy
Chief Harold Mackenzie, to say hello.

"Got a moment?" Orliff stood in the doorway.

Mackenzie waved him in, and Orliff took the chair by his desk.
"I'll be quick, Hal. This film guy I'm advising now, he made a movie
here about eight years ago, he says. He wondered what happened to
the guy who was advising him then. Said it was Salter, Charlie Salter.
I said I'd pass on his compliments, but Salter never worked with a
film company, did he?"

"Sure he did. That time the scriptwriter was knifed by the girl
from Czechoslovakia, as it was called then. Remember?"

Orliff, who remembered every detail, said, "Yeah. Vaguely.
Where is Charlie, by the way? Not in your office anymore?"

"Still works here. Left for home already."

"What have you got him doing these days? He's just about retired, surely?"

"Just about. Nothing much. Helps me out with this and that."

"How about you, Hal? Ready to hang up your skates yet?"

"Another ten years, I hope."

"That long? Will you keep busy? I hear the homicide rate is down. Marinelli's boys are looking up old cases."

"You don't want to believe the papers. We're busy."

"Nothing you can't handle, though."

"Biggest problem is bank robberies. We're getting there."

"No interesting homicides?" And then, to establish a connection in Mackenzie's head, he continued. "I just bumped into Calvin Gregson in the food court across the street. You noticed the way he's dressing these days?"

"Top of the line, you mean? Always was a snappy dresser. He can afford it."

"This is something different. He seems to be dressing *up*, not just looking sharp." Orliff mentioned the suit and the riding shoes. "Why would he worry about getting his feet caught in the stirrups when he's in court?"

"Maybe he goes for a gallop before he comes to work." Mackenzie giggled. "Anyway, you didn't drop by to talk about Gregson's boots. Know him well?"

"Everybody knows Gregson."

"He know *you*?"

"He remembered me. Why? A problem?"

"He's trying to put a little pressure on me about the Lucas case. Some lawyer got stabbed by a hooker."

"That right? What's Gregson's interest? Is he representing the hooker?" Orliff smiled. "Where's the money in that?"

"It's not her. Gregson came to warn me about some reporter who's sniffing around. But there's more than that. Says we don't seem to be taking the case very seriously."

"What does he mean by that?"

"I think he means that Lucas isn't like some kid killed in a fight on a subway platform. He was eminent, distinguished, all that shit. Him and his sister were pals of Gregson's."

"What are you going to do?"

"I could stick a firecracker up Marinelli's ass, I guess, but I think he's at a dead end. Next step will be to assign it to one detective so he can pick away at it, see if he can find another thread. Like Merton did, remember?"

Orliff remembered, mainly because Mackenzie was so fond of telling the story of the unsolved case of the woman murdered in her apartment. He would recount how Detective Merton *in his spare time* (Mackenzie always put the phrase in italics) knocked on every door in the neighborhood for three months until he found someone—an insomniac old lady who was sipping tea and looking out of her window when she saw a man come out of the fire-exit door of the apartment block next door. A rather dapper-looking man, she said, with blond hair like Alan Ladd, her favorite actor. She hadn't said anything before because she didn't take a newspaper and didn't know they were looking for anyone. No one had asked her. Mackenzie quoted the case whenever someone like Marinelli questioned the usefulness of going over old "open" files.

"That won't keep Gregson happy. But never mind Gregson. Be nice to see him unhappy. What did he say about Flora Lucas? That the MPP?"

"That's her."

"They're going to win next time, Hal. You know what she'll be doing?"

"Attorney general, according to Gregson."

"That's what I would guess. She could give you a bad time."

"Gregson said she's the rare case who wouldn't use her position to dump on me in a personal matter."

"Hal, Hal. Don't be naive. Anyway, she could be a saint but the press will make a story of it. 'Attorney general's brother: Still no clues to his killer.' That kind of thing. She won't want that. And who is this reporter you mentioned?"

"Guy named Chapel, works for this new paper."

"Him! Christ Almighty. You giving Marinelli any backup?"

"Where would I get 'backup'? You think I've got reserves?"

Orliff looked around the room. Following his glance Mackenzie said, "Yeah, I wish I had someone like Salter to give him."

It took Orliff a few seconds to realize that Mackenzie meant exactly what he said. He no longer considered Salter to be on active service, but he still wanted the idea of Salter, as it were. This was too easy. Orliff affected puzzlement. "So give him Salter. He's just counting paper clips until it's time to go, isn't he?"

Mackenzie shook his head. "Can't do that. They resent Salter over there, especially Marinelli's number two, Stevenson." He leaned forward, his stance confidential. "They don't like the idea of some kind of legend, you know, Salter of the Yard, that bullshit. And I don't want to give Salter a lousy time. He's practically got his slippers on. He doesn't need to slog around after a case like this until he retires."

"You don't think they'll ever find the hooker?"

"No. Nor does Marinelli. She'll turn up, in jail, probably, charged with possession. But not tomorrow. Maybe next year."

"Does Marinelli agree?"

"He doesn't have any other ideas."

"So tell him about Gregson and Flora Lucas and this reporter, and give him Salter."

But this was too quick for Mackenzie. "I've just finished telling you that Salter is the one guy Marinelli doesn't want around."

"Sure. But you've also been telling me that they'll never find the hooker, which is going to be a problem with a hotshot lawyer, a politician sister and an ace reporter all putting pressure on the unit. So tell them you've appointed a special investigator, special because of his high rank, and assign the case to Salter. Marinelli can explain to his boys that Salter's there to take the heat, not to solve the case."

Once again Orliff had gone too fast. "What heat is that?"

"The pressure from Gregson and Flora Lucas and the reporter, Hal."

Mackenzie gave it some thought, then nodded six or seven times. "Yeah. They'll see that, won't they? They've got to be glad to have someone take any heat, haven't they? I'll do it. Shit." Now he looked gleeful. "You always were a cunning bastard, Orliff. I'll clear it with Marinelli first thing. Hang on. What'll I tell Salter? I've just finished explaining to him why he should take it easy."

"Tell him the whole thing, exactly what his real assignment is, taking the heat off Marinelli—he'll know that, anyway. He'll be happy to have something to do. It's not as if he could screw up his career at this point, is it?"

"That's it. He's the only one around here with nothing to lose. Shall I tell him that?"

"I think he probably knows it. Don't make a big deal of it." Orliff stood up. "Gregson's going to a lot of trouble over Flora Lucas, isn't he? You ever notice that when you have a politician who is completely honest and public-spirited, the way they are *supposed* to be, everyone talks about their honesty and unselfishness, like it's a miracle. Now you can hear people's voices getting hushed when they mention Flora Lucas. Maybe that's what gets Gregson. Maybe she's his good deed. His real pro bono."

The next morning, Marinelli listened carefully to Mackenzie's suggestion. "I thought we'd just agreed to leave Salter out in the pasture."

"It's different now with this reporter sniffing around."

"You think this sister will be the next attorney general?"

"Everybody does. And things might get warm around here just with this goddamn reporter."

"Will you make an announcement?"

"What about? No, shit, no. I'll just put the word out. I won't even mention Salter by name. A senior investigator, I'll call him. What'll you tell Stevenson?"

"I don't have to explain myself to Stevenson. It looks kind of sudden, though. I'll tell them he's the window-dressing to satisfy some politician." Marinelli smiled. "I could kill two birds here. I've got a new man I haven't teamed up with anyone yet. He needs a wise old mentor to break him in."

"That doesn't sound like Salter."

"He *is* old, by our standards, and he's nobody's fool, is he?"

"Still, 'Wise old mentor'? Salter? Don't tell him *that.*"

Orliff's ideas were always clear as he explained them, but the deputy chief often found that in going over Orliff's suggestions later, he could not think through the possible ramifications. He kept losing track. In this case he felt uneasy about telling Salter the whole truth about Gregson's intercession, because Salter might ask if Marinelli knew it, and he wasn't sure what he would say. And should he tell Marinelli that Salter had been told? Mackenzie was no Machiavelli, nor was he meant to be. Just give Salter the direct assignment, he decided.

"Now, Salter," he said when he found him. "Don't go behind my orders, all right? I'm assigning you to Marinelli to help out with the Lucas case. All right? Don't get into it with Marinelli."

"What are you talking about, sir?" Salter asked, genuinely mystified.

"Never mind. Just report to Marinelli. Take it from there."

He's up to something, Salter thought, but what do I care? I've got the job. He said, "I could start this afternoon."

"Do that." Mackenzie nodded. "Give me anything else you're working on."

"He doesn't mind?"

"Marinelli? He looked happy to me."

"He's probably happy to have someone take the shit. This might be politically sensitive."

"That's the thing, Charlie," agreed the deputy chief, relieved to be on easier, more truthful ground. "If it was easy, Marinelli would have done it. It may not be doable."

"Then I can't lose, can I?"

"That's the way to look at it. Marinelli's waiting for you in his office." Mackenzie considered briefly telling Salter about the reporter, then decided that the reporter, like Gregson, was irrelevant. Might even inhibit Salter.

Salter's scheme for conducting his own investigation had not gotten off the ground. He had thought about it until his brain hurt without seeing how he could get to first base with no one aware of his actions. Now he had been handed a walk. So, more or less to propitiate the gods, he felt he ought to acknowledge his good fortune by telling someone he was grateful. He closed the door and called Orliff.

Orliff said, "Are you pleased? I thought you were twiddling your thumbs."

"Yeah, I was. As a matter of fact, I *am* pleased. I've got a little notion about this case, something about it that struck me at the beginning."

"That right? Did you tell Mackenzie, or Marinelli?"

"I tried to a couple of times, but I got the feeling I was butting in."

"So now's your chance."

"I didn't tell you my idea, did I?"

"No, you wrote it on a piece of cigarette paper, and I swallowed it so it would stay imprinted on my brain. What idea?"

"Sorry, sorry. I was thinking aloud. So you think I should accept this assignment?"

"Do I think *what?* You're a staff inspector, Charlie, not a special agent. You do what you're told."

Orliff put down the phone and dialed Calvin Gregson's office. The lawyer's secretary told him that he was on his way to Hazelton Lanes to see a shirtmaker, but she could reach him on his cell phone.

"Tell him to meet me in Holt Renfrew in thirty minutes," Orliff said, thinking how nice it was to be able to give orders to a guy like Gregson when you had something he wanted.

Gregson had added a dark blue brocade vest to the suit and the riding shoes. The two men found a place to drink coffee on the lower level.

"I think you're fixed up," Orliff said. "I've got them to put Salter on the case."

"Who's he?"

"A staff inspector, not a regular member of Homicide, but he's handled a couple of sensitive cases successfully. He's his own man."

"A lone wolf?"

"More of an odd duck. But he's the one *I* would want if it were me."

"Knows how to tread carefully, does he?"

"That's his nature. If he smells a cover-up, though, you won't be able to keep him quiet."

"I told you there isn't any cover-up. We just want the right answer as quickly and quietly as possible. Can you do one more thing for me? Ask Salter to come and see me as soon as he can."

"You want *me* to tell Salter to report to *you?* At your office, maybe? With his shoes shined? You hear what you are saying?"

"Right. Sorry. I understand. Right. Sorry. You had no hand in it. You really are a crafty bastard, aren't you? How come you're not a lawyer?"

"Poor guidance counseling in high school, I guess. Or the wrong high school."

"I don't need a teammate," Salter said. "When I need one, I'll ask you for one."

Marinelli shook his head. "We work in pairs, Charlie, remember? For a lot of reasons. Backup, mainly."

"In case of a fight? Who the hell is going to start something here? One of Lucas's Granite Club pals?"

"No, in court. You need someone to cover your ass, you know that, someone to testify you didn't use undue violence when you got that old lady in an armlock. We are getting too many complaints."

"If I see any trouble coming, I'll call for help."

"I'm serious, Charlie. The order comes from the chief."

"So assign someone to me, but keep him in your office until I need him."

"There's a guy just joined us. He's not long on the force but he had a lot of experience overseas before he came here."

"Let me guess: a visible minority?" Salter imagined a small Pakistani or Chinese, recruited in spite of the height requirements to quiet the demands for more ethnic representation on Toronto's traditionally white, Anglo-Saxon force. The West Indies had a presence on the force, but India, China and Sri Lanka were still underrepresented.

Marinelli laughed. "An audible minority, more like." He stepped to the door of the outer office. "Terry," he called across the room. "Come over for a minute."

A man in his mid-thirties, dark-skinned with acne-scarred cheeks, looked up from a computer, nodded, then stood up and crossed the room.

"This is Staff Inspector Salter," Marinelli said. "On assignment from the deputy's office to look after the Lucas case. I'm putting you with him. Charlie—Constable Terry Smith."

Salter put out his hand. Looking surprised, Smith responded and they shook hands.

Salter said, "Are you familiar with the case? I'll need to be filled in."

Smith said, "I'll need to fill myself in first, sir. I just arrived yesterday. I don't even know where the coffee machine is yet."

Salter said, "You're Scottish?" It seemed polite to acknowledge that he could identify the sounds he was hearing.

Smith said, "I am," and Marinelli, grinning, said, "See? An audible minority," and closed his door, leaving them to each other.

Salter said, "You just off the boat, you say?"

Smith shook his head. "I just came over to Homicide. I've been on the force for a year. I trained in Glasgow. I made detective and then decided to emigrate."

"Why?"

"My wife didn't like Glasgow. She's from Inverness. So we came over and I joined the Winnipeg police. Three years ago. Then we came to Toronto and I joined this lot. This is my first assignment in Homicide."

"Why did you leave Winnipeg?"

"My wife didn't like it."

"Did you?"

"I liked it fine. I liked Glasgow, too. Shall we get on?"

After a second to register that Smith was telling him to butt out, Salter said, "Let's go over the ground. I didn't ask for help, but your boss insisted. Okay? You say you don't know anything about the case, and I sure as hell don't. So let's make a start." He looked at his watch. "It's ten-thirty. Go back to your computer and read the file. I'll get rid of the paper on my desk and we can meet here at one-thirty, then you can tell me all about the Lucas case."

Smith was ready when they met again.

"The man's name was Lucas, Jeremy Baker Lucas. Fifty-five; a bachelor; lawyer; small, two-man practice, mainly in estate and mortgages; generally, looking after people with money, not problems. He was what I would call rich—belonged to three clubs, cottage in a place called Muskoka—you'll know where that is, sir? where he spent a lot of time in the summer; house in Costa Rica, where he spent much of the winter. You need a few shekels for that sort of thing, d'ye not? Actually, his law practice was more of a hobby. Hardly anyone came in off the street, and those that did usually ended up with his partner, but few as they were, Lucas's clients were well-heeled and the practice paid his rent, no doubt about that.

"In Toronto he rented an apartment, the place where he was killed. Not a luxury block, but what they call in Glasgow a 'guid address' "—Smith spoke the two words in dialect, and smiled to indicate that Salter should understand that Smith was aware of the quaint phrase—"near the intersection of Bedford Road and Prince Arthur." He looked up. "That's not far from Bloor Street. Bedford runs down to Bloor opposite the football stadium."

"You know the area?"

"Oh, sure. My wife works in a doctor's office nearby. And I've been to a couple of soccer matches at the stadium." He returned to his notes. "The rent for three bedrooms was three thousand five hundred a month. After his death his partner hired an accountant to glance over the books to reassure Lucas's clients that everything was in order, because he was managing a lot of money for five people, all old, well-fixed, who trusted him to look after their affairs, and in two cases to pay all their bills and give them an allowance. According to his partner, he handled the money very conservatively, no mutual funds, no second mortgages, and delegated the bill-paying to the secretary, which is fairly normal. He countersigned all the checks, and she kept some petty cash on hand for small purchases.

"In other words, he was exactly what he seemed—a well-heeled, semiretired lawyer who was in business mainly to have something to do and to have something to charge his expenses to."

"Family?"

"His sister, Flora, also comfortable . . ."

"Where did the money come from originally? I heard furs and liquor."

Smith shook his head. "There might have been a bit of that at the start, but Lucas's great-grandfather started a small office-supplies company selling sealing wax and string and so forth around the turn of the century, and when he was set up, went in for manufacturing paper clips and elastic bands, then went on to printing diaries, calendars, cards, invitations, all that kind o' stuff." Here Smith seemed to take a breath and resumed in a louder voice. "He made lots o' money, his sons more. Lucas's father carried on with the gold mine, so by the time Lucas and his sister came along naebody had to work again, but they carried on anyhow because they were from good lowland stock, the kind that couldn't be doing nothing. But he soon left the trade and became a gentlemen, a solicitor, and his sister went in for charitable work until she became an MP."

"MPP."

"What's the difference? I should have found out by now."

"An M.P.P. is a member of a *Provincial* Parliament," Salter explained, as he waited for Smith's explanation of why he had spoken the last sentences in an accent like an actor welcoming a stranger to the glen.

Smith looked up from his script with a slight flicker of knowingness around the corners of his mouth. "Am I going a bit fast for ye?" he asked, in the same accent.

"What's with the Harry Lauder impersonation?"

"Actually, I'm just giving you what I got from one of our colleagues who heard me speak, then went into the whole Rabbie Burns bit. Bloody Constable Macbeth, he called me. Claims the same tartan himself. Can you believe it?"

Salter leaned back, waiting for more.

"Professional Scotsmen," Smith explained. "I can't stand them."

"What are you, then? An amateur? You've still got an accent."

"I'm aware of that, but I still try to stay away from highlanders—sorry, *heelanders*—when I'm away from home because they piss me off and I'm sure they piss off everybody else, too. I'm from Glasgow. I've never eaten a haggis, or worn a kilt, or done any Scottish country dancing, and I don't know the words to 'Charlie Is Me Darling.' I'm a respectable working chap. Clan Smith, and the tartan comes from the wrapper around the toffees I ate as a wee lad."

"Well, well. That seems clear."

"Good. Shall we move on, sir?"

"In English."

"Aye. The accent was Hollywood Scottish, by the way, the language you people think we talk. If I talked like that around Drumchapel, they'd think I was speaking pure BBC English. Drumchapel is a district of Glasgow where they speak a language you would not understand a word of. Don't go there without an interpreter."

"I thought that was the Gorbals."

Smith looked irritated. "My grandmother grew up in the Gorbals and she claims she never heard a woman swear until she moved to Govan. Bobby Cairns's granny, it was."

"It must have gotten its reputation from somewhere."

"I suppose so, but my sister lives there now, and she's very particular. Shall we get on, sir?"

"Where did you get all this information about the Lucas family?"

"From the reference books. You left me a lot of time, and the Lucas family is pretty well-documented."

"What else do we know? Lucas was a bachelor. Was he gay?"

"Not if we make assumptions about the nature of his dealings with the only suspect in the case so far."

"Who is?" Salter knew well what he was going to hear, the tiny bit of information he had overheard Marinelli telling Mackenzie.

"There's a hoo-er in the case," Smith said, grinning, emphasising the word and the pronunciation so that Salter had to ask about it.

"Hoor? What's that? A scotch whore?"

"That's right, sir. Well done. I like the sound of it, don't you? It's different from 'whore.' A whore sounds to me like some poor girl without any knickers, shivering on a street corner under a gaslamp. It's an ugly word, don't you think?"

"And 'hoor'?"

"Nice and warm, a belly-dancer on the side."

Salter laughed. "Tell me about our hoor."

"The neighbors reported one lurking around the block the night Lucas was killed." The remnants of Smith's accent dwelled fondly, comically, on 'lurrrking'.

"What did they mean?"

"One of them saw her getting into the elevator, and the other one spied her on Lucas's floor."

"How did she get in the building? No security?"

"The usual. Either you press the buzzers until someone responds without asking, or you walk in, smiling gratefully, with one of the tenants. It's a rare body who will challenge you. But in this case, there's probably a simple explanation—he was expecting her and buzzed her up."

"Expecting her? Oh, right. I was thinking of something else. What made her seem like a hooker? A hoor. How did they know?"

"Silver boots; skirt up round her arse, a blouse that showed off her titties, and she was made up like Cruella, one said. Who's Cruella, though I can imagine?"

"A Disney character in a film called *101 Dalmatians*. I saw it about twenty-five years ago. A terrific movie, but make sure not to see the remake. So she was dressed for work, was she?"

"That seems to be the way of it."

"What do you make of it? Her."

"It's fishy. I would have thought that a poo-bah like Lucas could have paid for a bit of discretion."

"Maybe she just forgot her coat. Maybe the rest of the costume was contracted for on the assumption she'd cover it up until she got inside. You know, maybe Lucas *wanted* a 'hoor,' not a whore."

"I never thought of it like that, sir."

"What did you think?"

"Just that it was fishy, strange, incongruous. I didn't arrive at any conclusions."

"But on the surface it looks like a hooker who lost it, and stabbed him with a . . . what?"

"A kitchen knife. A Victorinox."

"A what?"

"That's the make. A big one. From his own kitchen."

"His?"

"Apparently."

"So she didn't plan to stab him when she arrived?"

"Not from the look of it so far."

"Did she rob him?"

"All the desk drawers had been tipped out. The cleaning lady says Lucas always paid her in cash, and I understand a Toronto tart costs mebbe a couple of hundred. It's a bit less in Winnipeg and around Argylle Street where I come from. I doubt they take American Express, these ladies, except the ones that work for regular escort services. So he mebbe had a few hundred on hand. Except for cabs and tips and the barber, though, little things like that, he did everything with plastic."

"His wallet?"

"Empty of cash. Everything else was there."

"Was there a sign of any fight?"

"Forensic said he was clean. No skin under his fingernails, that sort of thing. They collected a few hairs and fibers from his bathrobe, but they will all be his, probably."

"So he allowed someone to get close to him and they stabbed him. Who found him?"

"The janitor and the police. It was Saturday morning and on Saturday mornings Jerry Lucas—his friends called him Jerry—always went for a walk with a friend he had known in law school, a widower. It was their weekly constitutional. On this morning the friend waited at home for Lucas's knock, but Lucas, usually so punctual, hadn't appeared by ten-thirty and he became concerned. At first he was concerned that he had forgotten that Lucas had told him he would be away in Greece or somewhere for a couple of weeks. He was afraid he was reaching the age of forgetfulness, as he put it."

"How old is he?"

Smith consulted his notes. "Fifty-five, sir. But he was more concerned because he belongs to the school of psychology which says that if you forget an appointment you are making a statement about your feelings for the person you are meeting. Some such crap. But this was a regular date, so to speak, so he phoned Lucas's apartment and got no answer. He went off on his walk alone then, because nine times out of ten these things have a simple explanation, nothing psychological at all.

"When he returned from the walk, he phoned Lucas again, and when he got no reply he phoned Lucas's law partner, a man named Derek Fury, who would know if Lucas had gone away, but he knew about nothing like that, so the partner asked the police to rouse the superintendent to take a look, and that's when they found him. You don't want the patrol car's report, do you, sir? What I've told you is my own amalgam of all the reports I've read so far."

"I'm getting the story. Keep going."

"Now we move on to our investigation, starting with the scene-of-the-crime boys, I think. We found no signs of a struggle, some evidence of a minor robbery, nothing much in the way of other evidence beyond the knife."

"They got fingerprints?"

"The knife was wiped clean. They got some from the knife block on the counter, but they don't match any on file. So if they find a suspect they'll be able to say pretty clearly if she held the knife, but not having the prints on file rather damages the idea that it was a whore, doesn't it? It would in Glasgow."

"I don't think every hooker is on file. You can check it with the Vice Squad, but these girls come and go. New ones arrive from the country every day."

"This one must have been here long enough to get connected to Lucas. She came to the apartment, he was waiting, so he must have ordered her up. It sounds to me like a regular appointment."

"Suppose she's just a girl he ran across in a bar, making a little extra on the side, a student, maybe."

"We're dealing with a 'hoor,' though, are we not? It's hard to fit the painted image even onto a theater arts student, say, trying to earn her tuition."

"Keep going."

Smith returned to his notes. "The Homicide Unit obviously had to begin by looking for this woman, and they've spent a long time and a lot of manpower. They had a description of her. Did I tell you she had blond hair with silver streaks, maybe to match her boots? It all adds up to a striking picture.

"They had lots of pictures of Lucas, of course, though he wasn't so memorable, the kind of face you see in the business section every day having just been made chairman of some company: heavy jowls, grey crinkly hair, white teeth.

"They showed his picture and her description around, but they found no one who recognized them, and they did not have the feeling that the ladies on Jarvis Street were clamming up, either. The other women on the street had no ideas, and none of them had been cruised by Lucas, so the squad came up blank. Either the woman had disappeared after a very short stay, or she had never worked in the area." He looked up at Salter expectantly.

"That's it?"

"Somebody else thinks she worked the street. Several of the women interviewed by the squad reported that someone else had been around, asking the same questions, with the same description."

"Someone who knew what she looked like?"

"Apparently so."

"That doesn't make sense."

"Of what, sir?"

Salter knew he looked confused and tried to make light of it. "I have a feeling about this woman that she was no hooker at all, but someone dressed up to kill Lucas. Maybe even sent by someone else."

"A *plot*, do you think, sir?" Smith gave the word an ironic resonance."

"The last time it happened, it was, yes."

Smith waited for an explanation.

"This reminds me of another case I had." Salter swallowed his embarrassment. "Come on, Smitty. Think. If I'm right, who would have been hawking her description up and down Jarvis?"

"Someone who thought she *was* a hooker and had her description? Someone not acquainted with your theory that she was just dressed up for the night?"

"You think I'm full of shit?"

"I'm trying to grapple with the problem, sir. There's only one answer, is there not? It was someone who saw her that night who hasn't told us about it."

"Keep going."

"Lucas's killer, in fact."

"Why is he looking for her now?"

"He thinks she can identify him. That right?"

"It works, doesn't it?"

"We'd better find her before he does."

"If I'm right, then she's disappeared, or her costume has."

"So while he's looking for her, we'll look for him?"

"Let's keep thinking about it."

"In case you're wrong, you mean? In case she is a whore, like the squad believes."

"Then who is this guy?"

"Her pimp?"

Salter wasn't listening. "*Now* I'm glad you're here, Smitty, because you can cover my ass, see. While I follow my hunch, you will go the regular route. Assume she's a hooker, and go find her."

"We'll stay in touch, will we? You and me?"

Salter grinned. "Oh, sure. Let's get back to your report now. You finished with the homicide investigation?"

"Nearly. They've interviewed everyone except the sister, Flora Lucas, who was away at the time of the homicide, and hasn't found time to talk to them since she returned. They interviewed Lucas's law partner, who is mystified as to why anyone would want to kill Lucas, and feels sure it was a random act. He says he knows nothing about Lucas's sex life. He was surprised by the idea of a prostitute, though in the absence of a girlfriend or mistress he had always assumed that Lucas had an 'arrangement' as he called it, though nothing as flashy as a 'hoor.' "

Salter said, "What's all this about Flora Lucas being too busy to see us? Since when did homicide detectives take that kind of crap? Her brother's been stabbed, and . . ."

"She's an MPP, sir. Her appointment book is crammed, especially after she's been away. She didn't get back until a couple of days ago, because when she got the news she was sick, in a Costa Rican hospital. She came back as soon as she could travel."

"Call her office and tell her I'll be there at ten, or eleven or twelve, whatever is the least inconvenient for her. But I will talk to her tomorrow morning."

"Aye, so you will. In the meantime, will I . . ."

"Talk to the detectives who had the case—Barlow and Jensen?— about the net they put out for Miss Silver Boots. See if it's worth following up. Maybe you and I should have a look at the area. But tonight, when the tenants are home, go around the block again, find anyone who saw her, that night or any other time. Especially Lucas's neighbors. Were they aware of hookers calling on a regular basis? Did they see any other visitors? Ever? Did they know anything at all about him? Did they hear anything through the walls? I'll catch up with you here tomorrow."

A feeling that he had not been fully briefed ought to have made Salter wary, but it was having the opposite effect. He was fairly sure now that if Marinelli had thought the case was easily wrapped up, then he, Salter, would not have gotten it. The reason that he *had* gotten it was the probable difficulty of solving it—homicide investigations decay rapidly after the first day—and the possible peripheral involvement of politicians. If he blundered he would make headlines.

Having come to the conclusion that he could wind up as the goat, Salter considered his position calmly as he confirmed to himself that, this close to retirement, he didn't care, and certainly had no intention of proceeding cautiously.

8

S alter watched Joe Lichtman tuck himself into the corner of the back court, ready to spring forward and smash back his serve. For twenty-five minutes (about as long as he could play these days) Salter had been hitting his right-hand service as hard as he could to the same spot on the wall so that it came back to Lichtman at shoulder height. It gave him a big advantage over Lichtman for the first ten minutes. Then, as always, the serve had slowed down, just enough to give Lichtman a chance to hit it, but not so easy as to make Salter need to search for a different serve to finish the game. So far they were even in games, and he was ahead by two points in the third and final game, and needed a point to win. Salter decided that now was the moment to see if Lichtman was watching carefully.

They had been playing together for fifteen years. Salter's partners had steadily diminished in number, through death or retirement from the game—retirements that were usually a giving in to age, or obesity, or the fear of a heart attack. Only two men were left with whom he played regularly, only two who were prepared to die with their sneakers on: Lichtman, the lawyer, and Toogood, the chartered accountant. Toogood had become egg-shaped and bald over the years, but he remained light on his feet and retained an extraordinarily hard backhand—it was his only decent shot—which Salter couldn't return. They also were about even.

If anything, Lichtman had lost weight over the last ten years as he had become absorbed in the pastime of exercising his body, a pastime which had become a preoccupation. Nowadays when Salter arived at the club, he found Lichtman in the exercise room stretching himself, and after their game he moved on to the rowing machines to work on his stomach. Unlike the swelling elliptoid of Toogood, Lichtman in the shower looked to Salter like an arrangement of various-size balls, joined with rope and covered with skin. His biceps and his calves were fist-size iron balls, jiggling up and down. His buttocks were two cannonballs that looked as if they would hurt to sit on. Two lines of ping-pong balls rippled down the center of his stomach on either side of his navel. Balls appeared on his shoulders when he raised his arm to soap his head, and recently he had completed the effect by shaving his head, claiming it was more comfortable in the summer; but Salter suspected it was actually because Lichtman liked to present the image of a hard iron ball growing out of his shoulders.

Lichtman was fit; it was his big advantage over everyone in the club over fifty (he was sixty-four). So far he had never beaten Salter decisively; that is, never twice in a row. Today he hoped to.

Salter had more modest ambitions. He didn't mind if Lichtman, who had been gaining on him steadily since Salter's easy victories of ten years before, finally beat him, he told himself. He would satisfy his own long-held ambition simply by continuing to play. When he had learned to play, late in life as he thought then, in his early forties, he had read in the club magazine of a member of seventy who "still played twice a week." The phenomenon was referred to in the same admiring way people used to speak of the old king of Norway, who continued to play tennis at ninety.

Salter had no idea at the time whether the seventy-year-old member had achieved something of real significance, but as the years passed he remembered the story of that old member and set himself the lifetime objective of playing two games in the week after his seventieth birthday. In the meantime, his day-to-day ambition was to continue to keep Lichtman and Toogood at bay.

Now Salter lifted his racket, Lichtman crouched ready to spring, and Salter patted the ball just hard enough to make it plop off the wall into safe territory three feet in front of Lichtman's racket, as the lawyer waited for the fast smash at shoulder height that Salter *always* served. Lichtman sprang, but not in time; he connected, groveling, so poorly that the ball banged into the tin.

"Motherfucker," Lichtman said. (He was the exception among Salter's partners, using obscenities lavishly and with relish.) "Prick," he added in a conversational tone. "Try that again."

"I don't need to," Salter said. "That's game."

"Cocksucker!!" Lichtman agreed, then leaned on his racket for a second, smiling. "All right. I had you, you know that?"

Salter affected a look of puzzlement. "When?"

"The whole game. Right from the first couple of points. You know that. I had you. It was my game right up to the end."

"I got lucky then, I guess."

"That's *exactly* what happened. You got lucky. Fuck-pig. I was playing *way* better than you today." Lichtman smiled again. "Ah, shit. Still, if you don't take it seriously, it's just a game, isn't it? Come and buy me a drink."

In the health club's bar, Lichtman sipped on a large glass of orange juice while Salter swilled his beer. "When do you allow yourself a beer?" Salter asked.

"I *allow* myself one anytime. I just don't drink the stuff."

"Or any other booze, or coffee, or tea, eh? What do you eat, Joe? Are you a vegetarian?"

"I don't eat carcass meat, if that's what you mean."

"What other kind is there?"

"I don't eat fish, either. Eggs are okay once in a while. I'm not rigid about it."

"Yes you are. You're a fanatic, you know that?"

"That's what my wife says, too."

"She has to cope with you."

Lichtman shook his head. "She left me when I stopped eating chicken."

"What's it in aid of, Joe? Are you a Buddhist? Or trying to live forever? Or just want to improve the quality of the few years you have left?" Salter assumed a mock-solemn tone for the last few words.

"I'm doing it for its own sake." Lichtman's fatless, knobby face grew dark with shyness. "I'm interested in my body. It started out with just getting in shape, but I got involved in it. I'd like my body to work as efficiently as possible, so I keep it tuned up and try to provide the best kind of fuel."

"Why? You thinking of winning the seniors' marathon?"

"I just want to get nature's best performance out of myself. The marathon would be too much of an overload. Think of it like this: for me, my body is a garden, something I cultivate. I fertilize it, water it and keep the soil receptive to new growth. I'd no more feed it liquor or meat juice than I would feed them to a rose bush. They are poisons. Am I making sense?"

"You're mad, you know that? We've been playing for twenty years, so I'm entitled to say that. Why do you play squash, then? There must be a more efficient set of exercises."

"Two reasons. One: the real test of a garden is what it will grow. Squash allows me to test my body, to see if the latest modifications of exercise and diet have measurably improved my game."

"And the other reason?"

"To eventually beat the shit out of you."

Salter laughed. "In the meantime, I, sack of putrifying carcass meat laced with chemical additives that I am, will continue to whip your ass, even when I'm hung over. So cultivate your garden, and much good may it do you."

Lichtman smiled, knowing that in the end he must win, all of it. "I hear you're investigating the Lucas murder," he said.

Salter, slightly jolted, said, "Where would you have heard that? I thought you stayed away from criminals."

Lichtman nodded. "I do contracts, mainly. Actually, I picked it up at a lunch club I belong to. Mainly retired lawyers. One of them was asking did anyone know you. I told him we played squash. He said Calvin Gregson had asked him about you, and then it came up that you were on the Lucas case."

"You know Gregson?"

"A little bit."

"He seems a bit of a dandy."

"How do you mean?"

"The suit, the tie with horses on it . . ."

"Tie? With horses? What color?"

"Yellow, I think."

Lichtman laughed. "That's new. I haven't seen that. Is he still wearing riding shoes? Yes? I've got a theory about Calvin. He reminds me of a character in a story somewhere who is slowly being transformed—what's the word? metamorphosed?—into someone else. You know the story."

"Pinocchio?"

"No, but that's the idea."

"A werewolf story? You know—one day he looks down and his hands are sprouting hair."

"Maybe that's what I'm thinking of. Whatever it is, I'm convinced Calvin is changing his shape, bit by bit. We'll have to wait to see where he ends up. At the moment it looks like 'English country gent.' "

"I'll let you know if he gets there when I'm watching."

"If he buys one of those flat caps, that would tell you."

The two men enjoyed Lichtman's fancy for a few moments, then he resumed. "Maybe he's just bored. You know, reached fifty with all the money he'll ever need and not getting a kick out of it anymore.

"There are people you can go to, consultants who specialize in remaking you from the outside in, kind of the opposite of psychiatrists. They start by changing your wardrobe. They've analyzed Gregson's problem and come up with a new image for him. If you see him walking through the Eaton Center with a pack of foxhounds, give me a call." Lichtman sipped his juice. "Actually, I kind of like the guy. He's fun to watch, in court or out, and most of the lawyers I know are boring as hell."

"You ever meet Lucas?"

"Oh, yes, I knew him a little bit, too, but he was much more of a social type than I am. Moved in diferent circles, you might say. You wouldn't see him in a place like this, for example. But he used to belong to my book group, before I joined. I saw him at a concert once, talking to another member of the club, woman named Louise Wilder. They weren't together, just chatting.

"Is there anyone in your group who was there when Lucas was a member?"

"Most of them. I'm the new boy. But Sylvia Sparrow, our leader, is the one you might want to talk to. She's the one who organizes us. I think she set it up in the first place."

"Do you have her number with you?"

"No, but she works for the provincial government, something to do with the Human Resources Department. You know—personnel."

Salter finished his beer, but he was still sweating. He'd need to take a few more minutes if he was going to come out of the shower with his pores closed.

He motioned to Lichtman's glass. Lichtman shook his head, and they moved away from the bar and walked over to watch a game in progress on the adjacent court.

"This book group," Salter said. "How does it work? You all read the Book of the Month Club selection and talk about it?"

"More or less. But we choose our own books. Each of us puts in the name of a book before the season starts, and then we draw them out. I'm up next month."

"What's your book?"

"It's called *Elective Affinities*."

"By?"

"Goethe."

Salter said, "Gertha who? Sorry. No, I know the name. Famous old German, right? You do all classical stuff?"

"Last month we read *The Human Factor*, a Graham Greene thriller. Do you know it?"

"No, should I?"

"Some of them thought it was too lightweight for us. But the whole point was to discuss if a book like that has any meat in it."

"Has it? Did it have?"

"I thought so."

They were nearly dry now. "What do you do, then? Sit around in a circle while the leader of the discussion explains what to look for? Like in college?"

"Not in our club. What the leader of the discussion does in our group is prepare questions, maybe a dozen or twenty. Then we just see where we go. For instance, tell me the name of a book you've read lately."

"I can't remember the name of a book I've read lately. I'll come clean. I haven't read any books lately. How about a play? I saw *The Merchant of Venice* last summer."

"Perfect. So your first question would be, 'Was Shakespeare anti-Semitic?' If you've got any Jews in the group that could keep you going all night. What else have you seen?"

"*As You Like It*. Back up a minute. How about, 'Do you feel sorry for Shylock?' or rather, 'Are you supposed to feel sorry for Shylock?' "

"Great. Now. *As You Like it*. Got a question?"

"I overheard a good one in the intermission. 'Is Rosalind gay?' "

Lichtman shook his head. "In a mixed group you want to stay away from sexual interpretation. People start looking at the wall, or they get noisy to show they're not diffident. But you get the idea."

Salter stood up. "Next week?"

"Of course."

"Good. Don't eat too many prunes."

9

Flora Lucas was waiting in her office for him at ten o'clock the next morning. She was a rather large, soft woman with a pink-and-white complexion and light-brown hair caught up behind her head in a comb, or combs. She seemed to be wearing no makeup, but Salter wondered if she could have managed so smooth and finished-looking a surface at forty-eight without it. She had spent time on her hands and nails, certainly, and when she stood up he saw she was wearing very pretty shoes made of some kind of embroidered cloth. He found himself attracted to her, struck once more by how, entering his sixties, he had narrowed down the women he liked into two kinds—large, soft ones and small, light ones.

"This is a homicide inquiry, ma'am, but I'll be as quick as I can."

She stared at him. "What on earth is the matter with you? You called my secretary yesterday to arrange a meeting and fix a time and I accepted the first time you suggested. So here I am. I've cancelled my appointments for the next hour. I know it's a homicide inquiry. My brother is the homicide, remember. Now, why are you taking up this attitude?" Her voice was clear and penetrating.

"I understood you had difficulty finding time for my predecessor."

"I had difficulty being here. When Jerry was killed I was in Costa Rica, staying at his house, as a matter of fact. That is, I was in the hospital there, where I spent my whole vacation, laid low by a bug I think I caught on the plane."

"Maybe the water . . . ?"

"The water in Costa Rica is drinkable. I think it was the plane."

"I understand we had trouble finding you."

"My secretary had orders to say I was away at a retreat. The point was to be out of touch. My secretary took me a bit too literally. I should have said, 'Unless Jerry is killed.' " A tear formed and made its way down her cheek, a tiny leak in the dam. She made no effort to wipe it away.

Salter paused, more moved by that silent tear than if she had broken down. He continued, "So you didn't hear of his death until you returned."

"I got the news in the hospital, made some phone calls to make sure his partner was looking after things temporarily. My brother had no children; we had no other relatives at all. All I was needed for was to confirm Jerry's identity, and to get back to Toronto immediately I would have had to charter a plane, and I was still pretty weak. So I came back on the regular flight on Friday, and here I am."

Salter said, "There's a space on the form I have to fill out for the name of someone who could confirm you were in Costa Rica."

"You can leave it blank for the moment."

Salter looked at her skeptically.

"Until I trust you," she added.

"With what?"

"My personal life. They tell me I can, but I'd like to be sure."

And who are "they," Salter wondered. Lichtman's lunch club? "I may have to fill in the blank before that."

"Yes? In the meantime, what else do you want to know?"

"Were you close to your brother?"

"He has always been my closest friend from very early on. We were thrown together by an absentee father and a mother who devoted herself to a moral crusading movement. Nowadays we would say she was a member of a cult. She tried to bring me into the fold when I was in my last year at high school, but Jerry found an excuse to get me into McGill, away from her influence. She had tried to enlist him a few years earlier, but the effect was to cult-proof him.

"We, that is my mother and I, lived in Kingston then, and it would have been natural for me to go to Queen's, where Mother had a group going. Jerry had just begun work for a Montreal law firm and so I enrolled at McGill, moved into a dorm and spent the weekends with him, in his apartment. My mother wanted me to commute, so she could continue proselytizing, but she wasn't very pressing, because she was more interested in the movement than in me and spent a lot of time at international get-togethers, and as a sort of missionary. So Jerry and I remained very close.

"I'm sorry, this is turning into a speech isn't it? But when someone close to you dies suddenly you tend to think so much about them, going over and over it trying to get things straight for yourself, that it's all ready when someone asks a question."

"Didn't you get into his hair at all? I mean, swinging bachelor with kid sister underfoot. Look, I can come back. Tell me who his close friends were, and I'll come back later."

She had begun to cry again, lightly, a few bright tears. She pulled a tissue from a box on her desk and dabbed at her face. "I have to cry sometime," she said. "I'm actually doing rather well. If you don't mind, I'll be all right in a minute."

The door behind Salter opened and the secretary started to come in. Flora Lucas waved her away without looking up, and then, as Salter stood up to leave, signaled him to stay. In a minute she was done, her face mopped, and she was ready to face Salter again.

"Where were we? Thanks for sitting still. It makes for less of a fuss. Now. What were we on about? My mother. Yes. Every girl should have one. My brother, though. I think some girls have a relationship with their fathers like I had with Jerry. Extremely unhealthy, I'm sure any psychologist would tell you, but pretty goddamn wonderful all the same. And then I got lucky again when I fell in love with the man who became my husband. Then I got unlucky, because he died three years after we married. But now we are getting personal, aren't we? I want to talk about Jerry. The thing is, Jerry practically raised me; he guided me and counseled me through all that growing-up time until I graduated and knew what I wanted to do. His girlfriends helped—they sort of stood in for sisters, a couple of them. Jerry created a home for me and conducted his own affairs with—what's the word—decorum, when I stayed with him. His girlfriends didn't sleep with him when I was there, and it was a long time before I realized that they slept with him whenever I wasn't there. I think he felt I should be allowed to grow up without having adult life forced on me before I was quite ready."

Suddenly she let out a bark of laughter. "Some Sundays we even went to church. At some point, though, I grew up, and he relaxed and I started to find the occasional female at breakfast on Sunday morning. But it was his home, not mine, so I always made my boyfriends go home at night. All of which is totally irrelevant, I would think, but as I said, my head is full of him. What's your next question?"

"You've answered it. Did you know about the woman who was seen around the block the night he was killed?" Salter described her.

"That doesn't sound like Jerry's kind of thing. But . . . I don't know . . . you men . . ." She waited for his response.

"He never married?"

"Oh, yes. *His* marriage lasted five years. Nothing sinister, or even sad. She wanted a home, and he wanted a sexual partner. He shouldn't have married. After that he had a number of partners, but no one for a couple of years now. I assumed he was winding down, and that wouldn't have worried Jerry; he wouldn't rush about trying to reinflate his libido by hiring hookers. For him sex would just be something that had a season, like Old Farts' Hockey."

"Like what?"

"When he was fifty, he still played hockey with a bunch of men his age, hence the name."

The door opened again, and the secretary appeared carrying several sets of papers. Flora Lucas waved her away, adding, "Two minutes, Muriel." She turned to Salter, "Two minutes. Question?"

"Can you make any sense of this woman in silver boots?"

"I find it inconceivable that my brother had developed a taste for that kind of sex. I'm not speaking about the morality of it; Jerry didn't give a damn about private morality, his own or anyone else's, though he was fierce about public morality, behaving ethically in your relationships. As a politician, I felt his eye on me all the time, but he couldn't care less about who I . . . lived with.

"Now I'm rambling on, again, aren't I? I just had a thought. I think I know why he never married again. I knew one of his partners, not as a friend, just someone who works in the buildings here, some kind of editor." She gestured out the window to the legislature. "She told me once, in a drunken confidence, that she was hung up on Jerry still, after they split up, but she couldn't stand not being wanted. *Needed*, sure, as a hostess and in bed, but not *wanted*. I think Jerry didn't like women much, but he was normal and he had his needs. It wouldn't surprise me to hear of a discreet mistress, but not one with silver boots."

"What *was* he interested in?"

"Music. Japanese art. Canoeing. And gambling. Cards mostly, but he like to go to the track in the summer."

"A heavy bettor?"

"I thought so, but he could afford it. We inherited enough. I don't think he ever bet with bookies, though."

"Who did he play cards with?"

"Coming, Muriel." She waved to the opening door and stood up. "Now your two minutes are up. Ask Derek Fury, Jerry's partner. He'll know." She passed Salter on her way out the door, plucking the papers from her secretary's hand.

"What was the name of that girlfriend?" Salter asked as she was passing him. "Do you know that?"

She stopped, looking concerned, "All right. Jane Rudd. But, please, not from me. I hardly know her, but I don't trust her and I would sooner not have my name connected with her. Can you make her just one of the names on a list the police have compiled?"

"That's what she is. Just the next name on my list."

"Thanks. Now, I'm available any time you want, except right at this minute." She strode away down the corridor.

Muriel stood holding the door.

"Busy lady," Salter said.

"Woman," Muriel corrected, closing the door and trotting off in pursuit of her boss.

Salter approached the interview with Jane Rudd with care. She was a permanent civil servant, entitled to a large office with an outside window, but with no secretary to bar the door. She had a red-and-brown complexion and a weathered look, with large, flat, red cheeks, and a mass of dark, tangled hair messily caught up with a clip above one ear. Her blouse, or dress—she stayed seated behind her desk and it was hard to see—looked unpressed and was held at her throat with a large ornamental safety pin. On top of this she wore a knitted cardigan, the sleeves dangling loose. She looked as if she had dressed straight from her laundry basket. Salter wondered if being an editor gave her the license of the artist. He guessed she was about fifty.

Salter had anticipated that Jane Rudd would not be pleased to be part of the investigation, and that he might expect some hostility. But when he identified himself and told her his mission, she said, "I was intending to get in touch with you myself."

"Why?"

"When you are as close to someone as I was to Jerry . . ." She left the sentence in midair.

"Were you his partner once?"

"We were lovers. In the fullest sense."

You went all the way, Salter thought. Aloud, he asked, "When did your relationship end?"

"Does real love ever end?"

Salter had now established that he was in the presence of some kind of hysteria, perhaps an obsession, and that her answers would be filtered through her need to confirm her love for Lucas. He decided to shelve his questions about the hooker.

"When did you last see him?"

"It seems like only days."

"In real time? Weeks? Months? This year?"

She waved the question away. "Some weeks, I suppose," she said eventually.

"But not recently?"

She shrugged.

Now Salter put the question he would have preferred to avoid. "Were you aware of any other woman in his life, before you, after you, or at the same time?"

"There was no 'after.' We never separated. I just hadn't seen him lately. And there was no other woman before who mattered. Except his sister, that is."

Salter heard the suggestion in the remark, and saw it in the bold and sideways glance that accompanied it, but ignored it. What Jane Rudd was implying would make no difference to his investigation, as far as he could see, and he judged that if he even acknowledged that he understood her hint, she was capable of denying any knowledge of what he was talking about and bending her hysteria into an attack on him.

"Do you know of any women who *didn't* matter?" he asked.

She shook her head violently and turned to the window, her hand at her throat.

Salter gave up. The woman was being ridiculous, and he doubted that she had any real information that he could not get elsewhere.

Still looking out the window, she said, "I won't come to the service."

"The funeral? Why not?"

"I couldn't bear it."

"Nobody likes funerals. Would they . . . expect you?"

"I have no idea. I imagine so."

"It's your own choice entirely, I would think." Salter stood up. He wanted to get away from her and return when she got her balance back. "I'll leave my card in case you want to get in touch."

True to the little scene she was acting out, she remained staring out the window.

Back in the office, Salter found a message from Calvin Gregson, asking him to call.

The lawyer answered immediately. "I'm told you've been put in charge of the Lucas investigation, Staff Inspector. I'm very glad. Jerry was a friend of mine and I hope you catch the bastard who killed him soon. I just called to say that, and if there is anything I can do, any question I can help you with, don't hesitate to call."

"Thanks for the offer. You mean his habits, do you? Whether he wore a hat, stuff like that?"

"Anything."

"That's very public-spirited of you, Mr. Gregson. I'll make a note of it." He hung up.

10

"Are we off, then, sir?" Salter's new assistant asked him.

"Smitty, why would one of Toronto's leading criminal lawyers make himself available to provide information about Lucas, information he knows perfectly well we can get from a number of people?"

"They were pals, mebbe?"

"Yes, but he knows I've got Lucas's partner, and his sister, and others. I don't need him."

"Maybe he needs you."

"Sure he does. He's trying to insert himself into the information loop about the case."

"That's solved, then. Shall we be off?"

"By the way, a little job for you. Check up on Flora Lucas. She says she was in Costa Rica until last Friday, staying at her brother's house, but most of the time in the hospital. Confirm that, would you?"

"You mean get on the blower to Costa Rica? I don't even know where it is."

"Start with the consul. He'll be in the Yellow Pages. Find out when she entered the country and when she left. The address of her brother's house will be there somewhere. Ask the local police to confirm she was there, if you can find someone who speaks English. Check with the hospital how long she stayed there."

"Sir, why? What's going on? Why are we doing this?"

"Proper procedure, Smitty. I told you, this is what we're supposed to do, how we are supposed to proceed, so I'm showing you the proper way. Covering my ass. Make a note of it. We must check up on the whereabouts of all possible suspects."

"You suspect her?"

"Smitty, close the door. Now. An unreliable witness has given me to understand that Lucas and his sister may have been involved in a taboo relationship."

"At their age? I've heard of it among poor kids in Glasgow, but not when they grew up. You think that's right? True, I mean. I know it's not *right.*"

"I don't believe it for a second, so I'm personally going to take no notice of hints like that. But there's you to consider. If I fall flat on my ass, I'd like to know we've followed routine. That's you."

"Sir, can I ask if something is bothering you? I mean you're talking a bit strange. A bit silly if you don't mind me saying it."

Salter laughed. "I'm following my hunch, Smitty, that's all. But let's clean up Costa Rica before we tick it off. Now, tell me about Lucas's apartment."

Smith said, "It's no' a big block of flats, not by Glasgow standards. I've spoken to all the tenants on his floor except two who the janitor says are on vacation. Two of them saw the woman. One of them lives next door and rode up in the elevator about seven in the evening, and saw her knocking on Lucas's door."

"Wearing all the gear?"

"Aye, but here is the thing they didn't tell us before, she was wearing a raincoat over the rest, a slicker, the chap called it, but I think he meant raincoat. He said she was wearing a white slicker and holding the front closed, as if she had nothing on underneath. Now this chap thinks she didn't see him in the corridor, because when she turned away to go into Lucas's apartment she let the slicker fall open and he got a glimpse of a lot of leather straps. Her costume."

"So it looks as if Lucas had an arrangement with a tart who knew his apartment number. She was dressed for work with a white slicker on top. Maybe Lucas told her to wear both, the slicker for the neighbors, the costume for him."

"That fits."

"So we just have to find her. By now she'll be in Winnipeg or Vancouver and she won't be wearing the outfit, or the slicker, I guess. Could he describe anything else about her?"

Smith looked at his notes. "He said he caught a glimpse of Alice Faye under the makeup, but when she spoke it was more like Gloria Grahame. Who would they be?"

"Film stars. How old was this guy?"

"He looked about eighty."

"That figures. Alice Faye goes a long way back."

"What do they look like?"

"I've no idea. I just know the names," Salter said. "Did you try to put her description on the computer?"

"Barlow and Jensen already did that, with her costume, anyway. There's been no response yet."

"What did the autopsy say?"

"The knife entered the front of his chest between the second and third rib, severing the . . .

"Yeah, yeah. What about sexual activity?"

"Yes, within the previous eighteen hours. That's as far back as he could go."

"So she serviced him, then, and killed him?"

"Or both, at the same time. The old praying mantis trick. That where we're going?"

"Right now, let's go back over to the apartment. Have you had a chance to talk to the neighbors about anything else they saw that night, any other strangers, maybe?"

"The only thing I picked up was from a tenant in an apartment on the Bedford Road side. He's more or less confined to his home with arthritis, and he looks out the window a lot. He said that several times lately he's noticed a woman in a toffee-colored car—that's his description, sir—parked near the block, within sight of the main doors. She got out once and walked a few yards down the street but she had a headscarf on and all he could say was that she wasn't old and she wasn't young, and she wore a raincoat with a belt. He said she would stay there for two or three hours, then just drive off. Unfortunately, the one thing this old boy is sure of is that she wasn't outside on the night Lucas was killed, because when he heard the news he thought of her. But he's quite clear, not that night. What do you think, sir? Not much use?"

"It helps. If he's reliable—you think he is?—we know now that there weren't any strangers lurking about that night."

"Then what's this woman all about?"

"Surveillance, Smitty. She probably calls herself a private investigator, and what she is doing is keeping tabs on someone, either for an insurance company or a spouse. A red herring. Nothing to do with us, but useful in a negative sort of way. Let's go. You got the keys?"

"Oh, there was a call for you from another lawyer, a man named Holt. He calls himself the family lawyer."

"What did he want?"

"Just to know if he could be of any assistance."

"What's *he* really want, I wonder? To know how soon he can wrap the estate up, I shouldn't wonder. I'll call him back."

"Music, Japanese prints, canoeing," Salter said. "A friend of Trudeau's, maybe? No, there's no sign of politics, except his sister."

They were in Lucas's apartment, looking down on the Annex. Salter said, "Nice location. Half the restaurants in Toronto are at your doorstep, there's a liquor store across the street and a bookshop around the corner, movies, the lot. There's even a Japanese print shop a couple of blocks away. Where do they buy their groceries, I wonder?"

"The Manulife Center. My wife shops there on her way home."

"Yeah? Okay, I'll look around here, you take the bedrooms."

The living room and kitchen were worth only a glance. As expected, the walls were covered in Japanese prints; some stereo equipment, along with several hundred CDs, LPs and tapes, nearly filled one end wall. There was no television set in the living room, and Salter glanced into the main bedroom expecting to find one mounted on the wall above the end of the bed, but there was none there either.

The furniture in the living room consisted of two large couches covered in grey tweed and a matching armchair and two leather club chairs. Five tables of different sizes supported vases, cups and glasses and at least a dozen magazines. One of the vases held long-dead, white daffodil-type flowers, the kind that Salter disliked for their stink, but balancing those was a fragrant vase of still-living freesia. One huge Middle Eastern carpet covered most of the floor, a thin, pale expensive-looking thing. There were no Western paintings on the walls to compete with the Japanese prints except one, of a beautiful girl in her twenties with frizzy orange hair—a slimmer, younger Flora Lucas.

On a side table, a group of framed photographs testified to the history of Lucas's relationships. Salter noted several parental-looking couples and two pictures of heavy, balding men and pioneer-type women who were probably ancestors. The rest featured various combinations of Lucas, his sister, and assorted strangers, covering the span of the siblings' lives from infancy up to each one's marriage. There the record stopped.

Smith came out of a bedroom. "Nothing of any interest at all," he said. "It's all as Barlow and Jensen said. There's nothing unusual about the contents of the bureau or the closet except that he had two sets of long silk underwear. Folks in Glasgow would find that strange."

"Canoeing," Salter said authoritatively, the old Canadian explaining to the young immigrant. "You wear silk underwear canoeing if you've got plenty of money."

"Aye? I haven't come across it before. 'Course, there's not a lot of canoeing in Glasgow."

"Give me a hand with this lot. Marinelli's people would have taken the appointment books and such. I've seen a letter addressed to his sister he never sent."

"His last words?"

"His last wishes, I imagine, plus a list of his assets and where to find them. And any little donations or bequests he wanted her to look after, but weren't worth putting in the will."

"How do you know? Have you read it?"

"I just went through the same thing with my lawyer."

"Why wouldn't you put stuff in your will?"

"It's easier to keep a running list of intentions. If you put them in a will and change your mind you have to keep adding clauses and getting them witnessed. But if you change your mind about, say, who you want to leave your collection of *Hustler* to, you can just cross them off your list and write in another name. This way you leave everything to one or two people in your will, asking them to do all the little things on the list."

"How the rich live, eh? I don't think anyone in our family left a will. What if the heir doesn't want to do it? Maybe your wife doesn't like the man you've left your fishing rod to."

"Then she doesn't have to give it to him. You have to trust them a little, though. If not, put everything in your will."

"Have we found the will?"

"Probably deposited with his lawyer, who is also probably the man he was in partnership with. We'll find out this afternoon. Lucas's office is on Prince Arthur. I'll go over and talk to the partner now. Stay here, keep poking around, and I'll pick you up when I'm done."

Lucas's partner, Derek Fury, a small, polished man in his early sixties whose every hair, nail and tooth had been clipped, filed and buffed as if Fury had a loving owner, beamed his goodwill alternately at Salter and at the room behind Salter as if to an audience watching the two men put on a performance. He was not dressed in the height of fashion, nor was his hair the right length for the year; his glasses, which fashion said should be narrow and steel-edged, were huge, like oversize windows tacked onto an old house. Together with his bow-tie, his waistcoat and the large dots on his shirt they showed him to be an original, a man who dressed in the things he liked. His outfit, like the decor in most people's homes, could be accounted for as the steady accumulation over thirty years of the fabrics and accoutrements that continued to appeal to him, even as fashion moved on.

Salter introduced himself and Fury extended a little shell-like hand, momentarily caressing Salter's fingers, then put his hands together on top of the desk and waited, smiling.

"I'm investigating the death of Jeremy Lucas," Salter said. He had to begin somewhere.

Fury smiled his understanding of what Salter had said, then hitched his body forward in a gesture of encouragement, but said nothing.

"How long had you two been partners?"

Fury referred to a note in front of him. "Nineteen years. In the beginning we were both junior partners in a firm with two other lawyers, but when the seniors died we re-formed ourselves and gave the partnership our own names. Just the two of us."

"You knew him well, then?"

"Absolutely."

"Did you socialize with him?"

"Oh, no. No. Oh, my, no. Not at all. I bought him lunch on his birthday, and he did the same on mine. Somewhere rather grand, usually. We used to compete a bit. Last time he took me to Canoe. Do you know it? I thought by the name it would be somewhere he patronized with his trekking chums, where they would serve pemmican and canned fruit—you know, a sort of bush meal." He smiled, a huge delighted grin at the idea of eating a bush meal in Toronto, retaining the smile until Salter smiled back. Then the light died as he remembered himself. He continued, "But actually it's very elegant. I was on the point of arranging something for his birthday at a new place I'd heard about, The Samphire, on King Street. Do you know it?"

Again Salter shook his head. "Just the two of you?"

"We took Esther, of course." Fury pointed through the door. "She's been with us from the start and she does most of the work. And on the day we generally gave each other a small gift. Last time he gave me this tool, The Leatherman, do you know it?" He opened a drawer and held up a small leather case about the size of his hand, and took out a folded steel instrument. "It's wonderful. Unfolds into about twelve different tools. I can repair everything that breaks around the office."

"Otherwise you didn't overlap. Your personal lives, I mean."

"We had nothing in common," Fury said patiently and earnestly, as if he had explained all this twice already. "He was a man-about-town who liked roughing it in the bush in his spare time. I live for my family."

"Who would I ask about friends? Do you know any of his close friends?"

"He belonged to several social groups. He played cards with one group and canoed with another. And of course he was invited out a lot to dinner parties."

"Did he do any entertaining himself?"

"Quite regularly. Always in restaurants, because it was less trouble than entertaining in his apartment. His sister, Flora, was often his hostess. He invited me occasionally, and he came to my house once or twice a year, but more out of politeness than anything else. My wife said it would seem odd if he never came."

"Did he ever have a hostess apart from his sister?"

Fury smiled roundly, looking over Salter's shoulder to the unseen audience. "A permanent lady friend, you mean? Not for the last couple of years, at least. Before that he had several, in succession, I mean, you know what widowers and bachelors are like. Some of them for years. But I had the impression he no longer bothered."

"He no longer had a regular partner, to your knowledge?"

"That's it."

Salter waited for more, arranging himself expectantly. Eventually, Fury said, "I think he had just inherited his own nature to the full. He was a natural bachelor, a dear sweet man who would do absolutely anything for you as long as it was no trouble, do you know what I mean? Mostly he avoided spending time on things or people he didn't want to. Money was no problem. He was very comfortably off, and he could be extremely generous if it meant he could avoid doing anything more. Any legitimate appeal had him reaching for his wallet, and he always picked up the check in restaurants. He was, I think, completely and absolutely selfish, and he showed it by his generosity. He wouldn't spend a minute doing what he didn't want to, helping out in a soup kitchen on Christmas Day, say, but he disguised his selfishness by giving them money."

Fury sat up and leaned forward. "Now that we are there, I think his late-developing selfishness might account for his changing attitude toward women—you know, this is *interesting*." Again there was the sudden flash of Fury's smile. "I never thought about it before, but he simply had no time to spare for what we used to call courting, you know—meeting ladies for cocktails, that sort of thing. When he felt the need for . . . the company of a woman, he satisfied it. Sounds like a monster, doesn't he? But he never misled them, I'm sure. And these days, people *are* more direct about these things, aren't they? I don't know."

Salter scratched around to find another entry into the same topic, then barged in. "On the night your partner was killed, there was a woman seen at the door of his apartment." Salter described her outfit. "What do you make of that?"

"I've already been asked about that. I suppose anything's possible, isn't it?" The smile flashed. "If I can imagine it, someone is doing it, eh?" He thought for a few moments before he continued. "At the same time, if you work with someone for nearly twenty years you must hang onto what you have come to know about him until you are forced to let it go. Everything I know about Jerry tells me that what you have described is not what it seems. It is bizarre. Why would he hire a creature like that? If he did pay for sex, he could afford the best, especially in these perilous times. As I speak I'm making sense of another possibility. This woman was a crude practical joke, played on him to embarrass him by one of his trekking friends. That's what I would bet on."

"Someone else suggested the same thing. I'll find out. Now, what do you know about his personal affairs? His financial affairs?"

"I'm his lawyer, and the executor of his estate, as he was of mine. Because of my children and an old aunt I support, my world is more complicated than his; he left everything to his sister, except for the residue of the partnership. He still hadn't come into all of his inheritance. His mother died a month ago and her lawyer was just about to hand over her estate to Jerry on behalf of the two of them, Jerry and his sister. I'll take possession of it now on behalf of Jerry's estate. I was looking at his desk calendar—he had an appointment with his mother's lawyer, Larry Holt, next week, so I suppose they were to wrap it up then."

"Can I have that book?"

Fury handed the calendar across the desk and Salter looked at the entry, then put the book in his pocket. "You want a receipt?"

"It's not *my* calendar."

"Do you know where Holt's office is?"

"On Church Street, just past Isabella, on the east side. It's in one of those huge old mansions."

"Maybe I can catch him on the way back. So he had no responsibilities, and it is likely that everything goes to his sister."

"His only real responsibility was towards Esther out there, and the partnership has made sure of her pension, which she can take any time she wishes. At the moment she prefers to work."

"And you? How will it change your life?"

"I will own the office furniture outright." Fury said. "This has made me wonder if I shouldn't take the opportunity to shuffle off myself, while I can. All my children are well on their way to being established. I'll be lonely here without him. It'll be like being a widower, and I don't want to get another partner. You know, he was the ideal partner . . ."

Salter interrupted. "If you don't mind a comment, sir, you don't seem very . . . well, sad about him."

Fury sat back in his chair and adjusted his glasses. "Let me see if I can explain. It was like having the perfect neighbor, someone who would do absolutely anything for me as I would for him without ever seeing the inside of each others' houses—that's a bit mixed, but 'perfect neighbors' is a good analogy. Nothing either of us did ever irritated the other, or got in the other's way. I know a lot about him because we chatted a lot over the garden fence, as it were, but left each other strictly alone. I shall never have another neighbor like that. I was shocked to hear of his death, especially like that, but there was nothing between us for me to grieve over, so now I'm just sad for myself. I shall probably start taking those cruises my wife has been wanting us to go on for the last ten years."

Salter referred to his notebook. "Do you know the people he canoed with? And the names of the card players?"

"Of course. Esther will write them down for you because she was his sort of social secretary, but I know them all, of course. Of the poker gang, talk to Bonar Robinson. His office is in the Toronto Dominion tower. Here's his telephone number. And for a sporting type, talk to Tim Baretski. He's a doctor, practically retired, but still works in a group practice on Bathurst Street.

"I've heard Jerry on the phone to his canoeing pals, and I gathered they were all free to go on a trip without much warning whenever they felt like it, all sort of working part time, like Jerry. The card players, on the other hand, are a more hard-faced lot—busy, busy, busy making money—who squeeze their cards into a very tight schedule. Prominent citizens all. If one or two of them couldn't make the regular Thursday, you would hear Jerry trying to find an alternative night, any night except Friday was good for him, but the others were usually all booked up."

"Why Friday?"

"I wondered myself once, then I assumed what now looks likely. But I still find this woman you've described incredible."

Salter put away his notebook and turned sideways in his chair. "The idea of a prostitute or call girl doesn't make any sense to you, then . . ."

"Certainly not the dressing-up thing. I think I met all his respectable partners over the last twenty years. None of them would have worn silver boots."

"Married men have been known to indulge themselves outside the house."

"Jerry wasn't married. He could respond to his sexual nature directly. All the signs say that he wouldn't have liked silver-booted women in bed. But perhaps I'm out of touch."

"What about his nonsexual life? What kind of lawyer was he? Should I be looking among his clients for someone who wanted to kill him for giving them bad advice? Maybe someone who is in jail because of him?"

Fury laughed softly. "Oh, no. First of all, his clients—and he had very few—were rich and lived their lives legally, or he sent them away. Upright citizens all. He wouldn't touch anything doubtful. And confidentially, because that's what it is, confidential, I've skimmed through his financial affairs, including the trust matters, and nothing odd has jumped out at me. If you want more than that, you'll have to turn his affairs over to a forensic accountant, but you would be wasting your time."

"He didn't have to, did he? Touch anything doubtful, I mean."

"That's right. Honesty is easy if you have plenty of money, so why aren't more of the rich honest? But as a lawyer, Jerry went beyond not responding to greed. You know he was a gambler, apart from the cards?"

"It's been mentioned."

"That was his only vice, unless you count the sex thing. He agreed that gambling was a social evil but it was one of his great pleasures, and he didn't want to give it up. So he went to the races, and played poker with a group of lawyers who could afford to lose."

"All lawyers?"

"That was the connection between them. But it was one of the few contacts Jerry had with his colleagues. Oh, he still had lunch occasionally with an old pal from law school, but he had no close lawyer friends, except me, I suppose." Fury ended on a note of surprise. "I think that fits with Jerry not having any shady clients. And he sat on the most important committee on ethics of the Law Society. I suppose it sounds odd, but apart from gambling and, I suppose, sex, and his hobbies—canoeing and music—the thing he cared most about was the law. He loved it and he hated those who brought it into disrepute. On the ethics committee he could take up a fierce stance. It was Jerry's view that lawyers, like priests, had a responsibility to behave more ethically than others."

"He doesn't sound like someone I would have relaxed with."

"Oh, you'd have gotten along. He was good company."

Salter put away his notebook. "Now I have to talk to some of these people. Larry Holt is his family lawyer, I'm told. But you were Lucas's lawyer . . ."

"Holt is the *mother's* lawyer."

"What part does Calvin Gregson play? He seems to be in there somewhere."

"Really? Perhaps looking after Flora's interests." Now Fury's face was alight with mischief. "What's he wearing these days? I haven't seen him lately."

Salter again described Gregson's boots and suit and tie. Fury gurgled with joy. "He's still on that, is he? Perhaps he's found himself at last. One thing, he really brightens up the law courts, don't you think?"

On his way out, Salter called Larry Holt from the secretary's office and established that if he hurried, Holt would be happy to see him. Lucas's telephone was still connected, so he called Smith and told him to meet him outside Lucas's apartment building. "I want you to take me to Church and Isabella, then take my car back to my space at headquarters. I'll walk back to the office."

11

Larry Holt was waiting on the curb outside his building as they arrived, leaning on a walking stick.

"Staff Inspector Salter? I'm afraid I screwed up. I have a date in court in thirty minutes. Could we reschedule?"

Salter said, "In court? The provincial court? In the old Eaton's building on College Street? I planned to walk over there anyway, when we finished, and what I want from you won't take long. Why don't I walk with you, talk on the way. Won't take thirty minutes, surely."

"For me it will. I just got a new hip. I haven't learned to run with it yet." Holt buckled a strap on his briefcase, and the two men set off across Isabella. "I called your office, by the way. Did you get the message?" Holt spoke confidentially, his body slightly turned, apparently to prevent a third party from overhearing. It increased the difficulty of walking together on a crowded sidewalk.

"Yes," Salter said. "What for?"

"To offer my services, I'm Jerry's mother's lawyer, you know. But actually I was using it as an excuse to find out if you're making any progress. Are you?"

"We don't have any suspects in custody. That what you mean?"

"More or less. From my point of view, the sooner the better. I can finalize the estate, then, you see."

"I see. We've only got thirty minutes, you say. So let me ask you about Lucas."

"I'll walk in front. People see my stick and get out of the way. Oops, sorry, Miss. Let's cross over. This sidewalk's too crowded. Now! There's a gap." The two men scrambled across the street, Holt's face showing the effort, and resumed walking more or less side by side, though Holt stayed confidentially close to Salter.

"Let's start at the beginning. You're Jerry Lucas's mother's lawyer, right?"

"I was. Sorry." This to another pedestrian he had shouldered as he tried to stay beside Salter. "I was. She died recently."

"So I heard. What happens next?"

"In what sense?"

"What do you do now? You have control of her money, right? What do you do with it?"

Holt waved his stick at three teenagers who were barging along the sidewalk toward them, parting the group to let the two men through. "I take steps to dispose of her estate to her heirs," he said when the two men were side by side again.

"Have you done that yet?"

"I'd made an appointment with Lucas for next week. Now I guess I'll sort it out with Flora Lucas, or Derek Fury. It's fairly simple."

"A lot of money?"

"They are a well-established family."

"Why wouldn't Lucas have managed his own mother's affairs?"

"He didn't want to and she didn't want him to. She didn't believe he knew anything about managing money. Anyway, Jerry had very high principles—sorry, Ma'am—and insisted himself on a third party for his mother. As for Flora, he didn't want to be accountable to her if he managed it badly, I suppose."

"Surely she wouldn't have held him *seriously* accountable. I heard that she and Jerry were very close."

They had reached the corner of Yonge Street. Holt steered Salter's elbow south towards College. "They were. Very close."

"You must have been very close to Lucas yourself."

"I played poker with him, that's all. You don't have to be close to play poker. Better not, in fact, then you can feel good when you win. We lived in different worlds. Let's cross here now."

"Did you meet his sister?"

"Once or twice. She was very beautiful when she was younger. There's a portrait in the art gallery by Augustus John that's very like a painting of her that Jerry had."

Finally, by the elevators that connected to the courtroom, Holt looked at his watch. "We did that in twenty minutes. A record for my new hip. There's almost time for a coffee."

"You okay? Maybe we'll just sit down for a minute."

"Good enough."

"I'll be quick. Did you know anything about his sex life? Specifically, did he use prostitutes?" Salter told him about the woman in the silver boots.

Holt appeared to give the question a lot of thought, then started to shake his head. "All I can tell you is that I don't know the opposite. I never heard him mention the name of any woman for months. Before that I think there was someone he referred to as his regular date, but I don't think he'd lived with anyone for years. I don't know. I just knew him as one of a group of lawyers who got together to play cards. The others are all married, all except Jerry Lucas and me. I have a girlfriend who will marry me one day, I hope. I was lucky once, why not twice?" He looked at his watch.

"So you don't think the idea of Lucas and a prostitute in dress-up is unlikely?"

"I hardly knew the guy. Now, you know where my office is. Any time you want me. I have to run, in a manner of speaking."

In other words, thought Salter, you're one crony who dodges the question because he thinks it is possible that Pussy-in-Boots was just that. Because, as his mother's lawyer, you must have known him a little, surely.

Back in his office, Salter made an appointment to see Dr. Baretski, Lucas's canoeing pal, the next afternoon, and drove home early enough to eat dinner with Seth, if that was possible.

"Mom called," Seth said when he entered.

Salter had found him in the basement, apparently tidying it up. Salter said, "Did Mom ask you to clean it up?"

"Sort of," Seth said. "I just thought I'd see what's down here."

"Make a list of what we can throw out. Have you thought about dinner?"

"I was going to get some pizza and eat with Tatti."

"Fine. I'll send out to the Swiss Chalet for some chicken for myself."

"Hang on a minute. Let me call Tatti and put her off. Why don't we walk over to the Swiss Chalet? You and me."

"Bring Tatti. Take the car and fetch her up."

"She doesn't like Swiss Chalet."

"She doesn't like Swiss Chalet? Have you given serious thought to your relationship with this woman? Swiss Chalet chicken is the one thing left this family all agree to eat."

Seth laughed. "Tatti is nearly a vegetarian. No, it's okay, She won't mind a night off. Let's go."

After the "medium halves" of chicken had been consumed, the fries dipped in barbecue sauce, after the ice cream and the single bottle of Upper Canada Lager, after Salter had ordered coffee, Seth came to the point. "Dad, we were wondering, Tatti and I, if we could move into our basement. And now I'll go pee to give you a chance to think about it." He stood up and made his way to the stairs at the back of the restaurant.

The proposal was one he ought to have seen coming, but hadn't crossed his mind. The Salters' house was narrow and three stories high and had a finished basement lined with knotty pine by the previous owners; the basement contained a bathroom of sorts that had last been used regularly when the boys were small and had their friends in to play in winter.

At one time the previous owners had rented out this basement as a separate apartment with its own access at the back of the house, and the rudiments of a kitchen still remained—a small electric stove, a sink, some cupboards, and a counter. Annie used the sink now to wash out paintbrushes, and the cupboards were full of the jetsam that all basement cupboards are full of, and the counter was scarred by Salter's using it as a workbench when he wanted to saw something, or hammer something flat. But the damage was superficial, and it would take only a few days to restore it to a living space for a homeless couple.

"You can't have the laundry area," Salter said, when Seth returned.

"I was thinking, we could put up a partition of wallboard at the foot of the stairs with a door so we could access the laundry area, too."

"Who's the 'we' who are putting up this partition?"

"You and me, Dad."

"You know how to build a wall?"

"No."

"Well, the time has come, son, to tell you that I don't, either. Get yourself a carpenter to help you. I'll pay for the material. What about the stuff we have stored? My golf clubs, the suitcases, the old cans of paint, your mother's bike."

"We should chuck out most of it. Some of that paint dates back to before I was born. The rest can go in the laundry area."

"You have it all worked out."

But it was Annie who was in charge of living space, she who would know immediately if this were a good or bad idea. And Annie was on the Island. "We'll have to wait until your mother gets back."

"I already asked her when she called to see how things were going. She said great, but she said I'd have to ask you."

"I'll ask her again, myself, now she's had time to think."

"Is there a problem?"

What Salter was actually feeling was a relaxation of his wariness in this area, his natural caution that saw change in terms of the problems it might bring, and the replacement of that wariness, in this instance, with the pleasurable thought that his household, far from shrinking into an aged couple listening for the telephone to ring, waiting for the children to call, was expanding into a multifamily unit, one that would include a neo-daughter-in-law that he liked. But he had a role to play.

"I don't know if there's a problem. If not, I'll talk to your mother and figure one out."

But when he called Annie that night, she really was all for it, her pleasure like his at the idea of starting a family compound outweighing any qualms she might have.

He found Dr. Baretski late in the afternoon in an office on an upper floor of the Toronto Hospital on Bathurst Street: a small, fit-looking bald man wearing sandals, blue jeans and a khaki work shirt, all made respectable by the white coat hanging off his shoulders.

Baretski said, "We've known each other a long time, all four of us, but apart from the odd Christmas party I never saw the others except to plan a trip. I think it was the same for them. We got along very well together—you might say we'd achieved compatability over the years, and we were so used to each other we could trust any of us to buy the supplies. I'm not Orthodox, so the meals were no problem as long as they didn't bring hot cross buns." He had a tiny speech impediment, a lisp held at bay, expressing itself not in esses turned into *th* but in occasional slightly stressed sibilants. He was also highly energized, speaking and moving in quick little bursts. "We met at Jerry's club for dinner to plan the year's trip, the big one. We sometimes went for a weekend late in the year, but the big one was for a week at the end of July, after the worst of the flies."

Salter asked once more about Lucas's private life.

"I know more than most, but less than nothing, really. I'm a doctor, so he asked me a couple of things. Look, I'm not going into the witness box to talk about Jerry's sex life, am I?"

"That won't happen."

"Good. He asked me recently, in a general sort of way, about Viagra, like half my patients over fifty. I told him I would get him some if he wanted. It wasn't legal here then yet, but I'm a urologist." Baretski grinned. "I get samples that I distribute to needy cases. He backed off, saying he was just curious. I asked him once if he'd ever thought of remarrying, and he said he wouldn't inflict himself on anyone again."

"If he did have any sexual problems, he'd have been likely to confide in you, wouldn't he?"

"No. You know what he would have done? He would have asked

me the name of another urologist. But he never did."

Once again Salter described the woman in the silver boots, adding Fury's comment that it was so out of character that it must have been a practical joke. It occurred to him to jolt Baretski in case the canoeists had played the gag, which seemed possible. Horseplay, he guessed, was more likely to come from canoeists than card players.

Baretski considered. "As I said, I'm a urologist, not a psychologist, thank God, but I would have thought that it *was* possible that Jerry had hired her himself. Experimenting maybe? Thought maybe a prostitute would help? Who knows? Poor guy."

"So you think it's likely she was . . . real?"

"No. I think it's *possible*, and if you were a doctor, let alone a urologist, you would know that's what I'm bound to say. But with Jerry, knowing him as a friend, I would vote against it. We talked a bit about AIDS a couple of times, and everyone agreed that the days of casual sex were behind them." He grinned. "In a manner of speaking."

"Let me ask the question in another way. Would you say you *didn't* know him well?"

"We've been canoeing together, four of us, for about twenty years, believe it or not. All of us married except Jerry, and our wives have the sense not to try to talk us out of our annual canoe trip. Now if you canoe with guys for a week, share a tent and all that, you hear, and maybe overhear, all about them. We'd talk about everything, sex and death for starters, of course, God, Spinoza, literature, morality. On a canoe trip with the right person you get back to talking the way you did in college, and the way you never do the rest of the year. The word is 'intimate.' "

"So you *do* know him, you think?"

"I could tell you what he thinks about all of the above, and about his politics, too."

"Try giving me a sketch of him."

"Lives lived, sort of? Okay. Let's go across the hall to my other office. We won't be interrupted there."

In the other office, he said, "You want to take notes? Sit behind the desk. I can think better on my feet. We really need a canoe to do this properly. To begin, then, most of all, he had no secrets, no sad inner life. What you saw was what you got. He loved music and his sister. Have you met Flora?"

"Yes. No other people?"

"He had friends."

"But no one else he loved."

"He spent it all on Flora. That's what I learned in the canoe."

"He had women, though."

"Sure. He was happily married for a while. He loved his wife, too. But since her he has had a lot of ladies—women—what's the right term? He wasn't very interested in sex in the abstract, unlike a lot of my patients. I mean he didn't think about it much, or talk about it. It was just something he did. I imagine some of his women could have resented him for it. He wasn't very attached to any of them."

"Except Flora."

"Except Flora." Baretski waited and Salter picked up the cue.

"Was his relationship with Flora . . . did it ever seem strange to you?"

"Absolutely, in the sense of unusual, unique, even. They were devoted to each other, or maybe I should differentiate. He was devoted and totally protective of her, and he had always been the one she leaned on. The parents never figured much, you know that." He paused, then said, "I think some of his girlfriends resented Flora, because they all found out that those two had a private world that no one could enter. The same thing applied to Flora, but the difference with men is that her boyfriends probably felt content to be relieved of the full emotional responsibility for someone else."

"You've thought about this a lot, haven't you?"

"Over the years. Ever since I was sure there was nothing sexual in their relationship. And now, because I knew you would ask about just that, so that you could leave that out of your inquiries."

"And you guys. Was he a—what's the word, a nature lover? a naturist?"

"It's obvious you're not."

"I like fishing, when the mosquitoes have gone."

"Jerry was at home in the bush, and on a lake, but he didn't yearn after it the way I do all winter. He had all the skills that you want at the other end of the canoe, but for him canoeing was a fishing trip in the closed season. I'm not doing a good job of this. Try this: by the beginning of April I'm down on Front Street in my lunch break, in and out of the outfitters' stores along there, looking for stuff to make the next canoe trip better. I can hardly wait. For Jerry it was an event on the calendar, to be thought about the weekend before."

"Did he get excited about anything? Gambling, maybe?"

"His passion, in that sense, was music. He got from music what I get from nature, I would say. Have you ever considered the different kinds of pleasure that different kinds of experiences—physical or aesthetic, for example—provide you with, and whether the experience of canoeing on the French River is primarily physical or aesthetic, or perhaps a kind of synaesthesia in which the aesthetic blends with the physical? And with music, whether it's the emotional content or the aesthetic pattern that you are responding to?" Baretski had become very animated, his face alight and his hands trying to shape his words, and he spoke as if he had said these things often.

"No. No, I haven't." Salter hoped he had chosen the right verb and tense to conceal the fact that he had lost track of what Baretski was saying.

"We used to talk about it a lot. About the different kinds of pleasure, the pleasure of paddling down an unexplored river compared to the pleasure he got from—who was that woman he was just crazy about, played the cello—yeah, Monica Huggett. You know her?"

"No."

"Don't misunderstand me. He *liked* canoeing, and I like music. I'm just getting on to Mahler, some of him. And as I said, the four of us were very compatible, but there was a day last fall when Jerry and I clashed over all this. He went too far." He cleared his throat and got to his feet.

"We were on a weekender in Killarney Provincial Park. Do you know it? It is without doubt the most beautiful park in Ontario. A lot of people must agree with me, because if you want to camp there on a weekend you have to book a site months in advance.

"On this weekend, Jerry was looking after the cooking and I

pitched the tent. We were only out for two nights so we kept every-thing to a minimum—we ate chili that night, I think—and by the time I had the tent up the supper was ready.

"It was a terrific moment. As far as we could hear or see there was no one else in the world: the fish were jumping, a wolf howled, then the bullfrogs started up, but all these sounds just emphasized the *purity* of the silence they were part of." He looked pleased with him-self. "The sounds of silence, that's what they were. It was what I came for. And then, right in the middle of it, a trace of the aurora borealis appeared in the sky above us. Too much. Then Jerry said, 'Hold on,' and ran up to the tent. A few minutes later he came back and sat down, and out of the tent came this fucking *background* music. *The Archduke Trio*, it was. Beethoven. You know it?"

"No."

"It goes like this." Baretski mouthed the opening, loudly, harshly, in a crashing way, and waved his arms, conducting: " 'DA da DA da DAAA!' and Jerry said, 'Now it's perfect.'

"I wanted to kill him. Once, up in Algonquin Park, in the days when people who didn't know any better tried to have an outdoors experience there, we finally found a place to camp—we had been paddling for hours in the dark as every campsite we came to was full—and the traffic on the lake slowed down to like the four-oh-one on a quiet Sunday as canoeists in their hundreds trekked by—as I say, we finally found a spot, got the fire going, took our first drink and began to feel less sorry that we had come, and out of the night, from a tent maybe fifty feet away, came the sound of a ghetto blaster at full volume.

"They were just a gang of young kids; when I went over to throw their ghetto blaster into the lake, and them after it, they apologized and turned it off. Well this was a moment like that, only with the *Archduke Trio*. My world—the loons, the fish, the bullfrogs, the aspens playing with their leaves—all that disappeared behind 'DA da DA da DAAA!' I went to the tent and found the machine—it was a portable CD player—restrained myself and just unplugged it. Then Jerry and I had a chat.

"We started a long way apart in every sense, and very noisy, but eventually we agreed that he wouldn't play fucking Beethoven in the camp if he could play what he liked on the drive up and the drive back. See my point? I think, for him, everything was secondary to, or enhanced by, music. If the four of us had ever gotten into one of those 'What-was-your-greatest-sex-experience?' conversations—as I said, sometimes on a canoe trip you can go back to the dorm at college—which we never did, and maybe that's because Jerry wasn't very interested in talking about it, but if we had, I doubt that Jerry would have said it was the night a hooker wore her silver boots in bed. No, he would have said it was the night he got laid to the sound of the first movement of the 'Archduke Trio.' "

He paused, then added, "I'm getting carried away, aren't I? Well, I won't deny that was a strong experience, up there in Killarney, but we didn't let it upset twenty years of—what? I loved the guy, and I'll miss him. There was no one else I'd rather be in a canoe with."

"Was he your lawyer?"

Baretski looked surprised. "For wills and stuff? No. I did ask him to be, but he just said he found it hard to be really professional with friends, and recommended the guy I have now. Afterwards, I kidded him about not wanting his friends to know the size of his fees, but I let it go."

12

S alter descended, after the longest wait for an elevator he had ever experienced—how would one of those emergency response teams on television respond if they had to use an elevator like this? he wondered—and found a telephone on the ground floor, where he called Bonar Robinson and established that Robinson would wait for him if he came right away. He called Seth to synchronize the dinner hour.

"Mom called again."

"To find out when you two are moving in?"

"Not really. There is a lot of stuff to do in the basement before I can bring Tatti here. No, I think she has other things she wants to talk about."

Annie was still staying with her mother at the family home on Prince Edward Island. From the time Salter and Annie married, old Mrs. Montagu had never ceased pointing out how nice it would be if the whole family were together; that is, in her view, the natural thing would have been for Salter to have given up his job and taken his place in one of the family businesses on the Island. Gradually, over the years, the pressure had weakened without quite going away, until the situation was temporarily resolved by Angus, Salter's elder son, who, upon graduation from business school, had been offered a job in the business and moved east with his girlfriend. Salter thought that old Mother Montagu would be unhappy at the prospect of having a grandson on the Island living in sin, but his mind had been trudging along conventional and dated lines. Mrs. Montagu not only ignored Angus's unmarried state, but welcomed the couple into her home. She had even welcomed the news that Linda was pregnant.

That first pregnancy had miscarried, as did the next, but now, finally, there was a baby girl, Salter's granddaughter and the old lady's great-granddaughter. Life on the Island was therefore idyllic, Salter assumed, leaving him in Toronto looking forward to being visited by Angus and his granddaughter at their leisure. And now with the prospect of having Seth and Tatti around. Perfect.

"If she calls back, tell her I'll be home in an hour."

The firm of Lollard and Lollard, of which Bonar Robinson was a partner, occupied a large section of an upper floor of the Toronto Dominion building.

From the elevator, Salter emerged into a space through the glass walls of which he could see people moving back and forth like fish in a tank, along corridors and in and out of glass offices. Looking down the length of the corridor in front of him, he could see Lake Ontario at the far end. On his left, one of the glass walls had a square hole to let a woman behind the wall speak through and find out what Salter wanted. She told him she would let Mr. Robinson know he was there, spoke the message into a handset, and told Salter exactly what he expected to hear, that Mr. Robinson would just be a few minutes, and would he take a seat and would he like a cup of coffee.

Salter wondered if the few minutes' wait was something learned in law school, or business school: "You will be issued a timer. Always make the client wait two-and-a-quarter minutes to show how busy you are." In this case, Salter was exactly on time and said, "Is he hiding the evidence, or just having a nap?" to the startled receptionist, but before she had to cope with him, a glass door opened near Lake Ontario and she looked up and said, "Here he is now."

Robinson walked quickly into the reception area, shook hands, and led Salter back along the corridor to his office. ("Once you've made him wait the two-and-a-quarter minutes, be sure to conduct him personally into your office to show that, busy as you are, an important client comes first.")

"Sorry to keep you waiting," he said. "I was desperate for a pee." (Try for a light remark to open the interview.) Before they sat down, Robinson led Salter over to the exterior wall, and showed him the view.

Salter tried to think of something that would please Robinson. "You get a real view of the lake here," he said.

"It's fantastic during a snowstorm."

"I'll bet." Salter turned firmly back into the room and sat down on the other side of the desk, sucking Robinson along in his wake.

"Coffee?" the lawyer asked, his hand moving toward an intercom switch.

Salter shook his head.

"Then how can I help you?" Robinson splayed out his hand on the desktop to examine his fingernails. He was a carefully groomed man who spoke over half-glasses and articulated his consonants with care. Pleased with himself, Salter thought.

"Tell me who killed Jerry Lucas."

Nodding, as if to say "Quite funny," but not smiling, Robinson said, "Some thug. Got interrupted robbing his apartment."

"Possibly, but that's not what it looks like, although they don't have very good security in that building. It's not hard to get yourself buzzed up."

"Really?" The lawyer sounded genuinely surprised. "I've never been inside the building. It's a joke among his poker crowd that none of us has ever been invited into his place. So it was someone he knew?"

"I was hoping you could help us on one possibility. How well did you know him?"

"I played poker with him, that's all. There are, were, seven of us in the game, though we usually only got six or even five out on a particular night. Below four we called it off."

"Friends?"

"Apart from the game, you mean? Some of us are. But it isn't a group of friends playing cards. It's a poker game. You play?"

"I have."

"Ever been in a big game?"

Salter caught a flicker of amusement in Robinson's voice. Did

Salter want to know what Robinson considered big?

"I lost a hundred dollars I couldn't afford once, thirty years ago," he said, handing Robinson the advantage.

"What was your biggest win?"

"A couple of hundred. Once."

Robinson said, "Our biggest pot two weeks ago was five thousand. That would be the equivalent of five hundred thirty years ago. Not so different," he added, graciously.

"The difference is you can afford it." Salter wondered how much Robinson made, and whether it compensated him for all the jokes, all the hositility, that were the lot of lawyers.

"You were over your head?" Robinson asked.

"In nineteen-sixty a hundred and twenty-five was the month's rent. Losing that much made a difference to my life, in the short term. Would losing five thousand make a difference in what you plan to do tomorrow?"

"That was the pot, not what I lost. No. I would probably spend any winnings on wine. Normally I don't pay more than twenty a bottle. My puritan streak. How about you?"

"Ten."

"You like the fresh roughness of the simple vintages, I guess." Robinson mouthed the words with a flourish to show he was making a wine joke. "Remind me not to eat dinner at your house. Apart from that, it's just like winning a lottery. Offhand, I can't think of anything I can't do now that winning half a million in a lottery would allow me to do. By the standards of some of our clients, I'm not rich, but I do travel first class. I can afford to lose. That's what you want to know, isn't it? Can any of us not afford to lose? No. That would put a strain on the rest of us, having someone at the table we had to be concerned about."

"Winning money isn't important?"

"It's not what the game's about. It's about cleaning the clocks of the other guys. Beating them. Whipping ass. The money is there to show the score. It defines us, for the night. But, yeah, it's just a friendly game for decent stakes."

"When did you play last? Two weeks ago?"

"The night before Jerry was murdered."

"Who won?"

"Jerry and Bob Pender. The money went back and forth until about one o'clock, and then it all shifted over to the two of them and they tried to have a shoot-out, but the cards wouldn't cooperate. They probably made a couple of thousand each."

"And you lost a thousand."

"About that."

"And that's about the way of it every week?"

"More or less. I bring a thousand to the table, just in case I fight a serious hand, but once I've lost five hundred I'm ready to quit. I've lost it all a couple of times, and once I made three. Thousand, that is. That's about everybody's experience. So I don't think any of us killed Jerry for the pot he was taking home."

Salter said, "Did you know anything about the guy?"

"Not much. He went paddling in a canoe, and to just about every concert that came to town."

"Did he have a partner? A woman?"

"Every time I saw him at a theater or some such lately, he had a different woman, sometimes his sister. So I would guess not. But once upon a time, maybe ten years ago, he had a relationship with a woman I know, and that lasted two or three years. You would still see them together sometimes, even lately, in a restaurant, or at an art gallery. That's all I can tell you."

Finally Salter came once more to the story of the woman in silver boots. Robinson listened, nodding to show he was familiar with the story. "I've no idea what she was all about. My guess would be that she was looking for someone else. But, as I said, I knew nothing about his private life, not even enough to guess at the answers you're looking for."

"You don't think he might have actually wanted a hooker?"

"I think he'd be a bit more discreet than that. But that's just my impression of the guy. I have no hard evidence for you. Ask the others."

"I will. Can you give me the list?"

Robinson pressed a button on his desk. "Sydney, print out the poker group, would you? And the schedule." He leaned back. "I agree it sounds weird; there's got to be an explanation that fits with the little I knew of the man. It's a question of taste. Jerry was particular in all his other pleasures, the quality of the whiskey he drank—in his case, vintage Irish pot distilled—that sort of thing. I would have expected him to have a discreet arrangement with a lady cellist, no mention of money, but lots of presents." Robinson smiled slightly. "At any rate, no Jarvis Street hookers. Ah, here they are."

A beautiful woman in her forties dressed in black and hung about with gold chains came through the door and handed him two sheets of paper which he glanced at and handed to Salter. "There's the names, and, let's see, we meet next Thursday. Christ, at my place. I'd better tell Marion to stay out of the way." Robinson paused, regarding Salter. "Why don't you come along, watch for a while, if you like. We could maybe each drop out of a hand in turn and you could talk to all of us one at a time, that way."

Salter sensed that Robinson was up to something, perhaps simply wanting to show off in some way. But Lucas, his hunch told him, was probably killed by someone close to him, and since all homicides are rooted in sex, revenge, or money, then he should take a look at these guys. He said, "Maybe I could sit in for a couple of hands."

Robinson looked startled. Then, after a few seconds, said, "I don't see why not."

Salter stood up. "You play at a different house every week?"

Robinson said, "More or less. But we never played at Jerry's place. When it was Jerry's turn, he brought the wine and had some sandwiches catered. Yes, come and play poker." He was enthusiastic now. "Thursday."

"There's been a development. I'll need to stay a few days longer," Annie said.

"Now what?" He was immediately on edge. Any "development," he feared, would be bound to keep Annie on the Island longer. What could it be? Perhaps the family had lost all their money, and Annie was needed to cook while they looked for work?

"What's up?" he asked. This time he tried to sound jaunty.

"Linda has left Angus."

"Oh, Jesus. Poor Angus. Why? Where's she gone? What was wrong?"

"She ran away with a folksinger from Moncton. She's in Moncton now."

Salter laughed in spite of the distress he could hear in Annie's voice. "A folksinger? Where did she find him?"

"He played at a bar in Charlottetown for a week. She heard him the first night and went back every night afterwards. She told everyone she had decided to learn to play the guitar and wanted to watch a live performer while she got the chance. She did buy a guitar, and plucked at it a few times. Then she told Angus it wasn't just the guitar. She had become disenchanted with his life ethic, as she called it, and wanted to inhabit a more creative environment."

"That's bad. Sounds like more than a counselor could patch up. She become a hippie? That what she means? A bit late."

"There are new words for it, but that's the idea."

"She's found God, like."

"More or less."

"How is Angus responding?"

"Angry. The fact is, she's only been gone for three days, and he talks about how much he dislikes her. It sounds bad."

"Why didn't you tell me before?"

"I spoke to a psychologist I know in Toronto first, and she said it might be a temporary thing, that as soon as Linda realizes she won't have Charlotte with her, she'll come back and they can sort it out."

"She didn't take the baby? Christ! What's Angus supposed to do with it?"

"*Her*. Your granddaughter. Linda said in her note that it was only fair that Angus should have Charlotte because she meant so much to him, whereas Linda will have others, with the folksinger . . ."

"She just wanted out, didn't she? Didn't she ever seem attached to the kid?"

"You can look back now and see all kinds of signs that point to the fact that she was surprised to find herself a mother. At least that's what *my* mother's been doing ever since, pointing to the signs. But what does it matter? It isn't temporary. So Angus is here with no one to look after Charlotte."

"Your mother?"

"She's a bit past the hands-on care stuff."

"Your brothers' wives, until Angus can get something sorted out?"

"I'm testing the water on that. It looks cold."

"So how long?"

"I'll have to stay until we've found a nanny for Charlotte, probably someone to live in. At least a couple of weeks. How is Seth?"

"Tatti—I guess one day that'll sound like a nice French name instead of how it sounds now—anyway Tatti hasn't moved in yet. Seth won't let her until he's turned the basement into a palace."

"You helping, Charlie?"

"Don't start nagging, Annie. As you well know, I don't have any of the skills Seth needs. He lets me hold stuff, light things, so I don't rupture myself, but nothing requiring any expertise."

"Don't keep your distance. He might think you disapprove."

"He knows I don't. I smile warmly at Tatti every time I see her. That's easy to do."

"You know what I mean. Make them feel at home. Get an extra key cut so she can let herself in when you're both out. How's the work?"

"I'm on a case, a real case, a homicide yet, involving some of Toronto's movers and shakers. I've got a new assistant just for this case. Very ironic guy. Or do I mean laconic? Anyway, a Scotsman. But never mind him, is anyone listening on the extension? No. Well. You know of Flora Lucas?"

"Of course I do. Everyone does. I've met her at fund-raising events."

"Symphony? Ballet?"

"No, something noncultural, good works. Raising money for a hospice, that kind of thing. I remember one, a kind of private auction, where a lot of people donated something they valued and then all the donors were allowed to bid to get back their own thing, or someone else's."

"What did you donate?"

"Some books. The English Idyll series I've been collecting."

"Those litle green jobs with the gold lettering? I never noticed them missing."

"They were only gone for a few days. I bought them back."

"How much for?"

"They're my books, Charlie."

"Yeah. How much?

"Six hundred dollars."

"Jesus!" Salter felt a flush of pleasure that he was married to this woman. "So what do you make of Flora Lucas? Give me the dirt."

"I doubt if there is any. She made a speech about the need for hospices, about the care of the dying being a measure of civilization, and got passionate generally about how proud she was to be associated with the party that had introduced Medicare in the first place . . ."

"She isn't. It was Tommy Douglas and the CCF who did that."

"I know. You've often told us. Flora Lucas acknowledges him as the father-philosopher of the idea, but she was proud that the Liberals had written the legislation for the nation. Those were her words. She ended by saying that thing about pain being a form of evil, and anything we could do to get rid of it, we should. It was quite a speech; she's quite a woman. I'd have paid a lot more than six hundred to buy back my books."

"I can tell."

"What are you doing about food?"

"I bought a case of baked beans, and I heat two cans a night and Seth and I eat them out of the can with a spoon. Two spoons. One each. Don't worry about the food."

"Eat some salad!"

"I'll tell Seth. He buys the groceries. Tell Angus I'm sorry. No, don't. I'll call him, talk to him myself. Now I have to go and watch Seth work. Come home soon."

"Give Seth my love."

Salter hung up, collected two beers from the fridge, and walked to the head of the basement stairs. "Beer?" he shouted. "Want a beer?"

"Sure," Seth shouted back. "Who was on the phone?"

"Mom." And then, because it was better to deal with these things immediately. "Angus's wife has run away."

Seth reached out for the beer, laughing. "Run away? Who with? The raggle-taggle Gypsies, oh! Wives don't run away these days, Pop. They leave, is all. Good. Now Angus won't have to leave *her*."

"Was he planning to?"

"He called a week ago. Put me under a vow of silence which I guess I can now break. Those two have been in trouble for a while. Angus wanted to know if he could come back here, stay here while he looked for a job."

"Leave the baby on the Island? What did you say?"

"I told him to look after first things first. Sort out his life, then come home, maybe."

"What about this folksinger?"

Seth considered his words. "I doubt if Angus should be throwing stones."

"Jesus Christ. And Mom knows nothing about this?"

"You'll have to ask *her* that."

After a while, Salter said, "You think it's good, them splitting up?"

Seth put down his hammer. "Pop, Angus needs tent stakes, you know? Something to hold him down in a wind. He isn't as solid on his feet as he thinks he is."

Or as you are, Salter thought. "Don't you like her?"

"Angus needs someone solid, supportive. She was *creative*. He couldn't handle that."

"Creative is bad now?"

"In her it was a sign of instability."

Salter experienced a mild sense of diminishment at the realization that his second son was showing signs of wisdom, instructing him, no longer inhabiting any part of his shadow. It was odd. He would have to be more careful around the house in future, learn to treat his own family as a group of friends, no longer nodding in recognition of his omniscience, but listening to what he was saying and judging it. He was going to have to think about what he was saying as carefully inside the house as out. Or stop caring outside *and* in.

"I read your poem, by the way."

" 'Ulysses'?"

"Yeah. Sounded like Charles Bronson in that movie where he gets his old pals together for one last punch-up. Nothing to do with me."

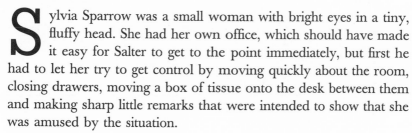

13

Sylvia Sparrow was a small woman with bright eyes in a tiny, fluffy head. She had her own office, which should have made it easy for Salter to get to the point immediately, but first he had to let her try to get control by moving quickly about the room, closing drawers, moving a box of tissue onto the desk between them and making sharp little remarks that were intended to show that she was amused by the situation.

"I've never been interrogated by a staff inspector before. You must excuse me if I get interested in the process. Oh, dear, I haven't asked you to sit down. Please sit down." She gave a little laugh. "Is there anything else you're too shy to ask for? Are you allowed to drink coffee on duty?"

When she had fluttered to rest, Salter said, "As you know, Jeremy Lucas, a onetime member of your book club, was found stabbed in his apartment."

She gave a twitchy smile around the room, then composed herself.

"Did you know him only through the book club?"

"Group. Not a club. Yes. We don't socialize. It seems better that way."

"How do you get new members, after someone drops out, say?"

"We have a waiting list, made up of people who have heard of the group and want to join. Suggestions are made, and if no one objects we put them on the waiting list."

"But if you don't know each other outside the group . . . ?"

"I didn't say we don't *know* each other. One of my colleagues was a member. I said we don't *socialize*. We don't recruit friends."

"Why? Why don't you recruit friends?"

"It's just something we instinctively agreed not to do in the beginning. I expect that doesn't make any sense to you, but that's our policy."

"You know what you're doing, I guess. Now, about Lucas. Did you know anything about him beyond his bookishness?" He wanted to say "book learning" or even "larnin" because her last sentence had sounded like a crack, but it would probably misfire.

"I believe he liked the great outdoors."

"In what way?"

"He communed with nature."

"How?"

"Physically."

"Hugging trees? Stuff like that?"

"I believe he *voyaged*." She pronounced it in the French way.

"He did what?"

"Like a *voyageur*."

"You mean he loaded up a freighter canoe with beads and whiskey and paddled to Winnipeg to trade them for skins?"

It worked. She stopped smiling at him. "I mean he went on canoe trips."

"Do you know what else he did in his spare time?"

"Concerts. He was extremely musical. Loved opera, except Benjamin Britten. He was an authority on Purcell. Dido's lament moved him to tears."

She was back again, making fun of him by pretending that he would know what she was talking about. Salter decided to ignore it. "Do you know who his companions were when he was doing these things?"

"The other people in his canoe? I'm afraid not."

"How did *he* get to be a member of your group?"

"Someone must have proposed him, I've forgotten who. Like all of the nominees, he came as a guest for a couple of meetings, then we asked him to join."

"What happens if you don't like someone who wants to join?"

"I can't really spell out our procedures, but they are designed to give the least offense. This is just a way we have of making sure people are in tune with us at the right level."

"Smart enough? Smart as the rest of you?"

"If you like. There are different ways of being smart, of course. I'm sure you are a smart policeman. Smart about literature is what we are looking for. Intelligent, thoughtful, undogmatic, widely read, and able to listen as well as talk."

"I understand he dropped out a few months ago. Any idea why?"

"I would guess he found another group more at his level. He was actually *very* smart. An intellectual quester, I would say."

"You don't have any idea who was in this other group?"

"I don't even know if there is one. I was just trying to acknowledge modestly that although ours is a good group, we know our limits. Maybe he went to look for a group to talk with about *Finnegan's Wake.*"

"That hard?"

"Very hard." She grinned, and Salter found himself thinking that she wasn't so bad. What he had read as her attempts to put him down were probably the signs of a larger than usual nervousness, an effort to get comfortable with herself in a new situation, that of being questioned by a copper.

She continued, "Actually, I can think of one person who might know. She dropped out of our group, too, a bit before Jerry left us. She was a musician, too. I mean she knew a lot about music and played the cello in an amateur orchestra. She hadn't been with us for long, about a year, and I have the feeling we didn't satisfy her. I sometimes caught her looking at her watch while we were trying to sort out an idea. Louise Wilder her name is. She and Jerry sometimes exchanged a remark or two about a concert they had both been to, or the latest singing star. Once when a countertenor came to town in an opera by Haydn, they explained to us what a countertenor was and how they retained their voices. Haydn? No, Handel. Anyway, they had that in common, and possibly bumped into each other more than the rest of us tone-deaf bookworms did."

Salter pricked up his ears. "Bumped into each other? No more than that? But they left the group around the same time. Did he drop out because she did, maybe?"

"I don't like that kind of speculation."

"No? I do. That's my job. Did you ever *wonder*, then, sort of privately?"

"As far as I know, Louise Wilder was and is happily married."

"And Lucas? What did you know about his love life?"

"I never thought about it. He gave off no vibes of any kind. Not to me, anyway."

"I'd better talk to Mrs. Wilder, I guess."

Louise Wilder lived on Sandringham Avenue, south of St. Clair, west off Yonge Street. The houses on Sandringham are worth a lot of money per square foot, and most of them have been transformed in various ways by people who want to live on Sandringham—but not in the style of a bank manager of the nineteen-twenties.

Not all the residents are rich. Some of the houses have been divided into apartments, or even discreetly into rooms to accommodate the lifestyles of the single apartment-dweller class—lecturers without tenure, young musicians, assistant editors—who prefer to live in the district rather than pay the same rent for a larger space in, say, Etobicoke, because of the easy access to bookstores, coffee shops, cinemas and the subway, and most of all, to other people like themselves.

Salter knew the street well. He and Annie had often walked it on Sunday afternoons, wondering if they could afford to move there. He thought he knew the Wilders' house, near the Avenue Road end where a higher proportion of the houses are still in their original condition, but when he came to it it did not strike a chord. It was a semidetached brick dwelling, and at a glance it looked to Salter as if it had been left alone, including retaining the original porch, but as his eye moved up to the second and third stories it was clear much restructuring had taken place, ending in a number of recently added skylights.

Louise Wilder was waiting for him on the porch. Somewhere between forty and fifty (it was getting harder and harder as he got older to locate them closer than that), dark-haired, plump, pretty—

Salter liked the look of her but regretted that she fell outside his two favorite categories.

"I had to leave school early for this," she said as she walked him into the house. "I suggested four-thirty so my husband wouldn't interrupt us."

"You teach, Mrs. Wilder?"

"I'm a secretary at a private school. My husband is an architect who specializes in renovation—you see his signs around here. You've come about Jerry Lucas, of course."

"I'm just ticking off names on lists, looking for information," Salter said. "This won't take long. A couple of people suggested that you might know Jerry Lucas better than anyone else in the group. They said you had been seen with him . . ."

"*Seen* with him? Where? Who said that?" She sounded genuinely surprised, and curious.

"Joe Lichtman, for one. And your leader, Sylvia Sparrow."

"Huh," she said, nearly grunted. "The human cannonball and, as you say, our leader. And where did Joe and Sylvia Sparrow see me?"

"I'm trying to remember. Concerts? Yeah. Roy Thompson Hall. I think so. Theaters, maybe. No. Concerts. They didn't say they saw you actually with him, like making up a couple."

"Good. I wasn't."

"Just chatting with him on the stairs or round the bar, something like that."

"If you live in Toronto and go to concerts, you are pretty well bound to bump into everyone else who likes music, at Roy Thompson Hall or the Ford Center or the St. Lawrence Center. The main venues. I went to hear *Xerxes* last winter and talked to six people I know well and waved to eleven others."

Salter had his notebook out. "What was that word?"

"*Xerxes*. It's got two exes," she added kindly.

"Thanks. Yes, that was the point they were making, too. But apparently you people in the group don't socialize with each other; you just get together once a month to talk about books. But because of the music, you and Lucas would have more to say to each other when you bumped into each other away from the group. That right?"

"More or less. But I didn't know anything about Jerry except that he liked Baroque opera, and he didn't like Brahms or Schumann. Like me."

"Many of you like that, are there? Who don't like those two, I mean?"

"I know a couple of others."

"Uh-huh. Now, let me ask a straight question. Did you ever see Lucas with a woman?"

"I never saw him any other way. He always had a woman in tow at the concerts where I saw him—which wasn't all *that* often. The only one I recognized was his sister, because he introduced her to me."

"So, apart from the music, you had no idea of his life outside the book group."

"No idea at all."

"Did he ever show an inclination to get to know you better?"

"Not in the least."

"You weren't too upset by the news, then."

"Of course I was. A man was murdered, a man I knew. But you can't stay upset, can you. I liked him, but we weren't friends. He wasn't part of my life."

Salter rubbed his hand over his head and yawned slightly as a sign to her that the interview was over and now he was just chatting. "He let someone into his apartment that night. A woman was seen."

"Where was she seen?"

"Getting out of the elevator. Do you know the building?"

She paused before she spoke. "I don't think we ever met in his apartment. Who saw her?"

"We? You said 'we.' You and him?"

"Of course not. I meant the book group. Who saw her?"

"A neighbor. Said the woman was kind of dressed up." Salter held onto the details, one of the oldest tactics in the book. Once in a while a suspect mentioned a detail they should not have known about—not often, but holding something back was instinctive.

"How do you mean, 'dressed up'?"

"Like, for a party. Of course, this woman may not be the person we're looking for."

"Surely . . . ?"

Salter shook his head. "I could give you six alternative explanations, all innocent. But I'd like to find her, because she might be able to point us down the right path."

"I can't help you, I'm afraid."

Salter stood up. "When did he drop out of the group? Why? Sylvia Sparrow called him an intellectual quester. That's a good phrase, isn't it? Is it accurate?"

"I don't know when he left because I was already gone. You see, the group always used to meet on Tuesdays, but Jerry had a strong lineup of concerts for that night, so he asked if we could switch to Monday, and they did. But Mondays are difficult for me, so I dropped out. I was looking for a new group, anyway."

"A bit of an intellectual quester, yourself, eh? Did you find one?"

"No, and I don't think I'll look anymore for a while."

They were at the door now. "How long ago did this happen, this change of nights?"

"Hang on." She returned to the living room and reappeared with a large leather bag from which she dug out her appointment book. "I dropped out in February. You'll have to ask Sylvia Sparrow or your friend Joe Lichtman about Jerry, but I have the feeling he lasted another couple of months. Wait a minute. I can do better than that. Yes, he called me and asked if I had found another group—I hadn't—let me see, a month later. He was nice enough to say that my going had made a hole in the old group. But that's all. Sorry. I thought I might have the exact date written down, but I don't. Sorry."

"If you come across it, or any other detail that you think might help, call me. I'm really collecting all the names I can get. Here's my card. Ask for me or Constable Smith."

"We're not making much progress, are we, sir?"

Salter slumped down to rest his chin on the desk and looked across at Smith, who had just sat down on the other side. There were several reasons why Salter preferred to work by himself, and now he had a new one: to avoid having an assistant for whom he had to find work and who made comments like that. It was like going fishing with Seth when the boy was eight and having the boy point out at the end of a long blank day that everyone else on the river was catching fish, so how come the Salters weren't?

"What have you been doing?"

"Knocking on doors, like you told me."

"Get anywhere?"

"No more news of our hooker. But a couple more people remembered the car, once I mentioned it."

"Car?"

"You remember an old fella with arthritis looking out his window saw a toffee-colored car parked on the street a few times lately, and once, the driver, a woman in a headscarf, walking along looking at the block," Smith reminded him.

"Not on the night that matters, though."

"No, still, I thought it was worth finding out about. I got a better identification from one person. He called it milk-chocolate colored, and said it was a convertible Volkswagen Golf with a sand-colored top. Sounds pretty distinctive, so I ran it past the parking enforcement office and they are going to get back to me if any of their patrol people remembers it."

"I told you, someone on surveillance, or even just someone trying to make up their minds whether they want to live on the street. A woman seeing if it feels safe at night. Any other ideas?"

"I think we should have another look at the girls on Jarvis Street."

"Barlow and Jensen never saw anyone who looked like Pussy-in-Boots?"

"No, sir. But I think it's like in Glasgow. Every tart on the street knows the Vice Squad, and the only time they will cooperate is when one of their own has been attacked. Even then they are more afraid of the pimps than they are of us. But if you get another Jack the Ripper, *then* they cooperate. But not for a simple disappearance, not until they know who is disappearing them. We need a new approach."

"Smitty, I'm sorry to tell you that I am playing poker with a bunch of lawyers tonight, but you go down to the red-light district by yourself. Make up a story, so they won't know you're one of us. With that accent, you could get away with any story. Tell you what, go down to Goodwill and buy yourself a coat, a foreign-looking one, tweed with a belt, make yourself look like an immigrant just off the boat. Then go down Jarvis looking for your sister.

"Did you ever see *The Picture of Dorian Gray?* The movie? In one part a sailor is going round the dives in Limehouse in Victorian times, looking for his sister who he believes is in the thrall of some filthy bastard who is having his dirty way with her. Try that." Salter sat back.

Smith said, "I don't think that would work, sir. Perhaps I could rent a kilt? Maybe not. I'm not sure which side the big safety pin goes on. You've given me an idea, though."

"Good. Tell me about it tomorrow."

"Oh, there was a call from a Jane Rudd. She's thought of something that might help us."

"What?"

"She said she preferred to speak to you herself. Here's her number."

Salter dialed the number unexcitedly. He did not anticipate that Jane Rudd had any revelations to offer.

"I've thought of something," she said. "After you left it came back to me that once Jerry and I had a conversation—can I speak confidentially? Privately?"

"I thought you wanted to tell me something. I can't promise to keep it to myself if it's useful."

"Wait until you've heard it."

"Try me, then. Our offices are regularly swept for bugs. We worry about the mob listening in."

"This is *personal.*"

"Go ahead."

"One night, after we had made love, we were exchanging lovers' histories. Do you know what I mean?"

"Like, when was the first time you did it, that kind of thing?"

"More or less. We got on to prostitutes, and I asked Jerry about his experience with them—I thought all men had some experience with prostitutes. He said he never had, and he never would have. He said he could not imagine rutting away for ten dollars a minute—that was his phrase, 'rutting away.' I think that's conclusive, don't you?"

"Of what?"

"It's at least an objective verification of what I said, that whoever this woman was, she certainly wasn't hired by Jerry."

"Sounds like it, all right. Thanks very much."

"Are there any other developments?"

"Not public ones. Don't hesitate to call me again if something strikes you." Salter put the phone down and looked up at the waiting Smith. "That was an old bedmate of Lucas's who says there's no way he would have paid for it."

"You believe her?"

"I believe she is giving an honest opinion, and I believe in this case she may be right."

"This part of your hunch?"

"That's right. I don't believe Pussy-in-Boots was a hooker, either. But what that one . . ." he pointed at the phone ". . . was really calling about was to find out how we are getting on. Trying to get into the loop, like Calvin Gregson, and everyone else."

"In the meantime, I should go back down to Jarvis Street and keep looking?"

"That's right."

"In case . . . ?"

"In case anyone asks if we looked properly. I'm keeping your nose clean, Smitty."

"And your own, sir."

"Me? I don't give a shit. With me it's just personal."

14

"We go to a different house each week," Bonar Robinson said, as he let Salter in. "That way we don't wear out our wives' welcome. Well, their acquiescence."

"They go out for the night? The wives?"

"They can stay home if they are very quiet." Robinson laughed to show he was joking. He seemed slightly excited, as if the presence of a policeman, even one more or less off duty, had energized him. "We're in here."

He led Salter through to a large room furnished like the lobby of a hotel, one of a superior chain. The two couches, the three armchairs, the broadloom, the shade the walls were painted, all fell within a narrow color range from wheat to cafe au lait. Even the pictures fell within the spectrum, all three scenes of a deserted seacoast in summer. Two enormous gilt-framed mirrors confirmed the impression of a traveller's rest. Half a dozen men were sitting around, waiting. There was no sign of cards.

"Introductions, then," Robinson said. He stood in the center of the room, looking over his glasses at each man in turn as he held Salter's elbow and revolved him slowly. "Scott Mercer; Larry Holt; Brian Davis; Andrew Cutler; Craig Lister."

The establishment, thought Salter. One of them, anyway.

"I told them you were coming and asked if anyone knew you, but our lawyers avoid criminals if possible and Scott and Brian work for investment companies and Craig is an investment broker, so your paths have not crossed, except for Larry, I understand." Salter and Holt nodded to each other but said nothing.

"This is kind of unusual, isn't it, Staff Inspector?" Andrew Cutler said. "We were questioned once before . . ."

Salter jumped in. "I'm new to the case, sir, and I need to make my own inquiries."

"No, no, I realize that. But I mean, isn't it unusual to see us all at once? Normally you take us one at a time, don't you, so you can compare our stories and see who is lying?" Cutler smiled genially, civilized, one member of the club to another.

"Is that what they did last time?"

The speaker looked around for confirming nods. "A couple of detectives came round to each of us at work. One asked questions and the other watched to see if we were pissing our pants."

"I could do that, but I thought I'd accept the report they already made. It seemed pretty thorough. What I'd like now is for you just to hear what I have to say, then respond by calling me tomorrow, if you can think of anything that might help me. I imagine you are as eager to find this killer as I am. And the sooner the better. The longer it goes, the more likelihood there is that all of you, and Flora Lucas, and anyone else who knew Lucas, will find themselves featured in one of the papers, and I assume you don't want that, so here's what I want to know. Do any of you know enough about Lucas's very private life to make sense of this hooker? You know about her?"

They all nodded, embarrassed.

"We heard," Robinson confirmed.

"So, question number one, do you have any confirmation in what you know about Lucas that he would have hired someone like that? Question number two is, if he didn't hire her, what was she doing there? She knew where to look for his apartment. Could it have been a joke? A practical joke? Nothing to do with Lucas, except that he got killed. I'm really just eliminating a remote possibility, because if she was hired as a joke by anyone here or known to you, someone would have come forward with her name and address. Wouldn't they? Now we have to find her, and we haven't any idea where to look.

"Finally, does anyone know how Lucas usually spent his Friday nights? Somebody told me that when you tried to reschedule an evening like this, Lucas was available any night except Friday but he never said why. Does anyone know why?

"Jerry might just have been going along with the crowd, Staff Inspector. The rest of us are married, except for Larry, who might as well be, and our wives don't like being left alone on Friday nights. I don't know that Jerry was unavailable. He just never questioned that Friday was a bad night for the rest of us."

"That's probably it, then. But would each of you call me tomorrow, even if you have nothing to say, so I can tick you off the list."

"You can't fool us, Staff Inspector. You have a message on Jerry's tape from the killer, don't you, and you want to compare our voice-prints."

Salter smiled. "Is that what they're called? So write me a note." He stood up.

"Care to stick around for a game, Staff Inspector?"

The question came from Robinson, but the others had been waiting for it. They sat watching him expectantly. Salter wondered if they had bet among themselves what he would say.

"There are clear regulations about playing cards with suspects, sir. But since none of you is under suspicion, then, yes, I'd like to."

The tone of mock pomposity Salter affected for this remark covered his excitement. It was a long time since he'd played poker, and he told himself that the reason he said yes was because he wanted to get a feel for Lucas's cronies, to get a feel for who would be most helpful. They were all smart and successful, but who were the sensible ones? Still, it was the prospect of a game of poker that was making him sweat slightly.

"Heigh-ho," said Mercer, the one who had joked about voice-prints. "Off to work we go."

Robinson led the group out of the room, through the adjacent dining room and across the garden by way of a covered glass corridor lined with gardening hardware and plants growing in pots, into a small separate building at the end of the garden. "My den," Robinson said.

All the equipment was laid out on a large table covered in green cloth. Seven chairs were placed around the table; a chest of poker chips stood on a side table.

"Be warned," Robinson said to Salter. "You are up against a bunch of sharks here."

"I know what you are," Salter said, "but can you play poker?"

"You'll pay for that," Robinson said. "Now, these are one-dollar chips, these are fives, tens and twenties. No, no, I'll just keep a tab. Three hundred each to start off, buy more when you need them." He issued everyone a pile of chips, and they sat down to play. It was dealer's choice, and they played a succession of different games, all the way from straight stud to "best five of seven: black twos, red sevens and the queen of spades wild."

Salter made no attempt to divine his opponent's minds, merely playing his own cards in the early part of the evening as erratically as possible so that if and when he got a really good hand it wouldn't be obvious. Thus very early he folded a full house as soon as someone else bet, clumsily throwing in the cards face up, and then two hands later took a single ace up against three hands that stayed in, which cost him eighty dollars.

Sometimes by accident he seemed brilliant, but on the whole he looked like someone who had never played the game before. By eleven o'clock he had been down as much as five hundred and up two hundred at various points, but now was fifty in the hole. Not a bad night, he thought. He had brought a thousand with him to make absolutely sure he had the wherewithal to sit at the table no matter what size the game was, and he was enjoying himself. He was playing poker again. And now he would start playing for keeps, fairly sure that he had not been sussed out yet.

Something else was happening. From the time the first hand was dealt, Salter had been aware of communication flickering about the group, messages below the level of speech. He had tried to brush aside the feeling, assuming it was a fairly natural result of his being an outsider. They did not exchange glances exactly; rather, they seemed to avoid each other's eyes as they worked to set him at his ease. It was the absence of family jokes that he noticed in the end, all the little joshing remarks you would expect among a group that had played together for a long time.

The feeling did not go away; by eleven o'clock it had jelled into a suspicion that he was being set up in some way, accompanied by the further feeling that the agreement among them had not quite jelled, or had not been adequately rehearsed. Twice two of them left the room, one after the other, apparently to visit the washroom, and returned looking as if they had had a meeting of some kind, speaking rather too loudly as if to blot out their unease. Whatever they're up to, he thought, they aren't much good at it.

Once, Salter asked, "Was Lucas a good player?"

Mercer said, when no one else spoke up, "I would say he was. I think he won more than he lost. We didn't keep close track."

"Jerry did," Cutler said. "He knew what had happened to the last dollar."

Salter said, "That sounds all right. I feel like I'm sitting in his chair tonight. I'd like to be worthy of him. Deal the cards. Let's see what I can do. I'm glad you didn't cancel the game, out of respect, something like that."

"We talked about it, but decided Jerry wouldn't have minded," Robinson said. "Then your deciding to come clinched it. Now, whose cards are they?"

About eleven thirty, Larry Holt made eye contact with Salter and hobbled out of the room, leaning on his cane. After a few minutes, there was the sound of a toilet flushing, and Salter, who had already folded, followed Holt through the door. A small kitchen, obviously no more than a wet bar for parties in the garden, led off from the hall. Beyond it, in an alcove, were two washrooms side by side, from one of which Holt emerged.

Just as he was about to speak to Salter, there were the sounds of someone leaving the den and coming their way, and Holt said, quickly and quietly, "The butter thing," and affected a cough as Mercer appeared.

Salter went into the washroom, peed, and sat down on the toilet to think. "The butter thing." What the hell did that mean? Maybe it was a code. Maybe "butter thing" was lawyer slang for "innocent" as in "butter wouldn't melt in his mouth" like U.S. President Bush, senior's "the integrity thing." Salter liked the idea of this, but he couldn't make any sense of it. Who was innocent? Of what? Or better, who looked innocent but was really guilty? Of what? But why would Holt betray his friends? What the hell was going on?

The toilet in the adjacent washroom flushed and Salter waited for the sound of steps to recede down the hall, then followed the sound into the card room, his brain squeaking with the problem.

Fifteen minutes later Robinson announced the last hand. "Dealer's choice," Robinson said. "I'm raising the limit to a thousand."

The limit had been five hundred. Salter tried not to look too interested. Robinson shuffled and got the deck cut, then jumped up saying, "Hang on, I left my drink in the kitchen," stepped out, and returned almost immediately with the drink. "Ready," he called and adjusted his chair to sit square to the table and dealt them all five cards.

Salter, antennae humming, couldn't believe what was going on. A dealer steps out of the room with the deck in his hand and returns and deals? Without asking anyone to cut the cards again? And no one else objecting? With the limit at a thousand, for Christ's sake? What kind of a fool did they take him for? He could call Robinson himself, of course, but now he felt a deep need to see what he could do to avoid being sandbagged, to turn Robinson's little game upside down, and he was forming an idea about where he would find the means.

Salter moved to pick up his hand. Before he could turn the cards over, Robinson leaned over the table and imprisoned Salter's hand on his cards. "One by one," he said.

"Sorry. Me to lead. I'll bet fifty." Now he had a third hint. Salter's mind was churning so hard he would not have been surprised if the other players could hear it.

"Blind?" Robinson looked surprised.

"It *is* the last hand?"

"Yes. Still. *Fifty*. Okay. Fifty it is. I'm in."

One by one the other players called.

Salter turned over the king of clubs. The four other cards turned up among them two picture cards, an eight and a six.

"A hundred," Salter said.

Once more they all matched his bet, and Salter turned up his next card, the king of diamonds.

Two other hands each revealed the beginnings of a possible flush. Robinson now had two jacks. Holt, with a nine and an eight of different suits, folded, catching a look of surprise from Robinson.

"Another king, please," Salter said, and sipped his drink. Something caught in his throat and he went into a violent coughing fit. After three or four paroxysms, he held up his hand, palm out, unable to speak, and hurried out to the kitchen for a glass of water.

He turned on the tap and looked around the kitchen, trying to identify the sounds he had heard Robinson make when he was supposed simply to be recovering his drink. The chief one was the fridge door; no doubt Robinson had added an ice cube to his drink, and Salter opened the fridge and peered inside. It was an old fridge, probably returned to light duties after a natural lifespan in the main kitchen; high up on the door was the butter compartment, the plastic door hinged on a spring that had become so weak that the door hung open slightly, making it not very effective for keeping the compartment the proper few degrees warmer than the rest of the fridge. The butter thing.

Salter pulled the door down, stared, said to himself, "Well, well," closed the fridge silently, gave a final cough and went back to the game.

He returned, apologized for holding them up, and turned up his next card, an ace. One of the two possible flushes broke and folded, another continued his suit. Robinson turned up a seven.

Salter, still high hand, said, "Two hundred."

The remaining flush, Mercer, called, and Robinson said, "And raise you two."

Salter said, "And two hundred more."

"Let's see your next card," Mercer said, writing out a slip of paper. "You're still high."

Salter turned up the king of hearts. Mercer broke his flush and folded. Robinson got the jack of spades. He now had three jacks and a seven.

Salter, who had three kings and an ace, said, "Five hundred."

Robinson called and said, "You can look at your last card but don't show it to me. Then we bet."

Salter lifted the corner of his card to peek at it, the six of diamonds, and waited for Robinson to do the same.

"You're still high," Robinson said. "Possible four kings to possible four jacks."

Salter looked again at his hole card and said, "A thousand."

"Did I hear a thousand?" Robinson asked, after a long pause. The others were all still, waiting.

"How much do we pay you guys?" Robinson asked, laughing a little, shaking his head in apparent wonder. "Call."

Salter said, "Four kings."

Almost before Salter had spoken, Robinson declaimed, "Four jacks!" and leaned towards the table, his arms extended to embrace the chips. Then Salter's words registered and he stopped in midgesture. "Wait a minute, *four kings!* You haven't got four kings, for Chrissake. Turn the card over."

Salter laughed. "Oh, not with *that* one. I don't even remember what that is. Let's see. The six of diamonds, that's right. No, no. Here's my other card." He reached into his pocket and pulled out a full deck, identical in markings to the deck they were playing with, shuffled through them, found the king of spades, inserted it into the hand on the table, said, "There. Four kings," and leaned forward to scoop up the chips.

"Hey, hey," Robinson said. "Hey!"

All the others except Holt made sounds of various kinds, looked back and forth between Salter and Robinson, and to each other, then fell silent again and waited for Robinson to move.

"What the fuck!" Robinson said, trying to laugh. "How long you been playing with two decks of cards? Eh?" He looked around for support, but the others, in various ways, retreated. Mercer found a handkerchief to blow into; Cutler pushed back from the table slightly and turned toward Davis, the two men seeking each others' support like two respectable matrons suddenly faced with a male stripper when they had been expecting a juggling act, or even a magician.

Lister leaned forward, fascinated by how Robinson was going to respond. Holt sat still.

Salter tidied the chips into a pile in front of him. "I guess the simplest way to sort this out would be for you guys to cash in whatever chips you've got left and the rest will be mine. You can write checks for your markers."

"Yours? Yours!" Robinson screamed. "You got that fucking king out of your pocket."

"You saw that, did you? Originally I got it out of the butter thing, where you put it. You want to know how long I've been playing with two decks of cards? Just for one hand, like you."

"You can't play with two decks," Robinson said. "Can he?"

"Listen to him, Bonar," Mercer said quietly, looking at the ceiling.

"I thought it was a house rule," Salter said, looking round the table.

"It was a joke," Lister said, also speaking very quietly. Davis nodded vigorously. "Just a joke."

"How do you mean? We aren't playing for keeps? We all give it back now, like at scout camp?" Salter grinned at them skeptically. "Ah, come on, guys. You wouldn't want *that* to get around, would you?"

"Just the last hand," Lister said. The others looked perplexed or worried.

"Yeah, but *I* wasn't in on the joke, see," said Salter. "That's my money in the middle. I had seventeen hundred dollars on that hand. Real money, which you could have kept if you'd won. Now you tell me it was a joke? *You're* the jokers."

"We were going to tell you after the hand. It was a gag. A practical joke."

Mercer said, "A joke that went wrong, though. I've got a suggestion. I think it's Salter's pot."

"Salter's pot!"

"Shut up for a minute, Bonar. Salter outbluffed us, and I hope he tells us how in a minute. We created a con—is that the right word?—and he beat us at it. He's earned the pot. What will you tell them down at headquarters, tomorrow, Staff Inspector?"

Salter had been thinking about this and all the other questions ever since he came across the spare deck in the refrigerator. "I'll tell them I took three lawyers and two stockbrokers for three thousand dollars. Which I have."

"Fair enough. Nothing about the butter compartment?"

"No, because it makes you look bad. People will wonder if you planned to keep my money. And also, because I *do* plan to keep *your* money, which may reflect badly on me, morally speaking." He smiled cheerfully. "I haven't figured it out yet. What will your story be?"

Lister looked around the table. "The same, I think." Everyone except Robinson nodded. "It's an interesting story that will be told around, no matter what we do. It could look bad, if someone, anyone, doesn't believe we would have given you your money back. *I* know we would because I'm the soul of integrity, as are we all, but I'm not going to get the chance to prove it now, am I, and some of our colleagues already have their doubts. So keep the money and we'll all shut up. But we're entitled to something. How the hell did you figure it out?"

This was the tricky bit. Salter smiled and looked around at them in what he imagined was Sherlockian fashion, catching Holt's eye to reassure him that he was not about to be betrayed.

"You made a couple of mistakes," he said. "The big one was using the fridge to stash the spare deck. Before we started playing that last hand, your colleague there slapped my hand down on my cards when I went to turn them over, by mistake, like. The cards were cold, real cold, like they'd been in the fridge. So I had a coughing fit and went out to the kitchen where I found the deck we have been using all night in the butter compartment. *Those* cards were still warm. I wish I had had time to go through the deck for the king and not have to look for it in front of you. I mean it would have been fun if I had been a real sharpie and been able to switch the card in my hand. Then your faces would have been something. But you can't have everything. This'll do." He started to pick up the money.

"You really going to take it?" Robinson asked. He looked around the table for support.

"Of course he is," Lister said quickly, cutting Robinson off. "Well

142

done, Staff Inspector. Don't come again." He laughed and put out his hand.

Salter shook hands all around, including Robinson's, and left.

As he crossed the street a few moments after he was called from behind. It was Holt. "I've just thought of something," he said, hobbling along quickly to catch up with Salter. When they were farther away from the house, he said, "Actually I just wanted to congratulate you, and thank you. I thought I was in the shit for a minute, but you were clever."

"Why did you do it? Why did you tell me, I mean?"

"I don't like practical jokes. Bonar set it up and it seemed like a good gag until we got into it. Then I realized that either you were going to look the goat when we told you, or it would cost you a lot of money if we didn't."

"*If* you didn't? There was some chance of that?"

"While you were in the bathroom someone suggested we not go ahead with the last hand because maybe you would be very pissed off and who wants a senior cop pissed off with him? The joke, in other words, had gotten out of hand. And someone, not seriously at first, I think, said maybe we shouldn't tell you. And then someone else felt that we should call it off, but Robinson was gung ho, and before we could settle it you came out of the bathroom."

"Why did *you* tell me? Oh, yeah, you don't like practical jokes. You're right. Got messy, didn't it? You think I should give the money back now?"

"As Davis said, it was our con, but you outconned us."

"And besides, if the story does get out this way, you'll look like assholes but like good losers, too, won't you?"

"That's a point."

"I suppose if I gave the money to the Salvation Army I could feel good, too."

"You could."

"But I don't have a bad conscience. Put it like this, for me this is just old-fashioned ill-gotten gains, just as much mine as anybody's. This is where Lucas and I differ. I understand that Lucas would not have dreamed of doing what I'm doing, right? The soul of integrity, as that one in there called himself tonight, although he was being jokey. That right? But Lucas really was, wasn't he? Would you have called him that?"

"Yes. He would not have taken the money. But he wouldn't have allowed the joke to develop, either. He was a very scrupulous man."

"Well, there you are. I'm not. I plan to spend it all on a trip to Vegas. Maybe I'm on a roll. Now, what's your excuse to them for running after me?"

"To offer you a ride. Someone said you walked here."

"I'll walk home, thanks. I don't live far away. Have a nice evening."

15

The next morning, Smith said, "Did Dame Fortune smile on you last night?"

"What? Yes, she did. How about you? Find any trace of Pussy-in-Boots?"

"You'll be glad to hear I didn't. But I'll keep trying. There's lots of hookers down that way; then there's Parkdale, is it?"

Salter said, slightly hesitantly, "I was only kidding about Dorian Gray."

"Och, I know that. But I'm not."

"What was your line?"

"Do you mind if I tell you later? If you're right, it doesn't matter, does it? Did you win much?"

"Yes. What did you tell them? The hookers. To get them on your side."

"How much did you win?"

"I promised the lawyers I wouldn't tell, to save them embarrassment. What did you tell the ladies on Jarvis?"

"Later, sir. How much did you win?"

"Three thousand dollars."

"That's a nice round sum. Is it evidence?"

"I don't see how it can be."

"Then you can keep it."

"I plan to, and Smitty, don't tell anyone. I promised these lawyers, remember."

By the time Salter stopped daydreaming, he was losing the second game 13–4, having already lost the first. Losing this one would mean losing the set, although they always played the third, anyway, since they were only playing for fun and for the sake of their health. Salter managed a lob that Lichtman had to scramble for, then smashed Lichtman's return into the corner to regain the serve.

Now he invoked the litany of phrases learned from sports commentators: "Then Salter dug down deep and found something extra"; "Salter concentrated fiercely, focussing on his opponent's weaknesses"; and his favorite, "Now Salter recited a mantra and invoked the ultimate umpire."

In fact he did none of these things. He was always amazed that sports writers and the professionals they wrote about seemed to know exactly what was happening on the court and in themselves when the game's fortunes changed. He had never caught himself in any act of conscious analysis and its consequence—an instant new battle plan. He was aware only of tensing up like someone preparing to jump on a moving train.

He brought the score to 13–13 before he let his mind return, and Lichtman sneaked back to win the deciding couple of points. Salter won the third game easily, but it was Lichtman's day.

At the bar, a rosy, grinning Lichtman said, as expected, "Christ, I thought you were going to turn the fucker over again. But I knew I just had to wait, so I kept a litle bit saved up for those last two points, then I blew you away. But you played well."

"Next time, Joe," Salter said, suppressing the urge to analyze the game in a way to diminish Lichtman's victory. "You played *really* well."

Then he had to listen for ten minutes while Lichtman explained to him how he had won—ten minutes was obligatory—but finally he was able to change the subject without seeming to cut off his opponent's victory chant.

"How's Go-ethe coming?" he asked.

Lichtman corrugated his forehead. "Ah," he said, finally, "Goethe."

"That's the fella. When do you have to tell them about him?"

"Thursday. Tomorrow. I'm all ready. A couple of them have already phoned to say they can't make it. That usually means they find the book too hard to read."

"Too difficult? I thought you were in one of the more upmarket groups?"

"Not difficult intellectually, necessarily. Just unreadable. Like *Over Prairie Trails*. And people have pet hates. One member only joined on condition we would never try Virginia Woolf."

"You miss Louise Wilder?"

"You've been talking to our leader. Yeah, they do. *I* don't miss her. I never met her. How about you? Found the guy who killed Jerry Lucas yet?"

Salter blinked, then remembered that although everyone closely connected to the case knew about the hooker, her story was not yet public knowledge, and it was natural of Lichtman to refer to the killer as a "guy."

"We've got him down at headquarters hung up by his thumbs in the basement. Every once in a while a couple of the boys go down and beat on him for a while, but he won't confess. Three days it's been."

Lichtman laughed. "There was a bit of mystery about Lucas, did I tell you? You've seen his apartment? What was it like?"

"Don't you remember?"

"None of them had been in it. When it was his turn to play host, they went to Sylvia's, and Jerry brought a case of wine and ordered in some gourmet snacks. I always assumed either he lived in total squalor like Walter Matthau in that movie, you know, *The Odd Couple*, or he couldn't stand people leaving dirty marks all over the place, like the other one, Tony Randall."

"I doubt if it was either. It wasn't just your book group he avoided entertaining; he did the same with his poker buddies. He was just giving himself the least trouble. He bought good wine, I bet, and the catering was gourmet, you say? But someone else cleaned up." And then Salter heard what he was saying. "How long has the group been meeting?"

"About three years."

"And all of you—Lucas, Louise Wilder, you, Sylvia Sparrow—you'd all been coming from the beginning?"

"Not me. I just joined, I told you."

"All of the others?"

"Beverly Potts is fairly recent, but all the others, yeah."

"And in three years you've never been inside Lucas's apartment?"

"Not once. They used to joke about it, making suggestions why. Apart from my idea of *The Odd Couple*, I mean. Someone thought he probably had a mad housekeeper, stuff like that."

"There was nothing like that. I think it was just the convenience, for him, of spending money to save energy. Same time next week?"

"Sure. I'll book the court. What's the rush?"

"I've just had an idea . . ."

"At my age that's like a hard-on: not too easy to come by. Don't let it get away from you."

The group always met at eight. Salter waited until seven forty-five. If Louise Wilder was at home he would ask her if she still had the book group's schedule around because he wanted to know where they were meeting next. But he did not expect to find her home.

A young man answered and Salter introduced himself and asked to speak to Louise.

"This about the—ah—Lucas case?" A noisy, slightly pompous voice, imitating the mannerisms of his elders.

"Yes."

"She's quite upset by it, you know."

"That's not surprising. When someone you know is murdered it's different from reading about it in the papers. Can I speak to her, please?"

"If you would leave a message I'll see that she gets it. She's out tonight. Wait a minute. Yes, it's her night for playing *Femme savante*."

"Playing what?"

"Her bluestocking night."

This time Salter did not even say "What?" but waited for the boy to explain himself. He was pretty sure that *"femme savante"* and "bluestocking" were terms being used to display the speaker's learning; Angus had done the same thing for a while in his last year of high school. He was also pretty sure that they pointed in the right direction, as he waited for the boy to say so. "It is her book group night. That's all it says on the calendar. So shall I give her a message?"

"Tell her to call me tomorrow, would you? At headquarters. Who am I talking to?"

"Her son, Derwent."

"Is your father there?"

"The last I heard he was working late at the office, as they say, though I don't think that's a euphemism in Papa's case. But I'm not here much, either, so I shall leave Mother an elaborate note."

She called at nine, shortly after Salter arrived at the office the next day. "I'd like to meet with you," she said. "As soon as possible."

"You want me to come to the house?"

"No. My husband may be home."

"So come down to my office."

"I don't much want to be seen in your office, unless I have to."

"Fran's is near the corner. You know Fran's?"

"I'm at school now."

"Shall I send a car for you?"

"No, no. Not to the school."

Then Salter grew bored with the problem. "Tell them you've got an emergency, and get a cab. I'll be in Fran's in fifteen minutes. You come, too." He hung up.

When she arrived at the restaurant, he was waiting, ready to continue to deal with her briskly, but she began with an apology. "I just wanted to speak to you before you phoned my home again."

"Because your husband might start getting curious."

"More or less. Could we get on with it?"

Salter decided to leave the point for the moment, guessing that she was concerned she might be tripped up when Salter compared notes with her husband. "Sure. Are you still a member of the group?"

"I told you I dropped out, and you've confirmed that with the others."

"So what's going on? A little hanky-panky."

"A little what! Oh, I suppose so."

"Nothing to do with me, then."

"No."

"So, after the book group changed its night, you dropped out and began an affair on the old book-group night."

"Yes."

"Didn't your husband wonder why you never met at your house anymore?"

"I told him we always met at Sylvia's."

Salter smiled. "Not easy, is it?"

"What?"

"Having an affair. I'm sorry you had to come down just to tell me."

"I couldn't speak on the phone at home or at the school."

"Right. You want to get yourself one of those mobile phones. Well, that clears that up, doesn't it. You could have told me earlier, though."

"It was none of your business earlier."

"When did it become my business?"

"It never did. But once you started . . ."

"Believing you? And calling you at home?"

She said nothing.

"Now that I know, I'll try to avoid making assumptions about where you are. To your husband, I mean."

She said quietly, "I'm looking for another group that meets on Thursday night. Until then, I shall just take the night off."

"It'll be our secret, Mrs. Wilder."

She did not rise to this. "If you need me any more, would you call me at the school, please. Here's a card with the number and my extension. Identify yourself officially, too, please. I don't want any gossip around the school at the phone calls I get from unidentified men." She stood up. "But with any luck, this is the last I shall see or hear of you."

Don't bet on it, thought Salter, as he watched her head move down the corridor, above the partitions. The little gavotte they had just danced confirmed for him what he had guessed on the squash court. He had taken a risk: she ought to have reacted at his interest in her affair, if it had nothing to do with the case. The absence of any sign of tension or embarrassment seemed to indicate that she had been expecting something like this and was trying to keep her head, to think clearly.

He returned to the office and gave Smith the keys to the Lucas apartment. "Get on over there and search the place again," he said.

"Sir, our people were pretty thorough."

"I know, but they didn't know what they were looking for. I do. Go over there and find a name, or a set of initials. Look for Louise, or L. W. If you find the name Louise Wilder, tell me, but I'll be disappointed. Using the whole name would be too impersonal. Now, where will you look?" In his excitement Salter was addressing Smith like a child, making him repeat his instructions.

The constable smiled. "I'll start with the personal books we took from the flat. The diary, the appointment book. Would he have used a code word?"

"Why?"

"In case someone came across it. Someone he wouldn't want to know that he knew Louise, or L. W. When you're writing up a diary, you have to consider the possibility of maybe getting into an accident, then someone reading your diary and finding out you are having an affair with the minister's wife, so you give her a code name. I give mine men's names. My last was Phyllis, so I called her Phillip, in the diary." He grinned.

"Did you start alphabetically?"

"What? Oh, no. Anyway, this fella Lucas was a widower who didn't have anyone looking over his shoulder. His sister wouldn't have approved, I would think, but she wouldn't be peeking in his diary, would she?"

"Where else are you going to look?"

"You think our fella was diddling the fair Louise?"

"I think it was likely."

"What is it I'm doing, then?"

"Proving it."

"So I'll search for fond postcards, that sort of thing. Gift tags with loving messages saved in his underwear drawer."

"Where else will you look?"

"I'll make sure there's no writing on the labels of whiskey bottles and such. Those cardboard cylinders that single malt comes in take a lovely message in grease pencil."

"Where else?"

"I've a feeling you have some place in mind, sir. A hunch."

"Once, about ten years ago, I identified a suspect by the flyleaf of a book which he had given to the victim. These are all bookworms, remember."

"Right you are, I'll check all flyleaves."

"Her husband is an architect, and she is the secretary of a very swish private girls' school. Keep your eyes open for identifiable notepaper. Off you go now."

"I shouldn't start with these books we have in the office?"

"No. Start with the books in the apartment."

Smith called back before noon. His voice was rich with satisfaction. "I am standing in the study of Mr. Jerry Lucas," he said. "And I have in my hand a book. On the flyleaf there is a handwritten message. "It says, To Jerry, from Louise."

"Not with love? Something like that?"

"Better than that. The message is completely enclosed within an amateur rendering of the outline of a heart, a valentine, as it were, done in red crayon. I think that's what you wanted, sir."

"That's the only one?"

"I came across it almost immediately. I thought it might be enough for you."

"What's the book?"

"*Elective Affinities*, by G-O-E-T-H-E."

"Goethe."

"Aye? I knew it would be tricky. That's why I spelled it out."

"It's not quite enough. That's on the book group list. He might have asked her to pick up a copy for him, and the inscription is a little joke. See what else you can find."

"Right you are, sir. It is *guid* though, isn't it?"

"Oh, yes. It is that."

———

"I asked you to come down again because I want to show you something to see if you can identify it."

They were in Fran's again. It was five o'clock, the earliest that Louise Wilder could get away from the school.

Salter drew *Elective Affinities* from his pocket, opened it to the flyleaf, and watched her try to calm down.

"So what was going on? Still just a little hanky-panky?"

She said nothing, her silence an assent. Her face was closed and hostile.

"When did you meet him?"

"The third Thursday in the month."

"How long had you been meeting?"

"About six months."

"Since you dropped out of the book group."

"That was the point of dropping out, obviously. It gave me a night when I didn't have to explain where I had been."

Salter said, "I was pretty sure this morning that you had been to Lucas's apartment, but it still might have been harmless without old Goethe here. It wasn't, was it?"

"We were lovers."

"Yes. That's not my concern, though, unless you killed him. What I want to know is, now you know you can talk, do you have anything to say that might interest me? Like who might have killed him?"

"Don't be grotesque."

"Didn't he ever tell you about his enemies?"

"I don't think he had any. We talked about music, we gossiped a little about the only people we had in common—the rest of the group—and so forth. He wasn't much interested in people, either."

"Where were you going?"

She understood him immediately. "Nowhere. We were lovers but we weren't in love. We didn't think of each other continually, and we didn't yearn to be together all the time. Once a month doesn't sound like much, but—" she shrugged "—We had both reached the age of enjoyment, which comes after the age of passion."

"The age of enjoyment. I must remember that."

"That was Jerry's phrase. The point is we weren't about to upset our other worlds."

Salter said, "The night Lucas was killed, a woman came to his apartment. She looked like a hooker. Dressed like one, anyway. Now you and Lucas were pretty easy with each other—the age of enjoyment: I like that—so you might have an opinion about what that girl was doing. The usual thing? Did he regularly entertain hookers, as well as you?"

She said, slowly and carefully, "I don't believe that Jerry would have hired a prostitute in a thousand years, if that's what you're asking, though it's not unusual for someone to harbor a secret like that until he dies, is it?"

"Go on."

"What do you mean, 'Go on'?"

"I mean tell me what you think. If you don't think he would use a hooker, then what was one doing in his apartment?"

Again, slowly and thoughtfully, she answered. "It could have been a mistake. Did anyone see her go in?"

"Like Pizza Pizza getting the wrong address, you think?"

"Or it might have been some kind of joke."

"That's a word that's cropped up before. What kind of joke?"

"A practical one. A group of his friends hired her to embarrass him. Did he let her in?"

"We're still finding these things out."

"Didn't anyone see her leave?"

Salter assumed an amiable expression. "You're not allowed to ask questions. That's *my* job. If you don't have any more to tell me, we can leave it there." He stood up.

"For good?" She had nearly recovered her poise.

"That depends. I may have to come back to you down the road a bit."

"Am I going to get dragged into this?"

"At the moment, all I can see is we might need a couple of hairs from you so that the forensic people can place you in Lucas's apartment, and cross the traces of you off the list."

"Will these do?" She reached up and tugged out a few hairs and handed them to him.

He opened the *Elective Affinities* at the flyleaf and she dropped them in. He said, "These will do. By the way, what's it like? The book."

"I've no idea. We hadn't done it before I left the group, but I'd bought it early to give to Jerry, as a present."

"Ah. I wondered about that."

16

S mith said, "There's someone else we should be looking for, sir. Talking to those dollies on Jarvis Street made me wonder. How did Pussy-in-Boots get to Prince Arthur that night?"

"By cab," Salter said. "I don't think hookers use buses, not when they are in war paint."

"Barlow and Jensen covered that. No cab driver has been found who drove to that address that night, or who had our lady as a passenger."

"So?"

"So she drove her own car."

"Or her pimp did."

"Aye. But assuming the first, I began to wonder where she parked. You know that area, sir?"

"I lived there a long time ago, with my first wife."

"Then you'd know there's not many meters in the area. There's a big parking lot that runs behind Bloor Street from Bedford Road nearly up to the back of the Park Plaza Hotel, with a pedestrian exit onto Prince Arthur. That would be pretty good for someone who doesn't want to be seen walking around in fancy dress. She could park up near the Bedford Road end, nip across the street and be in the apartment building in a jiffy. That was my reasoning.

"So I had a chat with the attendant, and wouldn't you know it, my luck was in, he was on duty that night and witnessed an altercation between Pussy-in-Boots and a man who accosted her. Perhaps another punter, sir."

"A what?"

"A customer. A john. What the attendant saw, then, was Pussy walking towards her car and then being stopped by this man. They talked for a minute and then she went on to her car. He went after her to stop her, it seemed, and the attendant looked out of his booth and shouted across the lot, and she stepped into the car and drove to the booth, paid her money and left.

"Did he get a look at her face?"

"He said he asked her if the guy had been bothering her but she didn't even look up, so he could only see the bit the wig left uncovered, and it was hard to tell. It was just a face, maybe not *too* young, but he's not sure."

"And the customer?"

"He had his car there, too, and a few minutes later he drove up to the kiosk and paid his parking fee. They had a few words: the attendant told him not to hang around the lot, and the man told him to go fuck himself, and drove off before the attendant could get out of his booth and thump him."

"A description?"

"Middle-aged. Pretty bald, but long at the back. Mouse-colored hair. Clean-shaven. Leather jacket. Driving a white pickup truck, with a fitted-cargo box behind the cab, like one of those that go around selling frozen food door-to-door. You know them?"

"Does it seem obvious to you?"

"The obvious interpretation is that he propositioned her, and she shook him off. Now if we could find this second bloke, we could get a better description of her, wouldn't you think? Face, voice, all of it, he must have gotten, even in a small argument. But how the hell do you go about finding whoever it was that was looking for a hooker that night?"

"You could start with the pickup truck."

"Aye, and probably end with it, too."

"What's that?" Salter pointed to the magazine Smith was carrying.

"Ah, yes. I brought this back from the apartment in case you thought it might be significant." He put it on the desk. "You know the magazine? *The Hogtowner*. Nasty name."

"It's the name the people who didn't like Toronto used to call it, once upon a time. Don't ask me why. Something to do with the meat-packing plants, I think. This magazine started as a scandal sheet, you know—gossip columns with rude names for the famous, faked-up photographs of homophobic politicians buggering each other, nothing was sacred; they were always being sued for libel. But it worked, because in a few years it got a glossy cover and began printing real scandal, and you started to find it in dentists' waiting rooms. Well, maybe not, because there was always something in it to offend some-body. Was this the only magazine in the apartment?"

"No, but it was in a drawer and I took that to be significant."

"So what's in it?"

"Nothing of any interest to an immigrant from Glasgow. But you may see something. And that woman called again. Jane Rudd."

"Shit. She has to speak to me personally, I suppose."

"That seemed to be the idea."

"Let's get it over with." He dialed the number and Jane Rudd, evidently waiting for his call, said, "I'll have to close the door. A moment."

What now? Salter wondered.

"I've just remembered another talk we had. He was telling me of an experience he had in Mexico when he visited a Canadian writer once, someone he had been in college with. They wanted a drink, and his friend said that the best bar in town was in the local brothel, so that's where they went. He said he felt like Graham Greene, re-searching a book. Again, there was no question of his hiring one of the girls." She stopped.

"Thank you," Salter said. "That it?"

"You told me to let you know if I thought of anything."

"Yes. Thank you."

"Are you still seeking information?"

"Whatever you think might be useful. Thanks again." Salter hung up. "She's still trying to find out what we're up to," he said to Smith.

He sat down and started to browse through the magazine, and came very quickly to the reason Lucas had kept it, an article about the trial of a crooked stockbroker who had borrowed money from his clients' accounts and been unable to pay it back before one of the clients found out. Someone had marked the place of the article with a little bundle of newspaper clippings. Nothing else in the magazine seemed to have been touched. Salter settled down to read.

17

He read the article twice, and then the little bundle of newspaper clippings. The article in *The Hogtowner* expanded on the facts related in the clippings by noting there would have been no arrest at all had not one of the victims persisted in harassing what *The Hogtowner* referred to as the "Dickhead Squad" until eventually they agreed they had a case to prosecute. Salter called the Fraud Squad and explained his request.

"You want Larson," the sergeant in charge of the squad told him. "He was the one who nailed that stock promoter. He's here. Hold on."

Larson had to be reminded of the details of the case, then he agreed, as long as no one was listening, that *The Hogtowner* might have had a point. "We'd have gotten around to it, but it didn't have a very high priority. At the time we had a rash of cases of senior citizens being conned out of their savings, so this Harry Cane seemed to me to be not so urgent. Frankly, I saw it as a bunch of greedy, rich bastards being taken to the cleaners by one of their own, and no one that mattered had gotten hurt—I mean, no one dependent on a seniors' pension. So I was inclined to—what's that saying, 'Let Greek eat Greek'? Is that the phrase?"

"That's not the original, but I like yours better. So what got you moving?"

"Pressure, like *The Hogtowner* said; that, and finding a victim who was really suffering. Preparing the case took a long time, because

Cane got himself a couple of high-priced lawyers, so we had to be extra careful in how we proceeded. But finally we were ready, and then, wouldn't you know it, Cane agreed to plead guilty on one of the charges and that was that. He went to jail for a couple of years. Actually about nine months, I suppose."

"Why did they concede?"

"They made an arrangement with us—I mean us upstairs, not at the level of you and me—on Cane's sentence and the minimum testimony to be heard in court. That's my guess."

"Who was it that put the pressure on you? To prosecute."

"The relatives of a woman named Vera Selina. I remember her name because Selina's my wife's first name. She made an impact statement that was read in court, about how she suffered from the fraud."

"By losing her money."

"That's it."

"And no other names came out?"

"Not in court. I made a list of the people who Cane swindled but who didn't want to prosecute, but I can't remember now who was on it. You know how it is. You do all the work to make a case and you send it off and they decide not to proceed. Why? Who the fuck knows? Or cares. I don't think about it."

"Is the list in your files?"

"I doubt it. I'll check. Call you back."

An hour later, Larson said, "Interesting. The whole file is missing. Or rather, the file is here but it's pretty well empty, except for a note saying the contents were passed to the attorney general's office. They needed it to prepare the case against Cane."

"You don't remember any of the names?"

"No, except the lawyers, Tannenbaum and Gregson."

"Which one defended Cane?

"Tannenbaum. He took over in the middle from a couple of others."

"And Gregson. Who was he representing?"

"I don't remember. I know he was involved. When you hear names like Tannenbaum and Gregson, you prick up your ears, don't you? Make sure all your evidence is under lock and key."

"Are they that good?"

"It's a matter of perception, isn't it? And money. Fact is, if you're from Rosedale you hire Tannenbaum, but if you're from Forest Hill, then Gregson's your man."

"Why?"

"If you're from Rosedale and you hire Gregson, then what the jury sees is Upper Canada College looking after one of the old boys, whereas if you hire Tannenbaum they keep an open mind. Same thing, if you're a Jew, and you hire Tannenbaum, then you can see the whisper going round the jury: 'Which synagogue do they both belong to?' But if you hire Gregson then they relax."

"Thanks." Salter hung up and dialed Gregson's number. "You said to call you anytime, Mr. Gregson. Something's just cropped up I didn't know about. Harry Cane. Remember him? Yes. Then why don't we have a cup of coffee tomorrow at ten. In the Food Court at College Park. Under the courtroom, okay?"

"I was working pro bono, you know. I do that from time to time. Makes me feel good."

"Mr. Gregson . . ." Salter began.

"Calvin."

"Calvin, then, if we are going to believe each other in future about the big things, we'll have to tell the truth now, won't we, over the little things. Who were you representing?"

"How do you mean? I had no status in the courtroom."

"Jesus Christ. Look. Feel under my jacket. Go ahead, no one's watching. See, I'm not wired, and we're all alone. Now, can we have a normal conversation in which I ask you a question and you tell me the answer? I know the list of possibles you could have been representing, or advising or whatever it's called if you don't have any stature."

"Status. It's a legal term. It doesn't mean the same to a layman."

"That right? Okay. Now, who were you protecting?"

"Charlie—may I? Charlie?—these people did not want their names made public, and they still don't. Give me a good reason why you should know. Or rather, give the attorney general's office a reason. He cooperated."

"In a cover-up?"

"Knock it off. No one is covering anything up, just protecting their reputations."

"Who actually hired you?"

"I told you, a group of people, Cane's clients."

"Who? I need to know."

"They were just a group of friends who would look damn silly, gullible, if this came out. They had had a little flutter and they were prepared to pay for it, but not with their reputations."

"Lawyers?"

"Yes."

Salter wanted to laugh. He said, "Let me guess." He named each of the lawyers he had played cards with. "You represent guys like this for free?"

Gregson sighed. "One day, Charlie Salter, I'll get you in a court-room and make you pay attention. I was there to keep their names out of it. Not Larry Holt. He wasn't sucked in. I didn't make a move, officially. A number of people could have looked very foolish; when an old widow is shown to have been gullible, that evokes our sym-pathy, but when you show a gang of lawyers being gullible, then the public finds that funny. More than that, if a lawyer shows himself to be a monkey's uncle, that's far worse in the eyes of his clients than if he is slightly crooked or likes to suck his stenographer's toes. Who cares anymore about lechery, or graft, or corruption, but you don't want a fool to represent you in court, do you?"

"This guy Cane must have been good."

"Oh, he was. We'll hear from him again."

"Not promoting stock? I mean . . ."

"No, no. That would be illegal. No, he'll find something else. He's always thinking up swindles. That it, then?"

"I'm going to have to talk to some of these people."

"Why do you have to? What do you need to know?"

"You still their lawyer? They're not under suspicion. I'm just curious."

"What about?"

"Calvin, I'd just as soon keep it confidential in view of their prominence. And this is the last of *your* questions I'll answer. I'm curious to know who introduced them to Cane. You don't know? Nor do I, and I'd like to. In some way, maybe the obvious way, Cane was connected to Jerry Lucas. Maybe they can help me."

"I doubt it . . ." He broke off as Salter stood up.

The policeman was staring at the escalator, where Constable Smith had just gotten off and was walking toward them at the same time as a trio of drably dressed women wearing no makeup, looking like extras in a European movie about a famine, ran together across the court, shouting and waving at Smith and then surrounding him. Salter began to go to Smith's assistance, but he saw they were not hostile, just excited, keen to tell him something important. The group chattered hard for a few minutes, then the women ran off to the elevator shouting good-byes to Smith.

Salter took the constable by the arm and sat him down at the table as Gregson also stood up.

Smith said, "It's you I was looking for, Mr. Gregson. Your office called. If you can get there in ten minutes, Keith Miller can fit you in this morning."

"Christ." Gregson gathered himself together. "That's my barber. I need a cab. We finished?"

"Yes. Thanks, Calvin."

As Gregson hurried off, Salter turned to Smith. "What was that all about? Who were those women? Street people? You been giving away your money?"

"I'm embarrassed. I was going to tell you before, but we were cut off."

"Tell me now."

"They're hoors, sir."

"Those three? What kind of a living can they make looking like that?"

"They're appearing in court this morning." Smith pointed to the ceiling. "They were booked for—what do you call it—propositioning?"

"Soliciting. So why do they look like that?"

"The idea is to look pitiful on the stand. Selling their bodies to get bread for their children, are they not? They are the three I got into conversation with the night before last."

"On Jarvis Street."

"No, one street over. On Church. There's a coffee shop there near the college where we had a chat."

"The four of you."

"Aye."

"What about? I know, but you tell me. First of all, did you have any trouble getting them to talk?"

"No, I didn't. I'd like to ascribe that to my winning personality, but I think it might have been my story that made them laugh."

"Jesus, you didn't really tell them you were a sailor looking for your sister?"

"Oh, no. That was *your* idea. But it did give me an idea of my own. The trouble with your story is: how could I have a sister who didn't have a Glasgow accent, d'ye see? No, I told them I'd met this Canadian girl on holiday in Glasgow, and fell in love with her, never realizing she was on the game. When she went back to Toronto I wrote her letters, but I never got any answer so I came over to look for her. I told her I was coming and I went to the address she gave me, but she was gone. It was a lodging house, or a boarding house, on Sumach Street. When I asked her landlady if she'd left a forwarding address, she laughed at me. Then she took pity on me, and made me a cup of tea, and told me that my Mary—that's the name she gave me, Mary LaRue—"

"Mary what?"

"LaRue, sir. It was the first Canadian-sounding name that popped into my head. I think it must have come from one of the first stories I read about Canada when I was a kid, about a fight between a Mountie named McAllister and a trapper named Frenchie LaRue. It's a story about the Frozen North . . ."

"I'll read it for myself. What did this landlady tell you about Mary? I mean what did you make up to tell the women about what the landlady—oh Christ, just go on."

"To start with, she told me Mary was a tart, and if I wanted to find her I should cruise—that was her word—Jarvis Street. And I'd just done Jarvis and was starting on cruising Church when I stopped off for a cup of coffee and a doughnut."

"And this made these hookers laugh?"

"Aye. Then they told me to fuck off. They said they had figured me for a dumb copper from a hundred yards away."

"And then?"

"Then I told them the truth."

"Which was?"

"That I was a police officer, right enough, working undercover, looking for a girl who has disappeared. All we knew was that there was a killer in the area, looking for a prostitute with blond hair wearing silver boots, and we wanted to find her before he did. This got them on my side. They're all scared of maniacs: prostitutes are very vulnerable, and if one of them is killed they wonder who will be next. So those three promised to spread the word and keep an eye out for Pussy-in-Boots. So just now, when they recognized me as I got off the escalator, they had some news for me."

"Thay've found her?"

"Not that. But there has been a development."

"Come on, Smitty, for Christ's sake."

"They found the silver boots and the blond wig. They were in a garbage can by a coffee shop on Church Street. I know the place."

"Where are they now?"

"Right now some street person has them, an old bag lady. The girls know her. They're afraid that mebbe there's a body lying around in another garbage can. Mebbe cut up."

"Why the hell didn't they tell you before?"

"They said they tried to tell the guys on the Vice Squad who arrested them, but they just got laughed at. They were planning to tell me the next time I went down."

"What's with the Vice Squad?"

"They probably thought the girls had made up the story to get off the charge."

"Hold on." Salter ran to the closing elevator and disappeared. He returned ten minutes later with the three prostitutes. "We'll use my car, Smitty. It's in the lot."

The women were apprehensive, excited, and pleased to see Smith again. "Should we trust that prick?" one of them said, pointing to Salter.

"Did your case get put forward?" Smith asked.

"Christ, no. He got it *scrubbed*. What's goin' on?"

"We need your help."

"Doing what? Bit early for the other, isn't it?" The three women laughed.

Smith said, "If you get the car, sir, we'll meet you out on College Street."

"There she is," one of the women said. "There; there." She dug a hard finger into Smith's shoulder. "Stop. Stop. Pull over. Let us out."

They surged across the sidewalk towards the small hill of garbage bags surrounding an old woman sitting with her back against a tree.

"Nellie," the spokeswoman said. "It's me, Connie. This is a policeman. Him, too. Don't be frightened. We brought them. They won't hurt you. They want to know where you got the boots and the wig. You still got 'em?" She turned to Salter. "They're in one of her bags."

"Fuck off," Nellie said. "Won't go. Fuck off."

"Nellie," Connie said gently. "You don't have to go anywhere. We just want to know where you found the boots. Here!" She pounced on a bag, drew it away from the pile around the old woman and showed Salter the contents. "Where did you find them, Nellie?"

Salter stood back. Connie would do better than he at this stage.

"They're mine," Nellie said. "He left them. They're mine." She grabbed the bag and pushed it close to her outstretched legs.

Salter said, to Connie, "I need them."

"Here, Nellie, I'll buy them," Connie said. "Here." She opened her wallet and took out two twenty-dollar bills and wrapped Mary's hand around them, simultaneously taking back the bag and handing it to Smith, who just as swiftly stowed it in the car.

"You'll be compensated," Smith said.

"By your guys? Don't be an asshole," Connie said without rancor. "Now, Nellie. Upsadaisy. Show us where you found them."

Nellie struggled to her feet, then, taking a bag of garbage with her for company, led them across the street to an alley by a bread-and-milk store. "He put them in there."

The second time it registered. "He?" Salter asked. "A man?"

"He put them in there. I watched him. Then I took them. Fucking mine now. He threw them away."

"Old man? Young man? Bum? Black? White? Chinese? What kind of man? What did he look like?"

"He put them in there, then went in a car. I took them after. Fucking mine."

Salter turned to the three women. "Is Nellie always around?"

"I think she goes to a shelter at night when the cold weather comes."

"You talk to her?"

"Yeah. Sometimes. Poor old cow. That's where I'll wind up. I bring her a doughnut sometimes."

"Is she usually out of it?"

"Not all the time. You want this fucker's description, don't you? So do we. I'll keep after her, let you know if she comes out with anything else."

"Where will we find you if we need you again?"

"Right here when the sun goes down." And then, as he turned away, she said, "It's him, isn't it? The guy who was looking for her after the murder, the guy we told him about." She pointed to Smith. "Got to her first, didn't he?" She looked frightened and bitter. "You fucking assholes," she added and turned away to where the other two women were waiting to lead her away.

On the way back, Smith said, "What do you think? There's been no report of body parts turning up lately. They're hard to hide. Is this the same guy the squad reported at the beginning, going up and down Jarvis looking for Miss Silver Boots? What do you think? How's your hunch now?"

"I don't know, Smitty. I don't know. Make sure the Vice Squad are still keeping their eyes open for him. In the meantime, until they find him, I'm going to do what I was planning to do before your girlfriends appeared. Until a body turns up, that is."

"I'll keep my eyes open."

18

B ack in the office, Smith posted the alert for all patrols to look out for body parts, then started once more to look through the appointment book they had taken from Lucas's desk.

"It's very disconcerting for someone from the old country to come across places that are named after other places in Europe, especially the U.K., places that are nothing at all like the places they are named after," he said after a few minutes. "I expect you get used to it, but I'm not yet. Paris, Ontario, for instance. I'll bet it's nothing like the place where I lost my virginity to a dark-haired cocotte named Fifi."

"You did what?"

"I was speaking in fun. Actually I was in Paris, France, once, for a weekend, but that was just to watch a football match. I never had to do with cocottes, called Fifi or anything else, but three of us did walk round the Place Pigalle and got offered a group rate for a blow job by a large black woman covered in tribal markings. I'll bet Paris, Ontario, has nothing like that."

"There's no Picadilly Circus in London, Ontario, either."

"Aye. It's disconcerting. Windsor, Kingston, Brighton, Hamilton, they're all here, looking nothing like they should. Places here should have Canadian names—Toronto, Ottawa, Pickerel River—*those* are the names I expected to find, and place names ending in Rapids, and Falls, and River and Lake. Not Peterborough or Cambridge. I suppose there's an Oxford, too?

"What started you on this? What are you going on about?"

"Lucas's appointment book. Now that we've met some of the people he knew, I was going through to see if any of the names in it would mean anything, and I came across this appointment a few days before he died, in Bath. Now, I know the real Bath a bit; I went there once on a school outing. Our choir was going round England singing in the cathedrals, including Wells Cathedral in Somerset, as it was then, and we had an excursion to Bath. So now I look up the one here and it's near Kingston, for God's sake, and there's no mineral waters mentioned. Why would they call it Bath?"

"The first settler got homesick. Give me that book. Where is this reference?"

"There. Bath. The whole day. Now, how long to drive there, do you suppose?"

"Three hours. There and back would be a day. Well, well, well, well, well. Look at what else is here. He had planned to go fishing that day, and the next. Then he puts a line through that and writes in, "Bath," instead. Shall I tell you what's at Bath? Bath, Ontario?"

"Let me guess. The Jane Austen Curling Rink?"

"Probably. But there's also a prison. A minimum-security prison. You know, for nondangerous white-collar criminals, scam merchants, crooked managers of pension funds—people like that.

"Aye. Swindlers. We have them in Glasgow."

"So who is visiting Bath? Lucas? Why?"

"Strange, is it not? I understand he didn't deal with criminals."

"Not that we know so far. You'd better take a run down there. See what was happening that day."

"How d'ye mean?"

"Lucas visited Bath. We could check with his sister, make sure he didn't have an old aunt retired near there, but it looks to me as if he might have been visiting someone in the prison. This appointment book doesn't name any names, but you could look in the visitor's book for that day. See if a name jumps out. So, go and find out who Lucas was visiting, then talk to the prisoner and find out what the visit was about."

"If you don't mind my saying so, sir, this looks like something you ought to be doing yourself."

"I've got a full day, Smith, and I don't like prisons. And as I told you yesterday, I'm following a hunch. You are covering my ass, following prescribed procedure. This one should be all right. It's a nice drive down to Bath, once you get off Highway Four-oh-one. You'll enjoy it. Hang on a minute." He looked through his notebok and dialed a number. "Dr. Baretski? Staff Inspector Salter. Is anyone in the office there? I have a request. Could you close the door? No, I don't need a prescription. What? Then I'm the exception. I'm calling about Jerry Lucas. I've come across an entry in his diary for a fishing trip that was cancelled. Four days before he was killed. There's no name in his book. Yes. Good. You remember who he was going with? Thanks. He didn't tell you why? No, okay. By the way, does that stuff *work?* Uh-huh. If I do, I'll call you." He put down the phone and turned to Smith. "Where were we? Bath. Yes. I think I know what you are going to find. The reason for you going in person is to surprise him, catch him unawares."

"I couldn't do that on the telephone?"

"The visitor's book for the period is probably in a vault now. Or the signature is illegible except to the keen eye of someone who has seen it a lot lately, like you. If you try to sort it out by phone you'll have someone saying, 'No, sorry. No one of that name here,' because it's a lot easier to say that than to really look. So you have to go and do it yourself, or watch the attendant do it."

"And if I find Lucas's name, and the name of the person he visited?"

"Request permission to speak to him, if possible, without telling him who you are, and ask him what his connection with Lucas is."

"I feel a bit over my head."

"I'll tell you what he'll say. That Lucas came down on account of one of his clients. Off you go. Oh, yes, one last thing. If you can't find any record of Lucas's visit, tell them who he went to see and ask if you can talk to him."

"And you know who that is, of course."

"Harry Cane. Tell him that his name is in Lucas's appointment book, and we'd like to know why. And one last thing. Ask the guard to verify that Cane was locked up nice and tight the evening Lucas was murdered. By the way, did we hear from Costa Rica yet?"

"Yes, sir. I left a note for you. On your desk. There. Flora Lucas was there all right when she says she was, with a friend, mostly in the hospital."

"Who was the friend?"

"A male. That's all they know."

"Nothing to do with us, then. Interesting, though."

19

Salter judged that Calvin Gregson intended to waltz him around the block as long as he could, so he next called at the attorney general's office. There he explained his need. "There was a matter of confidentiality involved then," he said. "but now I'm looking for a killer, and one of the lines of inquiry has led to Harry Cane's trial. In preparation for that trial, our Fraud Squad sent over their file on the investigation, and it was never returned. I need it now."

"Your own file?"

"It was a while ago. Some of the contents need to be looked at again. We want to get a complete list of everyone involved."

"But if it's confidential . . . ?"

"Look, we made up the goddamn file; you made it confidential. It's still our file, if you've finished with it. I could request it officially, but that would just draw attention to what I'm doing, wouldn't it?"

"You think one of the people involved is the . . ."

"No, for Chrissake. I'm doing a cross-check. One of these people may be able to help me is what I'm saying. Do you know why the list is confidential?"

"I wasn't here then. Look, it all sounds fine as you put it, but for all I know there is some procedure I ought to be following . . ."

"To cover your ass?"

"I should have something in writing."

"From me?"

"From my principal."

"Then go and get it." Salter looked at his watch. "Please. Now."

The official disappeared and returned in ten minutes. "The minister's deputy is in conference at the moment. Can you come back in an hour?"

"That should give you enough time to dig a hole out there and bury it." Salter pointed out the window.

"I'm trying to cooperate."

"I think you are, young fella, in which case all I can say is now you know what it will be like for the next forty years, knowing that everybody thinks that *you* are the problem. I'll be back at eleven."

When he returned, the assistant was waiting for him. "I'm afraid you're out of luck," he said. "Here, come and see." He opened the little gate that kept visitors from getting to him, and pointed to a desk with a large red folder on it.

Salter sat down and found what he wanted as soon as he opened the file, a large buff envelope with a single sheet of paper stapled to the outside: a list of contents. Item 14 was designated as the list of names of those not pressing charges. The envelope was empty.

"It isn't there," the official said.

"Somebody in this office signed for it. Whose is this signature?"

"Angela Boychuck, a secretary. She's gone now."

"What was she like, careless and sloppy, or reliable and efficient?"

A small, neatly dressed man in his forties who was leaning against the door, apparently daydreaming (but, in fact, Salter realized later, placed there to monitor the conversation), said, "She could make mistakes, like everyone else. The human factor."

From across the room a small, fierce-looking woman whose face was as red as if she were sitting in a one-person tropical zone shouted, "She was the best secretary this department ever had. So DON'T, BLAME, HER!"

The official and his boss ignored her. "So there you are," the boss said. "No help for it, I'm afraid."

"I'll go up the line," Salter said, "It has to be somewhere." He wanted desperately to ask the brick-faced woman to keep an eye on them for him until he returned, but guessed that would provoke a reaction from the official's boss that would hold him up for days, if not for good. "If it should turn up, let me know, would you?" As the boss walked away, the portcullis closed, Salter gave the official his card.

"Of course," the official said. "I'll keep my eyes open."

On his way back to the office Salter crossed the corridor to speak to Larson. Before he could say anything, Larson said, "I was just calling you. I was asking the guys here who you were and someone said you were handling the case of the lawyer who got stabbed. Salter, right? Sorry, Staff Inspector Salter. It jogged my memory. That was one of the names in the case you were just asking me about. Lucas."

"Jesus Christ. Thanks."

When Smith returned, late in the afternoon, he offered some confirmation of Salter's guess. "It turned out to be straightforward. We found Lucas in the book, visiting Harry Cane, as you deduced—I nearly said 'guessed.' What a nice bloke Cane is! He claims he is innocent, by the way."

"Of what? He pleaded guilty."

"He said that was an agreement, to save embarrassment to people like Lucas, because his lawyer told him to throw himself on the mercy of the court. Do they say that here, too? Anyway, that's what they told him to do, and he did. He thinks one reason they advised him to do that was because he'd run out of money to pay them. They already had it all. But he's not bitter about them, or about anyone else. Extraordinary bloke. He said if he'd had six more weeks he would have recouped everything with enough to pay everyone back."

"What does he say he *did* do?"

"Just borrowed a little from the clients' fund, wrote a couple of temporary checks that he would easily have covered a few weeks later, but some accountant who was related to one of the people came after him and that was that. Apparently it's illegal for a broker to borrow his clients' money without asking them. But he wasn't stealing, he said, he wasn't going to take the money and run. While he was talking I was inclined to believe him. And he's still planning, shaking his head over the opportunities he's missing.

"Here is what he said about Lucas's visit." Smith drew a notebook from his pocket. "I didn't take any notes in the prison, but I wrote it up as soon as I was outside and could find a cafe. It comes to this: Lucas had two things in mind. First, he wanted to impress upon Cane that it was in his interest to stay quiet about the fact that Lucas's poker-playing friends were among those he had conned; second, he made an offer to Cane to help him when he got out. He assumes the offer has expired along with Lucas, by the way, unless Lucas's sister feels she should honor her brother's wishes."

"Not if Gregson hears about them. You say Cane sounded, acted, like a decent guy?"

"While I was there, talking to him, I had no reservations about him at all."

"And afterwards?"

"On the drive home I had time to think, away from the sound of his voice, mainly about the difference between borrowing and stealing, and about the hardship of that old lady whose evidence sent him down, and about this business of Lucas promising him a helping hand, which no one else knew about, and about how he will ask Flora to honor her brother's wishes, even if she never heard her brother mention them, and about how he's still full of ideas about getting back on his feet, because he knows now how to make his ship come in." He paused.

"And you changed your mind?" Salter prompted.

"I think he's the biggest fucking rogue and liar I've ever met."

"Minimum-security prison too good for him?"

"Well, no. No. I got to thinking about minimum-security prisons on my way home, too, and I came to the conclusion that they are a waste of money. There's no point in incarcerating people like Cane. What we should do is sentence them, sentence Cane, say, not to two years, less a year and a half for good behavior, but to ten years, although not behind bars. Ten years on parole, but they would have FC stamped on their papers, driver's license and so on . . ."

"Standing for what?"

"No, not that. Financial Criminal. So an employer would know before he puts an FC in a position of trust. Any employer who knowingly employs an FC anywhere near his money would have no comeback if the bugger swindled him. But most jobs, from garbageman to university president, don't involve that type of trust, so they could get work. Finally, I'd add another penalty, which is this. All the money a swindler earns after he's caught, except for a minimum wage, would go into a fund to pay off his victims."

"The real swindlers would immediately get hold of a forged ID."

"Aye, that's a point. So you would have to brand them. A discreet little FC, on the arse, so no one could see it except a potential employer who insists on all new employees taking a medical."

"Why not cut off one hand?"

"We're not Visigoths. This is a civilized country. Maybe a tattoo would do, a little purple FC you could have surgically removed after your sentence was up."

"What about rehabilitation?"

"Rehabilitation is for the poor misguided fellow who makes a mistake. You can't rehabilitiate the Harry Canes. Just defang them and let them learn what it's like to be poor, like me."

"What happens if they figure out how to do it again?"

"Add on another ten years."

"And a third time?"

"Hang the bastard. But we're just fookin' aboot, as they say at home. What do ye think of this Harry Cane now?"

"I think it's his part of the story I'm going after. My turn to talk to Mr. Cane. But first things first."

20

Where to start? Question: why did Lucas's visit Harry Cane in prison? Because the reason given so far, to reaffirm Cane's silence when he got out, did not account for the fact that the meeting seemed to be a sudden decision. Perhaps, if Cane's silence was so important, then Cane was taking the opportunity to get Lucas to *pay* for the silence. No. Salter had not known Lucas, but his impression from others was that he would not have submitted to even a hint of implied blackmail. To have been swindled would make one look foolish, but to have agreed to blackmail to prevent one's foolishness from being made public would make one look worse, if discovered.

So if Lucas had spoken to Cane, it would have been by way of warning him, and, to be fair to Lucas, perhaps he did actually offer Cane a helping hand once he was released. But he still had six months during which to visit Cane. Why choose a time when he had such a full schedule already? Why cancel a fishing trip?

The first question was still the most interesting. What was Lucas doing on the Fraud Squad list in the first place? Salter felt that he had uncovered Lucas's other secret life, and wondered how many more there might be. Thus far, beneath Lucas's armor of integrity he had found a man who spent his Friday nights dallying with hookers, apparently (although Salter still hung onto his own idea about *that* scene). And now (more serious, surely, to some of his clients who would not give a damn about Lucas's sex life), it seemed he was also a gambler who had sometimes, dangerously, moved beyond poker into risking real money—perhaps some of which was under his trust, on a scheme proposed by Harry Cane. It seemed inconceivable, but such things happened every week.

Now all kinds of possibilities appeared, all the "what if?" scenarios. The chief one, of course, was the possibility that some client whose money Lucas had misappropriated had come looking for an explanation that Friday night. This was crazy, and to dismiss it Salter presented himself to Derek Fury who, he remembered, now had charge of Lucas's affairs, as well as those of Flora.

Fury's reaction finally justified his name. After a dozen words, Salter felt as if he were facing a a tiny, lethal animal who had the capacity, and will, to tear Salter apart.

"The suggestion you are making is absurd, but it is more than that; it strikes at the heart of Jerry's character and reputation, and if allowed an airing will do at least some of the vile damage that rumors always do. I don't know what the explanation will be, but I am sure what it will *not* be, so I suggest you start making inquiries elsewhere."

This was a warning, uttered without any movement of the hands or the head, or even much noise, but it was full of intent.

Salter gave himself time to make his response just as firm and clear. "You believe in Mr. Lucas's . . ." he stopped for the word that he needed.

"Honor." The word came like a single shot from a pistol.

Salter nodded, nearly bowed. "Honor. But belief is a luxury that cops aren't allowed, sir. Belief is something you need when you don't know. I plan to find out. Then I won't need belief, and I suspect your own will be justified."

There, he thought. Philosophy 201 (incomplete) to the rescue. True, too.

It was also effective. Fury sat with teeth clenched for a long time, then glanced at his hands and up into Salter's face. "I intend to satisfy you. Today is Friday. I shall consult with a company of forensic accountants, ask them to examine Jerry's affairs as quickly as they can. It shouldn't take long. They've already glanced at them. Will a couple of days matter?"

"I ought to be be cross-checking in the meantime."

"In what way?"

"I came to ask you, among other things, to give me a list of those people for whom Lucas held money in trust."

"You plan to visit them?"

"As a matter of routine. Sir, someone killed your friend."

"A prostitute."

"No, sir." Shit, it was out.

Fury continued to sit still, but his face lost some color as the anger receded. "What happened to the prostitute?"

Salter tried to recover. "We are continuing a twenty-four-hour search for her, because, on the face of it, she is our most likely suspect and I'm obliged to follow the obvious line until it runs out, as I just said. I don't believe she is the one we are looking for, but the evidence says she is and I have to follow the evidence. What's most suspicious about her is that she has disappeared."

"I should have thought she was bound to, knowing you would be looking for her. But get back to the point, why don't you think she is the killer, and who do you think is?"

"I don't have an answer to your second question, but as to the first . . . Look, talking to you like this would finish me if it were known, but I need your help, I think. I need to know the list of clients in the same way that I need to find the prostitute, to cross them off the list of those I am investigating."

"What you need to know is if Jerry misused his clients' funds . . ."

"And if any of them knew it."

"First things first. I'll know the answer to the first question when the accountants finish with his books. I will ask them to work through the night until they find it. If the answer turns out to be, as I know it will, that everything is in order, then you won't need to know who his clients were, will you?"

"Apparently not, at this stage, but I don't know what's under the next rock."

"When you find something, you can come back. But this prostitute? May I know why you no longer feel she is the one you want?"

"I'm counting on your discretion, sir."

"I know you are, but you have to trust somebody, don't you? The prostitute?"

"From the beginning, even before I had the case, there was something not quite right about her. My strongest impression of your friend, apart from his continually testamented probity, is of his need for privacy. Now a man like that, living at such a respectable address, is he likely to have dealings, publicly, with a hooker? I know she was wearing a slicker over the major items, but the hair and the boots were on display for all to see. I don't believe it."

"But she was buzzed up, or whatever the term is, at the apartment building, wasn't she, by name?"

"That means he knew her, and was expecting her. So who was she? On an investigation I was on a few years ago, sir, an actor dressed up as an Italian gangster in order to to kill someone, and I got nowhere until I picked up a clue that he *was* dressed up. So I wondered if the same was true in this case. Was this, in fact, someone who was dressed up as a whore in order to create the story that Lucas was killed by a hooker he had arranged to come to his suite? But in fact, perhaps this woman was nothing of the kind. A whore, I mean. Then who was she? A disappointed lover? What else could she be? People keep saying maybe she was a practical joke, a gag, someone hired by Lucas's pals to ruin his reputation. Possible, but how did she get past the door? Still, presumably, by using the name of someone Lucas knew. And then . . . but see what I mean, sir? So I'm coming at it in another way. Just possibly, someone who wanted to kill Lucas had hired the prostitute, explaining to her what to say when she heard the buzzer, conning her into believing it was just a gag. But then, the real killer comes along and kills Lucas, leaving us all looking for Pussy-in-Boots. There is some evidence that supports this." Salter ended. "Evidence which has given us a whole new, urgent reason to find the hooker, if she exists."

Fury had changed while Salter spoke. He had not moved, but he no longer looked like an executioner. "I appreciate your confidence, Inspector, and I'll respect it. But I would still prefer to learn from the accountants if there is anything to worry about in the file first. Surely there is time for that."

"I hope so." Salter stood up, ready to leave.

Fury added, "And by the way, I don't think you can use 'testament' as a verb."

"No? Thank you. I'll be careful."

"The thing to do is to put in one of those drop ceilings—you know, those sheets of foam plastic you drop inside metal frames. I helped Joan Binder's da put one up a couple of years ago."

"Who is Joan Binder, Seth?" Tatti asked from across the basement where she was trying to scrape off seventy-five-year-old paint which was sealing the frame of the one small window that might let in some natural light.

"The one before you," Seth said.

"The one we met the other day, with the thick ankles?"

Seth walked over to her. "This is not a very economical use of time," he said. "You know that? When you get it unstuck you are going to have to clean it and repaint it and oil the hinges—all for what?"

"So that I can lie in bed when I am dying of consumption and watch the shadows of the night creep into the room past my one tiny window, and on my last morning I will feel a breeze of fresh air as I watch the sparrow who always comes to eat the breadcrumbs you put on the—whatdoyoucallit—windowsill."

"Ah, fuck," Seth said, coming up behind her and putting his arms round her, burying his face in her neck and feeling for her breasts.

"I'm still here," Salter said from the top of the stairs where he was sitting drinking a beer. "You won't . . ."

"Don't say it!" Seth yelled.

"What? Don't say what?"

"Don't say 'You won't get any work done like that.' No, but it helps to pass the time. Mom called, by the way. I forgot to tell you. She sounded concerned. Wanted you to call her back."

"What are you doing about dinner? Pizza?"

"Tatti wants to make dinner."

"What do you have in mind, Tatti?" Salter, in the fatness of his pleasure at watching these children play, risked a bit of ethnic stereotyping. "Pea soup? Tortière? Poutine? No, not poutine."

"I thought I would make a big cheese omelette and salad and bread. Is that all right? I could make porridge or boil you some sausages, if you would prefer."

"An omelette would be fine. When?"

"Half an hour."

"I'll be there."

Salter finished his beer and turned to climb back up to the kitchen to phone his wife.

She was waiting for his call, and sounded anxious. He eased off his shoes as he reassured her about Seth and Tatti, and asked her how far he should go in lending Seth furniture. "Some of it is his, sort of, from when he lived here," he pointed out.

"Lend him what he wants. I'll sort it out when I get home."

"When will that be? It's nice having Seth and Tatti in the basement, but I'm getting lonely above ground."

"Early next week, I think. Now, Charlie, listen."

"Yes, Annie. That's what I'm doing. What 'listen' really means is, 'You won't like this.' Right?"

"Let me tell you what's happening. The main thing is that I can't get the problem of Angus's baby sorted out. No one here wants to give her a home."

"I thought we'd agreed on that. Angus will have to hire a nanny. Don't they have Filipino nannies on the Island? This street's full of them."

"There's been a bit of a complication with that. Angus is not getting along with his uncles. They're treating him too young for his age. Maybe people grow up more slowly here, but his uncles are at him all day, mostly without realizing it. Constantly making sure he isn't doing something stupid, like driving to Charlottetown without any gas. I mention that because yesterday he *did* run out of gas on the way to Charlottetown, and one of the neighbors rescued him on the highway and took him to a gas station. By the time he came home his uncles already had the story from the neighbor. They kidded him, and he lost his temper."

"He doesn't have to stay. It was their idea to offer him a job. It was his idea to take it."

"I've said that to him."

"So tell him to come home. You, too. Bring the baby. All of you, come home. I'll retire and we can all babysit while Angus makes a potful of money on Bay Street."

And then, by the thread in her voice Salter guessed how much running back and forth, literally and metaphorically, Annie had done to keep her family relationships intact. "You mean it, Charlie? Not about retiring, silly, but bringing Angus and the baby home?"

"I'd come and get you but I'm in the middle of an investigation."

"You think you'll be all right with the baby?"

"Christ, what am I? Billy-Goat Fucking Gruff? We had babies of our own once, remember? Did I eat any of them?"

"Should we just think about it overnight?"

"You've been thinking about it for days, haven't you? Weeks? I can tell. I don't need to think about it. I've got an honorary daughter-in-law in the basement who, if Seth can keep his hands off her for half an hour, will shortly cook my dinner. You come home and I'll have a full set again. The baby will probably be a pain in the ass, but that will be your problem, and Angus's. Come home."

"Hold your breath."

"What? Oh, right. Something else while I've got you. You think I should join a book club?"

"Which one? Oh, you mean book *group*. A discussion group."

"Yeah."

"What brought this on?"

"I thought it might be interesting."

"It is."

"What? Oh, right, you used to belong to one, didn't you?"

"For the last ten years. Until this year. You should listen a bit more."

"Well . . . when you join up again, could I come?"

"No."

"Why? Ashamed of me?"

"No. I just don't want you sitting next to me when I'm explaining the hang-ups of the hero of whatever we are discussing."

"Do you ever hear of other groups?"

"That would suit you? I'll keep my ears open. You could put the word out down at headquarters."

"I could but I won't. Anyway, do that, will you? Keep your ears open?"

21

Salter had never liked movie musicals much. Neither Gene Kelly nor Fred Astaire had danced their way into his heart, and a legion of songs and singers had left him looking at his watch, wondering when the next comic bit was coming. Sopranos with nice tits well-framed in lace as in *The Merry Widow* were okay as long as they didn't shriek, but their male counterparts had him running for the popcorn concession as soon as June started bustin' out all over. The worst, in his experience, were the whimsical movies, the ones with elves. The only exceptions to his prejudice, formed in early adolescence, were *Kiss Me Kate*—in his view the first and only adult musical—and bits of *Guys and Dolls.*

He had never seen *Alexander's Ragtime Band.* The date did not seem promising, sometime before he was born, but he hoped for an antique quaintness that would make up for the inevitable corniness.

"What are you watching, Dad?"

After the omelette had been cooked and eaten, Seth and Tatti had gone out to get an ice cream, and he had not heard them return. "We were having a discussion at work," he extemporized, "About favorite movies. One of the sergeants said this was his parents' favorite. I thought I'd take a look."

"You like it?"

"It's short. Movies used to be shorter, then, didn't they?"

"It doesn't grab you, though."

"No."

"Can I have the car for the night?"

"Call me before ten tomorrow in case I need it."

"With you, Pops."

"Good night, Mr. Salter." Tatti from the hall.

Salter shouted back and the door closed behind him.

So far he had nothing. The movie had been pleasant enough; Salter enjoyed watching every device of the Hollywood musical unroll as the classic plot moved Alexander's band up from the roadside cafe to, finally, Carnegie Hall, and brought the boy and girl together, then apart, then together, managing to include what seemed like a one-minute version of World War One. Also, in the early part, set before the War, there were a fair number of vaudeville acts from an entertainment era he was sorry to have missed.

But the neighbor who had mentioned Alice Faye was more than ten years older than Salter, and it now seemed likely to him that the man was treasuring a memory of a night at the cinema, a memory that was gradually losing its definition. Alice Faye did not look like anyone he had seen. Probably the neighbor just meant she had a lot of makeup on. It had always been a long shot, the notion that Alice Faye or Gloria Grahame would look like one of the women in the case. He had retained a mild worry about Lucas's ex-lover, who had seemed slightly deranged, but Alice Faye looked nothing like Janet Rudd.

Gloria Grahame was another matter. He saw that movie through because he found *Oklahoma!* more watchable than most musicals, mainly because of Gloria Grahame's performance as the girl who couldn't say no, and because as soon as she appeared on the screen, he saw immediately what the neighbor had been talking about. Something about the way Gloria Grahame's upper lip stayed put while the rest of her face mobilized around the song, as if she had received a tiny local anaesthetic under her nose. The effect was unmistakeable.

"I spent a good part of the weekend at it, sir. I think I know every tart in Toronto, and I've talked to half of them, but there's no sign of Puss-in-Boots."

"She's disappeared, Smitty."

"Where to?"

"Up her own arse, as they probably say in the Gorbals. She never existed—just a wig and a pair of boots. Which, let-me-not-hide-my-light-under-a-bushel, Smitty-old-son, I kind of expected from the first, which is why I was pleased to get this job and why I'm pleased to find out I was right."

"You certainly sound pleased with yourself, right enough. Smug, I would say. So she was wearing a disguise? Kinky. Maybe even a 'he,' sir. Where have you got her now? You send a car to bring her in?"

"Not yet. I'd like to guess at a bit more of the plot. Any ideas?"

"Aye. Jerry Lucas was kinky himself. He couldn't get it on without she's wearing a lot of gear, ye know? So every Friday night she climbed into the costume and away they went."

"So she did kill him?"

"No, why would she? But you know the rules, sir. So far, yes, she killed him, even though she didn't. Right?"

Salter nodded. "So, does she know who did?"

"Mebbe so."

"How?"

"She saw him."

"Where?"

"In the parking lot. The fella we thought was a punter."

"But now he's the killer?"

"He's the only other suspect we have. A jealous rival, mebbe."

"Mebbe. What was he driving. Remember?"

"A white pickup with a lock-up box."

"Which we haven't found so far."

"Aye. We haven't."

"Now." Salter consulted the Yellow Pages lying open on his desk, noted and wrote down an address, and handed it to Smith. "Go up there and call me back when you find the truck. Quick now. If someone finds out I knew who the hooker was when I was farting around like this, my last years in the force will pass very slowly." He jumped up from his chair in excitement and crossed to the window. "There's a way to go yet, Smitty, but the road's a lot clearer ahead."

Forty-five minutes later Smith phoned him back. "It's here. Not even in a garage. There's a kind of yard behind the building shaded by a big tree. The truck is tucked away in a corner. You wouldn't see it driving by, either from Yonge Street, or the cross street. You'd have to be on foot."

"And we don't have foot patrols any more. Did you find out the owner?"

"I didn't ask anybody, sir. I didn't want to expose myself unecessarily because you seemed to be playing it very close to your chest."

"Come back to the office and we'll talk about it."

"I'll start, you listen. What we've got here on the surface is a woman dressing up to excite her lover and being suspected by her husband. He follows her one night when her excuse seems weak—a nonexistent concert, maybe—and figures out who she is visiting. He confronts her in the parking lot when she comes out but she brushes him off, so he goes back to the apartment block and kills the lover."

"But the parking lot attendant said he drove away."

"He could have come back."

"Right enough. I'll check the area again to see if I can find anyone who saw his truck parked somewhere while he was killing Lucas."

"We won't waste time on that just yet. We have to backtrack. We have to ask what happened to her after she was accosted in the lot, accused by her husband of screwing around, dressed up the way she never would for him."

"She probably went home and waited for him to come back and pound the bejesus out of her. That's how it would have been in Glasgow."

"These are solid burghers, Smitty."

"Solid what? Burgers? What's that the slang for over here?"

"No. 'Burghers,' with an aitch. Means upright middle-class citizens. The kind that don't pound each other. No, I think she went home and found him there, or the other way round, and they talked. No, that would be later. That Friday night they just . . ."

"What?"

192

"I'm not sure. One voice says she crept into his bed and said she was sorry. Another says that she said nothing that night, or the next day, waiting for him to explode. Then, on Saturday afternoon, during the opera broadcast from the Met, a friend called with the news. Right away she thinks her husband did it, then remembers he wasn't out of her sight long enough. Then her husband comes back from the office—he's self-employed, so he works all hours, including Saturday afternoons—and he's heard the news on the car radio and thinks she did it, or might have, but then he remembers that when he saw her across the parking lot she did not look like a killer, more like a woman who has just left her lover."

"What are the signs of that?"

"More preoccupied than distraught. So they talk long into the night. Saturday night. Have you read the *The Great Gatsby*, Smitty?"

"Aye, it reached Glasgow. We did it at school."

"You remember the scene at the end where Tom Buchanan and Daisy are talking—it was like that. But this time Gatsby was already dead. Louise and Wilder saw how bad it looked for them if they were identified. Because she was *his* alibi, but she had none for the time before he saw her. Wilder knew she had been unfaithful, but didn't believe she was a killer, but knowing how the cops—us—look for the obvious answer, they came together in a pact."

"That takes care of them, then, sir, so we'd better do the obvious thing and arrest them and charge them both."

"What with?"

"Murder and accessory to it. We'd better be quick. As middle-class citizens with access to clever lawyers, they'll know how to be on their way to South America by now, to join that bank robber."

"You serious?"

"I'm trying to get into the spirit of whatever the hell you are up to which I can hardly follow, by the way. We seem to be pissing about, imitating a couple of characters in a television series."

"Sorry. Yeah. The fact is, I think they're innocent, I *know* they're innocent, and I'm going to give them plenty of line. So let's prove I'm right, shall we? Back in the beginning, Barlow and Jensen took statements from Lucas's neighbors. One couple were in Florida, so we got the local police there to take a statement from them. This couple said they heard voices coming from the apartment during the evening, that they thought there was more than one man. The possible interpretation, if there were two men, to fit the theories at the time, was that one of the male voices could have been a pimp, and the hooker and the pimp killed Lucas together. Then the hooker left, and the pimp followed her after he'd ransacked the apartment. Now go over and talk to that couple again, find out exactly what they think they heard, and when. The times."

"Can we pin it down that close, sir?"

"Yes, we can. We know when she left the parking lot, because the time is on the ticket. If the couple heard voices after that time then she's in the clear."

"An accessory, though."

"Go talk to them."

"Will you be here?"

"I'll wait for your call."

Smith called back in the early afternoon. "I don't know if it's bingo, sir, but it's quite interesting. First, these people always go to bed at eleven sharp, so everything they heard took place before then. Second, they never saw the hooker, but others in the building have told them about her. This is what they're sure they heard: One, there was a man and a woman in the apartment until after ten, but after she left it was quiet until he turned on the television and they heard the voices in the movie or the play he was watching. This play went on until after they went to bed. That was all they heard. They were asleep before he switched off. Now here's the thing, see, Lucas doesn't have a television. He was one of those kooks who brag about never watching it, probably."

"The radio?"

"I checked all the stations in our area, sir. Did you know there is no radio guide here where you can look and see what's on? Like a Radio Times. Do any of the papers publish a schedule? How do you find out what's on?"

"I don't know. Word of mouth, probably. What did you find out?"

"They say the CBC puts one out, but I can't find it in the shops. I had to phone every station in Toronto."

"And?"

"Everyone including the CBC was broadcasting music at that time. Those voices were live."

"Well done, Smitty. Now come back. I've got some more errands for you."

"Are you going to pull them in now?"

"Who?"

"The Wilder couple. It's the other way round now, is it not? Him for murder, her for accessory, because, really, he went home covered in blood and told her about it."

"I have a few things to do first."

"For God's sake, sir, you'll get a rocket up your arse if you're wrong and they fly away."

"Smitty, I want to tie this up in a ribbon and drop it in the deputy's lap."

"Keep me in touch, won't you, sir. I have another twenty-five years to go before my pension kicks in."

22

"We've come across the name of a Harry Cane linked to your brother. Cane is in prison for fraud . . ."

They were in Flora Lucas's office. She cut him off. "I can guess what you found. What can I do for you?" Brisk, let's-deal-with-this attitude, consistent with treating her brother's foolishness as no big deal, although she would prefer to see it remain quiet.

"How did your brother meet Cane?"

"What is this, Inspector? Are we having a chat over coffee? I don't know. What does it matter when those two met? It's me we are talking about, isn't it?"

"Could you explain that, ma'am?"

"It's me that Harry Cane swindled, not Jerry. Didn't you know that?"

"I see," Salter said, one pleasant area of speculation withering on the vine, as he scrambled for composure. "I was coming to that. Let's forget about your brother for the moment. How did *you* meet Cane?"

"He appeared at a couple of functions, I think. And some private receptions. He helped out with a bit of fund-raising. When you go into politics, friends organize events, partly to raise funds, partly to get you known. It is an old principle that if you shake enough hands, kiss enough babies, you will get elected. Somehow in all this I found myself knowing Cane. First I had his card, then he was in my office, selling shares in a company that planned to replace Microsoft?" She smiled, like saying "cheese." "I lost twenty thousand."

"It was a straight scam?"

"*He* didn't think so. Have you met him? My memory is that he is a remarkable a man who ought to be in politics. No, he put my money into a trust fund specifically designated to buying this particular stock. But a better opportunity cropped up, and Cane spent the money on something else—a Malaysian gold mine, I think." She laughed. "Something like that. We lost the lot."

"And the company that was supposed to replace Microsoft?"

"It is now worth three times what it was worth then. I'm telling you this to show you how persuasive Harry was. He was a dreamer and a liar, but he really thought he would make a lot of money. He believed, and he made his clients believe."

"But one of his clients could stand the loss much less than you could."

"So I heard."

"Did your brother know Cane, apart from you?"

"God, no. Jerry would have nothing to do with a character like Cane. Jerry was one of the people who *didn't* buy into "Trivial Pursuit" when he could have. It sounded risky, and he hadn't gone to law school with the people involved. Two big strikes against it. Oh no, he was appalled when I told him I was one of Harry Cane's victims."

"Then why did he visit Cane in prison?"

She blinked. "When?"

"A few days before he died."

She continued to stare at him, but only out of surprise. There was no hesitation when she spoke. "At this moment I have no idea. I would imagine it had something to do with me. Perhaps he wanted to make sure that Harry Cane would continue to observe a vow of silence where I was concerned."

"But your brother never discussed this visit he made?"

"No. I was in Costa Rica, remember? He was probably just being protective, even there, sort of what-I-don't-know-can't-hurt-me. Now I remember who introduced me to Cane. It was one of Jerry's poker pals. Robinson, I think. Several of that gang were sucked in. But not Jerry. Never Jerry."

This time Robinson kept him waiting for fifteen minutes, without apology. To be fair, Salter had not arranged an appointment, but simply called his office to say he was on his way and hung up before Robinson's secretary could put him off. So Robinson might well have managed, with great effort, to create a space in his schedule in which to fit Salter. But Salter had the impression that he was supposed to understand that he had been kept waiting deliberately. That was all right with him.

Salter believed that he was bearing news of Robinson's humiliation, and that this was one occasion when the messenger's knowledge of the message was more important than the message itself, and that therefore every attempt would be made to kill the messenger. He decided, after a look at Robinson's tight face, to try a fake-jolly approach as the one most likely to make the lawyer lose his temper and drop his guard.

"Many thanks for finding the time to see me at such short notice, Bonar," he said. And then, "What's the trouble? You're not still pissed off about that poker game, surely?"

"What's the problem now, Inspector?" Robinson looked over his glasses and managed a small, mechanical smile, as if Salter were an clumsy oaf jostling him on a subway car.

"Same as before. Jerry Lucas. The name of Harry Cane has cropped up, and I was talking to Flora Lucas about him. She says she met him through you. She was one of the people he conned, you remember?"

"What was the name again? Harry what? Cane? I'm not with you."

Salter laughed in a friendly, knowing way. "I think you are, Bonar. Harry Cane. Swindler. Probably took you for a few thousand, right? But it's embarrassing to be known as one of his dupes, so you didn't join the prosecution. Right? Like with me and the poker game." He watched Robinson's body signal each hesitation as he considered his response, the hands lifting and dropping, the fake relaxation and then, at last, the throat-clearing before the resolve.

"You seem to have it, Inspector. I did join in Cane's little scheme. It seemed to me on a par with buying a lottery ticket. I was skeptical, of course, but it seemed worth a try."

"Did the others feel the same way?"

No hesitation now. "Absolutely. We all enjoy a gamble, as you know, so we made a sort of pool among ourselves, a little syndicate."

"For how much? Each?"

The hesitation returned as Robinson wondered whether to lie, then dropped the idea. "Twenty thousand."

"How many of you?"

"Four."

"Jesus Christ. He got eighty grand off you. And another twenty off Flora Lucas. Who were the others?"

"Scott Mercer, Brian Davis, Andrew Cutler, Craig Lister, and me."

"The gang. Who was missing?"

"Lucas."

"Why?"

"Because Jerry smelled a rat and we didn't. Give him credit. He did his usual thing. When I suggested we invite Cane on a Thursday night to explain his scheme—he'd already pitched me—Jerry did a little research and decided not to join us."

"Why? He found Cane had a record? Cane didn't have any convictions."

"A police record is only one kind of record, and not always the most important one. No, Jerry tried to find Cane's track record, if you like, his reputation in the marketplace."

"And heard some rumors?"

"He heard nothing. *That* is what made him suspicious. He couldn't find anyone who knew anything about Cane."

"But he worked for a company of stockbrokers, didn't he? Bonded, I would imagine? They would have checked up on him."

"Inspector, if you want to have a chat about how crooks get themselves trusted, into positions of trust, or how people in positions of trust turn into crooks, we'll be here all day. There are crooked lawyers, crooked bankers, crooked you-name-it, all of them totally trustworthy until they are caught. I understand from television that even the odd policeman is bent, so let us not be amazed that Harry Cane was employable."

"I guess all of us have a crooked streak, *and* a gullible streak, eh, Bonar. Now, how did he work it? First of all, there's one other name missing—Holt."

"Larry was there that night, but he stayed out of the syndicate. Though as I remember, he had no reservations about the particular scheme."

"So how did the scheme work?"

Now Robinson looked uncomfortable. "I'm not sure. I'd have to get the others to help me out on the details."

"Twenty thousand dollars bet blind?"

"No, no, no. Of course we were careless, but Harry Cane was a very persuasive man."

"Give me an idea."

"I'll try. Let me come at it from another angle. You know how currency traders work?"

"Not the faintest."

"You've heard of them, surely?"

"Oh, sure. They sit up all night sending money back and forth to Hong Kong, and in the morning they've made a quarter of a cent which translates into half a million dollars. Something like that."

"That'll do. Money is constantly changing in value, and a good trader knows when to buy or sell."

"And once in a while he loses the lot."

"Okay. Now you can trade fundamentals or you can trade momentum."

"Let me try. Fundamentals. You can sit tight, certain that dollars are actually worth so many pounds or yen, so if you wait, the fundamental value will come back, right?"

"Very good. And momentum?"

"No, Bonar. You hear a lot about fundamentals, but momentum I associate with politics, as in when to call an election."

"It's the same principle. If you trade the momentum, you are betting that a currency that has started to rise will continue to rise, so you should jump on the bandwagon."

"The same if it starts to fall?"

"Absolutely."

"But if everyone's doing it, who's on the other side?"

"That's the trick, of course, to get in and out at exactly the right moment, before the momentum expires. And to know when there is momentum in any change in price."

"You're losing me."

"Hang on to what you said. It's all about knowing when to jump on and off the bandwagon. Now Cane was very knowledgeable about the history of momentum trading in the securities market."

"Stocks and shares?"

"Yes. And he had devised a new factor. He called it the Inertia/ Disaster Index. He had done a lot of research to show that you could bet on the inertia of the general public to take a particular price change a certain distance, even in the face of very weak fundamentals. The Inertia/Disaster Index involved a lot of factors; the chief one was a very sophisticated psychological analysis of how the average man responds emotionally to a sharp shift in the price of his stock, even in the face of concrete information that should tell him exactly what to do.

"Let me give you a crude example. Margaret Thatcher privatized a lot of state industries while she was in power, and they invited the 'little man' to subscribe to a public offering of shares before the shares actually hit the market, all acording to the Thatcher social philosophy that everyone is a little capitalist at heart, or should be. In some cases, the shares went up when they went public and the little man made a profit, but in one case, at least, the advance shares were offered at a price that the market felt was too high, so when the day of offering came the price had gone down and you could buy the shares for less than people had agreed to pay.

"Now there was no legal obligation for the little subscriber to take up his shares, and it was nonsense to do so, because he could actually buy the shares, if he wanted them, for less in the market. But what happened? Many of the people who had signed up took their shares, paying the higher price, sometimes in installments. When they were asked why, the replies were astonishing 'Oh, well,' said one man. 'I still think it's a good company so I'm sticking with it.

I've made up my mind, and I don't like shilly-shallying around.'

"That's where Cane's Index comes in, knowing that such a reaction is possible. He undertook to apply it to any shift in price of a major stock to predict how much the inertia of the small investor would affect momentum. Cane claimed to have charted seventy-five years of the history of emotional response to share changes. But it gets more sophisticated than that so as to take into account the increasing sophistication of the small investor, who is himself instinctively slotting in his own Inertia Index, based on his knowledge of other people like himself."

"So, using this index, Cane got in or got out a day before everyone else, that it?"

"More or less."

"So you gave your money to Cane?"

"We bought shares in the partnership he set up among us."

"What did he need you for? If he knew what was going to happen, why couldn't he just make money for himself?"

Now Robinson smiled. "That, Inspector, is the great unaskable question in this whole arena. Roughly speaking, it asks, if the experts—analysts, tipsters, gurus—know anything, why are they telling us? Why don't they just make money? You'll have to answer that one yourself, but all of us forget from time to time that the answer is that there must be more money in selling advice on how to make your fortune than there is in risking your own money, and it is entirely risk-free.

"In Cane's case, someone actually asked him your question, and the answer was that for certain strategies and maneuvers he needed more capital than he had—he pretended to be quite honest, saying he needed to be able to risk a lot and even lose it so that he could stay in the market and recover it and more.

"He called ours the Blue Chip Partnership, because we agreed that he should deal for us only in first-rate stocks, those that make up the Dow Jones average."

"You wanted to play it safe."

"If you like. And we wanted to know that if a call went wrong, price-wise, we would still hold options on some valuable stock."

"Options?"

"We didn't deal in the actual shares, but in options to buy or sell them. For the leverage. The thing is . . ."

"Oh, shit, let it go. What happened?"

"We were wiped out almost immediately."

"But why send Cane to prison? You knew you were gambling."

"Because, Inspector, the scheme, the Inertia/Disaster Index, was in fact a con, a scheme to make money for Cane. He never invested our money as he reported; he really gambled with it."

"And you didn't know what he was doing?"

"We got fake statements almost daily, the way you do when you are trading a lot, statements showing the profits we had made out of specific trades. But it was all, all fake. And Cane's market instincts were no good. When they caught up with him he was broke."

"What kind of con man is that?"

"Exactly. He believed in what he was selling, even in the Inertia/Disaster Index. But he believed even more in his other schemes, and they let him down. He didn't line his pockets, though, and they tell me he still thinks if he had a little more time and a little more money, which he was working on, he would have made our fortunes."

"When the Fraud Squad called, did you tell them you didn't want to proceed?"

"The money wasn't worth the embarrassment, frankly."

"You looked like assholes. For prominent lawyers, I mean."

"We would have, yes. But there you are. I still think Cane is a very bright guy who got into the wrong company."

"What company is that?"

"His own, chiefly."

"And Lucas was the only cool head among you."

"Steady on, now . . ."

"It's hard to see it any other way, Bonar. You were a real gang of suckers, classically conned by your own greed."

"All right. We should have known better. Jerry was the only one with his head screwed on. When his sister came to him, that was the first time he realized that she was involved, but he acted quickly enough to keep her name out of it."

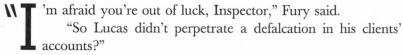

23

"I'm afraid you're out of luck, Inspector," Fury said.

"So Lucas didn't perpetrate a defalcation in his clients' accounts?"

"What?"

"A case I was on, the accountants talked like that. I memorized that one."

"These accountants have given me a preliminary oral assessment of Jerry's clients' affairs, and they found no reason to suspect that they will be surprised when they weigh the supporting data."

"All on the up and up, eh? No truck with Cane?"

"That's what they said. I will confirm it as soon as I have their written report. I've told them to make a routine check of everything that Jerry was involved in. He dabbled in arts management—two or three times a year he raised the money to put on a concert, arranged for the ticket sales, paid the artists, and so forth. He was also raising money for a hospice, there's a trust fund for that; there's his mother's trust fund that he took over from Larry Holt. I found that in order, but I want them to look at everything."

"He didn't have a Stradivarius worth getting killed for, did he?"

"He played the piano."

Cane was everything they had promised: with his dapper air, even in prison; yellow hair brushed flat across his head; and slim, he somehow managed to look like an old-time tap dancer in his rehearsal clothes. He was charming, affable and *sincere,* and as far as Salter could tell, completely convinced of his own probity. He did not set out to swindle his clients, only to use their money for a better purpose than the one agreed upon.

"It's very simple," he told Salter. "I got into currencies, where the real money is. There's a joke there: the real money was about to save me when you guys walked in."

"You're talking gibberish, Harry."

"I'll explain in a minute. See, I was betting against the ruble, and the Russians squeezed us by manipulating the exchange rate and by making it very difficult for us to borrow rubles to cover our positions. Then, when we were all bloodless, they took off the squeeze. I was wiped out."

"It's still gibberish, but it sounds like you came up against a sharper operator than yourself. They're learning fast, aren't they? Was what they did illegal?"

"That term doesn't make any sense in currency trading. A lot of central banks try to manipulate their currencies, but the Russians did it successfully. In effect, they made their money worth twice as much for a day, long enough to kill off the speculation. I imagine they're still laughing.

"But there's no crime in this game. The *sin* is guessing wrong. Anyway, I figured I had one more chance before my clients asked to see their money—the Brazilian *real.* It would have worked, too. No, screw it, it *did* work, but before I could raise enough money to make it pay off, one of my clients called for his money and it wasn't there. Next time it'll be different."

"There'll be a next time?"

"You think the stock market can go on for ever? Talk about momentum. And I think I have created exactly the tool to figure out when the final drop has started. I hope they let me out of here in time."

"You won't be allowed to trade, will you?"

"Not under my own name. Have to be a partnership." Cane laughed. "And that's enough of that. What did you come for? Not to hear my story, I bet."

"Oh, yes. That, too. But you know why else, don't get cute. A man came to see you and was killed a few days after. We know he came on urgent business. What was it?"

"I lost his sister's money. Twenty thousand. He came to tell me to downplay her name if any reporters wanted my story. She's a politico, you know. It would look bad if . . ."

"I know, I know. And that was all he came for? What was the urgency about that?"

"That's it, though he did add he would try to help me when I get out."

"Nothing in writing, I'll bet."

"I thought his sister might want to honor his word." Cane looked earnestly at Salter, then shrugged. "But I won't pester her."

"Good. Now. That's a nice story you just told me, Harry, but it's pure bullshit. I think Lucas came for something else. I think he found something in the woodshed that stunk a lot worse than it should have. Maybe he found you had a lot more than twenty thousand off his sister. Maybe you got her signature on a piece of paper you could take to the bank. I don't know. I'm floundering. Maybe it had nothing to do with her. But right now we've got five forensic accountants scouring Lucas's books, and the Fraud Squad is putting everything else in the X-ray machine to find some new trace, a name that we don't know about, especially anyone associated with you. Because there is money involved, money and you.

"I'm groping around, Harry, and I'll get you by the balls eventually, and the other guy, too. Lucas came to see you and got killed, because of something you told him. Now, what did Lucas come for?"

"I told you, his sister . . ."

"I'm going to find out in the end. There are only so many possible connections between you and Lucas. I'll start with anyone who lost money with you that Lucas knew. I have the list."

"For Christ's sake . . ."

"See, you may be the only person who knows who killed Lucas, or at least, why Lucas was killed."

"For Chris*sake*, Inspector."

"I've been looking through the transcript of your trial, too. You were very cooperative, then. If you stay a good boy you'll be out of here in no time. If not, not."

"I'm *still* cooperating. I don't know who killed Lucas. What can I say?"

Salter stood up. He had done what he came to do. This one could be left to simmer while he talked to Louise Wilder. "You're very loyal to your friends, Harry. But you'd better tell this one it's a waste of time. I'll get to him soon enough. Don't be there when I do."

"Should I have a lawyer present?"

Louise Wilder spoke steadily but not lightly.

"I don't think you'll need one. I plan to ask you to have dinner with me. I don't want to feed your lawyer, too."

"Is that allowed? Taking a suspect out to dinner?"

"I'll put it on expenses, make it official. I'll tell them I was trying to put you at ease. You're not a suspect, but you may be a witness."

"Where are we going?"

"You didn't say, 'Witness to what?' Some people would find that suspicious. You know the Purple Orchid, just south of Woodlawn? Meet me there at six. If you're there first, go upstairs. At that time we should have it to ourselves."

The Purple Orchid cooperated. Salter and Louise Wilder got a table in the back of the room, shielded by the wall at the top of the stairs. Even when the room was full this table was well protected from prying ears.

"You will be very private here, sir," confirmed the owner-hostess, a pretty woman in her forties wearing a black pantsuit, her blond hair hanging over one eye.

"They think we are having an affair." Louis Wilder said.

"Yeah? At my age it's nice to be under suspicion."

Louise Wilder had adopted a slightly formal manner, as if she were being interviewed for a job, but the remark, a shade bold in the circumstances, suggested she was trying hard to be on top of the situation.

Salter ordered a glass of wine for her and a scotch for himself, straight with no ice. Most of the time he drank beer, but when he did drink whiskey he liked to taste it.

When the drinks came he ignored his, leaned back and said, "I'll come to the point right away. What were you doing in silver boots and a blond wig in Jerry Lucas's apartment the night he was killed?"

She scrambled to her feet, knocking over her chair. "Some kind of game?" she muttered as if to herself. Then loudly enough so that Salter was glad they were shielded by the wall, "Well, fuck you, Inspector Smartass. I'll sure as hell have a lawyer along when we meet again. And the first thing I'll want to hear from him is whether a meeting like this is legal, or whether you are in for a major goddamn reprimand at least." She gathered up her purse by the strap, dragged her coat off her chair and pulled it around her.

Salter, on his feet, reached across and touched her arm. "Hold on. Bear with me. That was stupid, what I did. I'm sorry. You're right. I was being cute. Please. Sit down. I'll tell you what I should have said. Please."

She slumped down and sat sideways on her chair, her purse still held up, as if to keep it from getting wet. She watched him, silent.

Salter cleared his throat, adjusted his chair, and sat back, the bearer of unthreatening news. "We know that Jerry Lucas was killed after you left the apartment. We have evidence that there was someone in the apartment talking to him, even while you and your husband were talking in the parking lot. You are not a suspect. But you might be able to help us. So I'll go back to square one. What were you doing . . ."

"I still want to know first why we are having this conversation in the Purple Orchid."

"Because I wanted to talk to you, not question you. I don't have many questions, and I thought if we just talked you might tell me something I didn't know enough to ask for. You are the only one who was on intimate enough terms with him that he might have told you something, dropped a casual remark, revealed a worry, maybe, something I might find useful."

Slowly she faced forward and stopped gripping her purse so tightly. "You are sure I had nothing to do with it?"

"Yes. Yes, I am. I have to prove it, though, to make the question irrelevant."

"I always thought you might have to if it came to this."

"Did Jerry Lucas ever mention the name of Harry Cane?"

"Me first. How did you find out it was me in the fancy dress?"

"Someone identified you."

"Who? I don't know anyone in that building."

"The identification was arrived at through matching you with a third party you were said to resemble."

"In English, please?"

"Someone said you looked like Gloria Grahame."

"Did they? Do I?"

"I'd already met you. I rented *Oklahoma!* on video. And there you were."

Now she smiled slightly, her face still unsettled as if she had been slapped. "Yes, okay, I've heard that before. And James, my husband?"

"We tracked him down from his truck. By the way, do you keep your parking stubs, both of you?"

"James saves his for his accountant. Why?"

"They are time-stamped."

"That's good, isn't it? I still think it's a goddamn strange way to go about it. Surely once you identified me, you should have arrested me right away. I was half expecting it at any time."

"If I hadn't already met you earlier, I might have."

"You just *believed* in me, did you?"

"That's right. Then I confirmed it, so I didn't have to believe."

"Jesus. I guess I got lucky."

Salter watched as she put her purse over the back of her chair and took a sip of water. "Want to order?"

"First I want a glass of wine."

"There's one in front of you."

"So there is." She gulped, then sipped, then arranged her cutlery. "Right. Go on."

"There is a man Lucas was mixed up with who is now in jail . . ." Salter began.

"Harry Cane. The man who swindled Jerry's sister. You started to ask me about him."

"Was that all Lucas told you about him?"

"He visited Cane in jail. Did you know that?" She was calm now, chatting over dinner.

Salter nodded. "About his sister. About the importance of keeping her name out of his affairs."

She sipped her wine. "There was more to it than that. Sure, Jerry was concerned to look after Flora's reputation—more than *she* was, I think. Jerry was a little out-of-date about how untainted politicians have to be for the public to accept them."

"I had to have it explained to me, that no one minds a crook in government. I don't believe it, but the spin doctors might. So he went down to Bath to look after Flora's interests. You know he cancelled a fishing trip to go down to Bath."

"I was coming to that. Shall I tell you *my* story?. It's what we're here for, right?"

"Sorry."

"As I keep saying, I think there was more to it than Flora. On the Thursday, our regular meeting day—Friday was unusual—are we coming back to that?"

"Yes, but finish Thursday."

"He was agitated about Cane. Told me he had to go see him. I assumed it was about his sister, but he said it was much more important than that, that Cane had his fingers in everything and it was going to get very messy. He was afraid he would have to do something that would look bad, his motives he meant, but he couldn't help that. There were more than just Jerry and his sister involved."

"Who?"

"You never met Jerry, did you? He didn't talk shop, ever. No confidences in bed, that's for sure. What he told me was that he had to see Cane about something that went beyond his sister."

"He didn't mention any names?"

"Like who?"

"Read the menu. I'll make a list."

Salter took out a pen and recreated the poker game, naming all the players. He got them all just as she looked up. The waitress took their order and when she left, Salter said, turning the paper napkin around so she could see what he had written, "Do any of these look familiar?"

"Bonar Robinson, Craig Lister, Scott Mercer, Brian Davis, Andrew Cutler, Larry Holt—they were all his poker pals."

"Except for Holt, they were also Cane's victims, like Flora Lucas. Did he mention any of them that night? Or anyone else?"

"No, no. I've heard of all of these, of course. They all lost money because of Cane, did they? But it wasn't a big deal for them. I think I remember Jerry being involved in keeping their names out of the news, along with Calvin Gregson."

"Did they talk together, Lucas and Gregson?"

"Of course. Both of them were working on Flora's behalf."

Then the obviousness of it hit him. "Gregson and Flora Lucas?"

"Oh, shit, you didn't know? Well, you would have heard about it soon."

"But Gregson is a Tory?"

"And Flora is a Liberal. Interesting, isn't it? I think he's going to hand in his party card and work for her. Jerry said Gregson wouldn't give her up even if she were a Trotskyite."

"They were in Costa Rica together?"

"Gregson answered the phone when Jerry called his own house down there about this Cane thing."

"Well, well. Well, well, well, well, well. Nothing to do with me, though. I'm surprised, given Lucas's reputation for being discreet, that he would say anything at all to you about this."

"We were lovers. Lovers have to tell each other *some* secrets or they don't trust each other. In Jerry's case, interesting but nonlegal secrets."

"Which brings me back to my first question. Again, I'm sorry to be such a . . ."

"Oh, never mind. What was I doing in that outfit on a Friday night, you want to know. Does it matter?"

"If we find this guy."

"*If?*"

"*When* we find him."

"Will it be long?"

"As soon as I have everything lined up. In the meantime, when his lawyer examines my case, he will enter a plea of not guilty. Now a standard response of a criminal lawyer in this kind of case is to find someone else equally suspect who the police have apparently overlooked. It won't take him long to find out about you. Before then, I want a case so solid that it will be a waste of his time. So tell me about the silver boots."

"They were a joke. We used to have fun. Jerry was a larky guy, off duty. There was nothing sweep-them-off-their-feet-about him. I had no illusions about why we got together. We had things in common including sex. We went to bed one night, liked it, and then arranged to do it regularly." She paused and leaned back to allow the waitress to set the food in front of them.

"What about your husband?" Salter asked, when the waitress left.

"My husband had nothing to do with it, or with your problem." She waited for a response, and when Salter shrugged, she continued, "You want to know about the boots. I said, they were a joke. I bought them and borrowed a wig. All the rest I had or adapted from my own stuff. The idea was I would do a sort of 'Avon calling,' you know, flash him when he opened the door. "Hello, Stranger. Looking for a good time?"

"The deputy chief guessed something like that. Did it turn Lucas on?"

"It was a *joke!*"

"Sorry. That was it? Why Friday, by the way? Your regular night was Thursday, you say."

"Our regular night was Thursday, but we met on other nights sometimes, when I had a good excuse, and Jerry didn't have tickets to a concert. That night James said he had to meet a client in King City and he would be late. I immediately checked with Jerry. He was free, so I told James I would go to a movie, and the rest is . . ."

"But James didn't go to King City."

"He was setting a little trap. He had long ago guessed I was having an affair, so he followed me."

"And now?"

"This is no business of yours, either, is it? But as a matter of fact he has been very supportive. I told him the whole story and together we decided not to come to you with it unless we had to. This is getting cold." She picked up her knife and fork and started to cut up her steak.

"I've never been here before," she said. "It's good. Discreet." She grinned.

Salter smiled and set his plate aside. "Now that you've had a chance to brood, did Lucas tell you he was expecting someone later? No? Did you see anyone on your way in or out that you knew?"

"As I was standing in Jerry's doorway, waiting to flash him, a guy got out of the elevator and stared at me. I thought he'd seen the costume, as he probably had, so I put my hand in my raincoat pocket to pull it round me as a kind of screen. My memory is that he went off down the corridor, but I was too busy with Jerry to notice. It was probably just a tenant, surprised to see a tart in the building. Did anyone complain?"

"What did he look like?"

"Like a thousand other guys. I nearly said 'johns.' Professional-looking, an accountant or a lawyer, grey hair, his clothes fit properly. That's all I noticed."

"One last one. What did you do with the costume?"

"It's in a garbage can downtown somewhere. My husband got rid of it because I was panicking. So he drove down to Jarvis street and dumped it. He thought it would give you a problem."

The waitress came. Salter paid the bill and they walked down the street. "Shall I walk you home?" Salter asked.

"Where are you parked?"

"Near Avenue Road." He pointed up Woodlawn.

"I need a few minutes after you've gone, before I talk to James. Who is at home and knows all about *us*." She grimaced. "And is as puzzled as I was as to why you should buy me dinner. I'll leave you here. I've got a good exit line."

"Say it."

"You know who did it, don't you?"

"You always know, but half the time you're wrong. Yes, I know."

To Smith, he said, "She got a good look at him and he was afraid she could identify him. So he went along Jarvis Street, looking for her. Remember what your girls told you?"

"To kill her? Shut her up?"

"He was hoping to bribe her, I would guess."

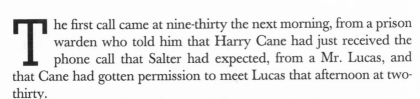

24

The first call came at nine-thirty the next morning, from a prison warden who told him that Harry Cane had just received the phone call that Salter had expected, from a Mr. Lucas, and that Cane had gotten permission to meet Lucas that afternoon at two-thirty.

"*Mister* Lucas? Mr. Lucas is dead. Was it a male voice?"

"Hang on a minute. Yep, no doubt about it."

"How long are visitors allowed to stay?"

"An hour in this case."

"Here's what I want you to do for me. When he arrives, park him in an awkward spot, then block him in so it takes him fifteen minutes to get free. Just in case the meeting doesn't last very long. Then get his license number and call me with it right away."

Next he called the Ontario Provincial Police, who agreed to have an unmarked car follow "Lucas" when he came out of the prison, and accompany him to Toronto, there to hand him over to the Metro Police. Bayview was his most likely exit from the highway, but Salter arranged for cars to be at Yonge Street and Avenue Road as well, in case 'Lucas' had an eccentric reason for using one of those to enter the city.

"Nearly ready," Salter told Smith as he put down the phone. "He's using an alias—'Lucas,' the guy he killed."

"Should I be making a note in case you suffer a sudden cardiac arrest, sir? You are over sixty, and I have no idea what the hell you are up to."

"Then listen. Yesterday I had dinner with Puss-in-Boots, just to cross her off our list—she was never on mine—and she confirmed all we already know and added a rough description that fits our man."

"Who would that be? In case of your sudden death. You know his name?"

"I think so. But I believe I'll keep it to myself until I've proved it. Puss-in-Boots, by the way, is Louise Wilder, Lucas's mistress. Or lover. Lucas wasn't paying her. They used to meet on Thursday once a month under cover of a book-group meeting they were supposed to be attending, and on any odd nights they were both free and Wilder's husband was out of town."

"What were the boots and the bum-freezer skirt all about?"

"They were part of a joke she was playing."

"Not a turn-on, then?"

"She says not. We have enough corroboration to tick her off the list."

"I don't think I'd go that far from what you've told me, sir."

"She didn't do it, Smitty. Look, yesterday I went to the jail and I talked to Cane for about an hour. He thought I was trying to find out why Lucas had visited him."

"You already knew why?"

"I think so. But it's got to come from him, the horse's mouth. All the time I talked, I wanted to make one thing clear, that we were getting close, and bound to get there soon. And I threatened to charge him with lack of cooperation, which would affect his parole."

"Is that kosher?"

"I doubt it, but I won't stick around for a reprimand. Cane stuck to his story, that Lucas was concerned only about his sister. I just wanted to get him going, give him a chance to think about it, which he did, and after I left, he changed his mind. He'd been loyal so far, but it was time to tell Mr. X, just in case *he* was the killer—which Cane didn't know—that he, Cane, planned to rat on everybody in a day or two because the police were breathing down his neck, and as long as they had Cane fingered, then he was going to be a good boy and cooperate. I'm guessing all this, but something like it is going down because right now, Cane is expecting a visit from Lucas . . ."

"But Lucas is *dead*."

"He's a code word now. The visitor doesn't want to sign in under his own name. Cane has told him how we found Lucas's name in the visitor's book, and he's panicking. Looking for a name to write in the visitor's book, Lucas is the first that jumps into his head."

"And you know who it is."

"They are going to call in his license number when he arrives. Then I'll be sure."

"Mr. Fury called, by the way, asked you to call back as soon as possible."

Fury said, "I want to show you something. I don't want to say more over the phone. You people tape everything. Can you come over now?"

"Should I?"

"Yes."

The folder, blue, an inch thick, was tagged with the Lucas name, this time that of Beryl, Jerry Lucas's mother.

"You know that Holt looked after Beryl Lucas's affairs?" Fury was trembling, but Salter could not tell why.

"And he's milked her. There's no money left. Right?"

"Not quite. The sum in the bank account is about what one would expect to find, but some other things one would expect to find are missing. It is impossible to trace the month-by-month growth, or the year-by-year toward the final figure."

"There's a backup file, maybe. That file was simply physically too big."

"You don't know what the hell you are talking about. A file that grew too big would simply be split by period. You would not weed out important material and put it somewhere else. The accountants found the answer. Although the final figure was consistent with the opening balance and several years of conservative investing, in between, the amount of money dipped much lower, twice nearly to zero, then it was topped up, most recently just before Holt was to hand it over. The crooked bastard has been playing fast and loose with his clients' money, Beryl's, and probably all his other clients', too. We'll soon know about the rest, but it is my gut instinct that Beryl Lucas's trust was topped up with money from Holt's other clients' accounts. Jesus Christ Almighty!"

"Did he expect to get away with it?"

"He had probably developed a last-days-in-the-bunker mentality."

"I imagine Beryl's account was very low and Lucas found out about it."

Fury had stopped trembling, and now turned white. "Larry Holt killed Jerry?" he whispered, his voice barely carrying across the desk. "I've been trying not to think it."

"I'll be arresting him this afternoon. Keep that to yourself until you hear it on the news."

Fury stood up. "I'm going home. Do you have my home number?" He pushed a card across the desk and stood up. "Esther," he called, "I'm sick. I'm going home. If those accountants call, tell them I'll be notifying the Securities Commission tomorrow, and the Law Society. There's no hurry, I understand. Not anymore." He turned to Salter. "How long have you known?"

"When I first met him he told me about a picture of Flora in Lucas's apartment. When the others told me that Lucas never invited anyone into his apartment, not the poker club nor the book group, I remembered that Holt *had* been inside. And it came back the night of the poker game, the night he ingratiated himself with me, even told me about the so-called practical joke they had planned. I wasn't really suspicious of any other of Lucas's card-playing pals, but Holt's behavior that night stuck in my head.

"After that he kept cropping up as the one who *wasn't* involved. Why wasn't he part of the little syndicate that Cane swindled? The answer is that he was mixed up in Cane's losses, but so deeply that he couldn't let it come out without someone wondering whose money he was using. So he made a deal with Cane to keep his name out of the case completely."

"The accountants will find it eventually."

"I think your partner had already found it. Now I have to go. Don't forget. Keep quiet until you hear the news."

Gregson was next.

"How was Costa Rica, Calvin?"

Gregson rose in his chair, his face tight. "I don't know what the fuck you think you are doing, Salter. I was told someone was inquiring about me. Let me tell you, putting tabs on a citizen just for fun lays you open to some serious charges."

"Up your ass, Calvin. Sit down and listen. You're here so I can help you, if I can. I knew what you were up to from the beginning. You were too involved. Naturally I was suspicious, so I did a routine check, proper police proceedure. To clear you. If you were that close to the sister you might have some reason to kill him I didn't know about. Never mind what I think, I have to check. So let's get on. This thing is nearly wrapped up and I thought you'd like an opportunity to keep that reporter happy. You know, the one we are all frightened of. You could give him an exclusive." Salter gave Gregson a summary of the story. "I will arrest Holt this afternoon. I'll do it quietly, but even if he doesn't protest, if he confesses, he'll need advice, because he's not a real lawyer, is he? I mean he's never been involved with criminals."

Gregson stirred himself. "I'll take care of him."

"He doesn't have any money."

"This too will be very public-spirited of me. His clients will want money and revenge, of course, and that the courts will have to deal with later. What about Cane?"

"I think Holt and Cane were still financially connected."

"Involving anyone else?"

"I don't know."

"But the clients will want to know what he did with the money."

"Let me arrest him, see what he has to say."

25

As Salter sat down across from Holt in his office he saw that the lawyer had given up. Salter made a brief speech telling Holt that he knew and could prove that Holt was the killer; he threw in gratuitously that he wasn't sure why, but that they had a lineup of witnesses who could identify him at the scene, and that the forensic people . . .

Holt threw up his hands. "Go ahead."

There were still things Salter wanted to know. What caused the confrontation? Beryl Lucas's death?

"He told me he was going to send my name to the Securities Commission, on the grounds that he had discovered a serious mis-handling by a stockbroker of a clients' funds. And then he mentioned the Law Society." Holt shrugged. "I didn't plan to kill him," he said.

"I don't think you did. You would have taken a better weapon. Remind your lawyer of that. So what gave you the idea?"

"We were moving around the apartment, arguing. I was sort of chasing him, asking him for more time to find the money. I just needed a few days. If she hadn't died I might have made it."

"Like Cane? Waiting for the Brazilian *real* to fall?"

"Oh, no. I was waiting for the stock market. I'd made a big bet on the futures market. I figured three or four days."

"And did it rise?"

"Not yet. But it will."

"But when Mr. Fury looked, the money was there."

"I bought some time with money from my other trust funds."

"Did you always deal with Cane?"

"At first. Not lately."

"What did you go to Bath to see him about, yesterday?"

"He called to warn me, after you had talked with him."

"But you weren't one of his clients, lately."

"We knew each other well, in a number of ways. He owed me a favor because I had sent him some clients, recommended them. The poker group, for example, and Flora Lucas, and a few others."

"For a commission?"

"More or less."

"You knew by then he was a crook?"

"Not at all. He seemed brilliant to me. Any commission, as you call it, I invested right back with him."

"And your clients' money."

"No. I thought I knew enough not to need Cane for that. I managed my clients' money by myself."

"And lost the lot."

"Nearly."

"But why did Cane warn you? What did he know of your own dealing?"

"Nothing concrete. But he knew I was dabbling. He could smell it. I had one or two little winners that I didn't keep to myself, and he heard about them. But we were on good terms, so he thought he would do me a favor."

"Now. What happened in Lucas's kitchen?"

"We got shouting, and I kept following him around and threatened him with my cane. He was facing the knife block and he turned around with the knife in his hand and told me to get out, and I knocked the knife out of his hand and then it got stuck in his chest. That's the best I can do for you."

"That was the time to come to us."

"Possibly. But when I calmed down I realized I had a chance of getting away with it. I'd seen that prostitute leave Jerry's apartment. It was quite a surprise, and I had mentioned it to Jerry and he got mad . . ."

"You said you would blackmail him? About the prostitute?"

"That's what he *thought* I was saying, but of course, I wasn't."

"Made him angry enough to keep waving a knife at you."

"Yes. Anyway, after Jerry died I thought I would wait to see if she had been seen by anyone else . . ."

"In which case, she might take the rap?"

"I knew they would never find her. So I washed the knife clean and left. I saw no one on the way out."

"How did you know?"

"She wasn't a hooker. I'd seen her face before. A very striking face."

"When?"

"At a couple of concerts. I saw them chatting once and walked over to say hello and she scuttled away before I got there. That happened again at another concert, in Roy Thomson Hall, and this time I felt sure he had signaled to her that I was approaching, so I thought it might be someone I knew, someone's wife, maybe. So I kept my eye on where she had gone, and after chatting for a minute with Jerry, I followed her. I caught up with her at the record shop in the lobby. I didn't know her then, but I remembered her face when I saw her dressed up, and I guessed what they were up to."

"They were just horsing around."

"It looked to me like someone acting out their fantasies."

"Never mind. Go on."

"So after the knife went into Jerry, I panicked at first, but then as I cleaned up I realized that there was the perfect suspect. Someone must have seen her, but they never would again. She would disappear, so nobody innocent would be charged."

"That was your first thought, was it?"

"Let's just say I did have the thought, all right?"

"Let's get out of here. You want a lawyer at the station?"

"None of the lawyers I know would be much use. You have any suggestions?"

"Gregson. He's the best."

"I can't afford him."

"Ask him."

Holt took down a directory of lawyers, found Gregson's name, and called his office. Then Salter took the receiver from him and explained the situation before handing the phone back to Holt.

Holt said into the phone, "I can't afford to pay you. Can I run a tab?" He listened, then looked surprised. "This is the first good news I've had all week. Why? I see, I just got the right number in your charity draw. We're leaving now. Thank you." He put the phone down and said to Salter, "He says the fee is irrelevant. He does pro bono work, and he says this is an interesting case."

Salter was so pleased with himself he never noticed that Smith was looking more excited than usual, but as he finished the story, Smith said, "There's a detail, isn't there, sir? If Holt wasn't looking for the nonexistent hooker on Jarvis Street, as the girls reported, then who was?"

Salter said, "I don't know, but let's keep that one to ourselves until the mystery is solved. We've got a full confession, but if Gregson gets hold of that thread he might find a way to unravel it."

Now Smith shook his head, his face shining. "Not to worry. While you were out the Vice Squad called. They picked him up last night." He looked at a note in his hand. "You know who it was?"

"Don't fuck about, Smitty. Who?"

"A man named Gavin Chapel, a reporter for the *Dominion*. You know him?"

Salter laughed. "I'll tell the deputy chief. He may want to have a word with him."

To his boss, Deputy Mackenzie, Salter said, "Holt is probably going to be advised to plead involuntary manslaughter. Gregson wants a quick trial—and so, surprise surprise, does the attorney general. He probably feels sorry for a colleague, wouldn't you think? And we don't give a shit, do we, as long as we've done our job? Anyway, if Holt decides to change his mind and plead not guilty, the whole case becomes circumstantial. There are no fingerprints on the knife, and no fibers or hairs of the kind that Forensics are supposed to find. Louise Wilder was panic-stricken and is not sure she could identify him, so we would have to rely on the financial evidence, and no one involved wants that stuff coming out in a manslaughter trial. Later on, while he's in jail, Holt will stand trial on the embezzlement charges, but lawyers embezzling clients' funds is so routine nowadays, the papers hardly report it."

Mackenzie said, "So you haven't really identified him except by a witness who will herself be under suspicion if we don't nail Holt. Christ, she's a likelier suspect than he is. All Holt's gotta do is say he never entered the apartment. He knocked, he could say, heard voices, then left. Just calling on a friend, he could say. Christ, yes, let's have a quick trial, quick and dirty, and get it out of the way. Still, you did a good job. When did you first suspect Holt?"

"When he told me about a picture he'd seen of Flora Lucas in the apartment. Later on, when I heard how private Lucas was, I got to wondering why Holt would have been in his apartment if none of the other poker players had."

"I'm glad you didn't go to town until you had something else. All he had to say was that he had visited Lucas once to pass the time. One Sunday afternoon, like . . ."

"That's why I waited."

"Good. Jesus Christ. When did you get something a bit more solid?"

"When he tried to kiss me in the kitchen."

"When he *what*? How old is this guy? Oh, I see, you're shitting me again. All right, all right. Finish it up, now."

"Yes, I was speaking metaphorically, sir. He came on to me like a soulmate. But he's a lousy con man. And I never believed in that hooker from the start."

"Right, right."

"And I couldn't smell any deep, dark secrets worth killing for. I thought all those lawyers had enough money, and Lucas was a perfectly normal, middle-aged, upper-middle-income heterosexual lawyer with no kinky tastes. Except for Puss-in-Boots, who I couldn't resist, it looked like a dull and difficult case, and I would have dodged it."

"Sonofabitch," the deputy said. He giggled. "Eh? Lucky and crafty, Salter, that's you. Jesus. Now, I've got something else I want you to look at."

"An investigation?"

"A very delicate case. One of us."

Salter shook his head. "I don't think so, sir. Time's up. If you try to get me to take this on, anyway, I'll call in sick."

"So this is it, eh? Good way to go. Scored a fucking goal in overtime, you have. I was talking to Marinelli this morning . . ."

"He pissed off?"

"Marinelli? Nah. Don't do it again, though."

"Good. I'll write out my resignation today."

"I'll lay on a dinner for you at the club. Okay?"

"A pair of silver-plated handcuffs would be nice, too. And ask Constable Smith if he'll play the bagpipes."

"We'll give you a good send-off."

Salter left him, and went off for his encounter with Lichtman.

Salter won the first game, and Lichtman was silent except for a hissing noise as he got his breath, so Salter knew the situation was serious. In the second game, the court felt like a large steel cage in which he and Lichtman had been locked to kill or be killed. Lichtman won, just. Salter said, "A tie?" Lichtman smiled for the first time at Salter's suggested temporary solution to the struggle. "Right," he said. "Let's play again, settle it, when we're younger."

Angus was waiting for him after the game.

Salter came out of the changing room and there he was, sitting in the lounge, where he had been watching the game through the glass wall, waiting to go home with his father. Angus, Annie and Charlotte, his granddaughter, had been home for a week now, home for good.

"You really play hard, don't you, Pop," Angus said.

"It's not just a game, you know," Salter said. "Want a beer?"

When he returned from the bar with the two mugs, Angus said, "How about teaching me?"

Salter immediately wanted to respond by asking if this was Annie's idea, but he bit his tongue. "Did you ever play tennis? I don't remember."

"In high school. I was nearly on the junior team."

"Then you should be all right. It'll take you two to three months to beat me, then you'll have to find a new partner."

"Make it a month. Tell you what. Let's make a deal. You teach me squash and I'll teach you fly fishing."

"You never liked fishing!" It was one of the failures between them.

"Fly fishing, not sitting in a boat with a worm on a hook. Real fishing. Uncle John showed me. It's the only way to go."

"Fuck off. I *like* sitting in a boat with a worm on a hook. Anyway I've never seen anyone do it around here. Fly fishing, I mean."

Angus nodded. "There's a place in the corner of Algonquin Park set aside for it. When the trout season opens next spring. All right?"

Was it all right? Not really. The way Angus had handled the breakdown of his relationship with Linda had left Salter feeling slightly disappointed in him, then judgmental, and caused him to wonder about his son. He found himself now slightly irritated at the boy's enthusiasm for a fishing trip while some large problems remained unsettled. He had begun to wonder lately whether he ought to have probed his brother-in-laws' irritation with Angus as an employee, to see their impatience as a sign of something lacking in his son as much as in them. All this made him a little sad, and not quite able to enter Angus's enthusiasm.

The receptionist called him over. "There's a call for you. Sounds urgent." She handed him the receiver.

It was Smith. "The parking control people have identified that light brown Volkswagen that was around Lucas's apartment building. A woman owns it. Someone called Jane Rudd."

That made sense. She had been stalking Lucas, besotted and slightly deranged. To Smith, he said, "I'm glad we didn't find out about her earlier. She might have become our prime suspect. Just make a note that we knew all about her, and she has nothing to do with the case."

"Who is she?"

"An old girlfriend of Lucas's."

"The one who phoned us a couple of times?"

"That's the one. With us she was just trying to get noticed, or to find out if she had been noticed. It doesn't matter now."

"Aye, then. It's been interesting working with you, sir. Very unorthodox."

"Yeah. You'll get on okay with Marinelli."

"Not for long, though."

"You leaving already?" Salter laughed, to show he was being flippant.

"Yes, I am."

"Why?"

"My wife doesn't like Toronto."

"Oh, shit, I'm sorry. What now? Back to Inverness?"

Smith drew a breath. "She's going back to Inverness. I'm going back to Glasgow, where I belong. I've been talking to a counselor. She says my wife is never going to be satisfied, because it's me, not the place we live in that she doesn't like. And that's all right, you know. I can see that. When I thought about it, I don't like her much either, so it's a weight off my back."

Salter was appalled. "Otherwise. You okay?"

"I'm fine." Again Salter heard the note asking him to butt out now, please.

"Fine. If I ever come to Glasgow . . ."

"Oh, Aye. We'll see you, then." He hung up.

Back at the table, Salter looked at the fresh mugs of beer Angus had ordered. "Who's driving?" he asked.

"You are." Angus grinned. "I figured you were bulletproof."

Salter looked at his watch. "Who's looking after the baby now, at this moment?"

"Mom. I wanted to talk to you about that. See, Dad, I've been offered a terrific job in Vancouver. Guy who runs the company is a very, very good friend."

"Then we'll have to postpone the fishing trip, won't we? Algonquin Park's a long way from Vancouver." Salter tried to keep his tone amused and dry as he realized that the talk of a fishing trip had been just that, talk, confected to induce a warmth between them as Angus prepared to introduce his Vancouver plans.

"What about the baby?" Now he felt slightly sorry for Angus. Not many fathers were left holding the bag. But if it happened, was Vancouver an option? It wouldn't have been for him. "Have you spoken to Mom about this Vancouver idea?"

Angus nodded. "She says she'll take care of Charlotte until . . ."

Angus turned his palms upwards. "Until I can, I guess. She was concerned if you would agree."

Now we know why you're here. Salter stood up and finished his beer. "What's the alternative?" he asked, this time allowing some of his mood to get into his voice. "Leave her on the church steps?"

Two weeks later, on a Sunday evening, Salter was carving ham and counting the plates he had yet to fill. "Seth, Tatti, Angus, Annie, me. And baby makes six." He sat down and contemplated the group. It was the last family dinner before Angus left for the West Coast. Tatti settled Charlotte in her lap, where she had spent most of the time since Annie had brought her from the Island, lowered her head and closed her eyes, expecting grace. But there had been no grace said in this house since Annie's mother's last visit. Salter said to Seth, "Your move, son. You know what to say."

Seth stared at his father, then became inspired. As Tatti opened her eyes to see why nothing was happening, he slid down in his chair until only his eyebrows showed above the tablecloth. Then, in the voice of Tiny Tim, he said, "God bless us, every one."